Coasting and Crashing

What Reviewers Say About Ana Hartnett's Work

Catching Feelings

"I have yet to read Ana Reichardt's debut, book one in this series, *Changing Majors*. That is something I will soon rectify after reading *Catching Feelings*. There is an ease to her writing, and I was quickly drawn to Andrea, the adorkable lesbian who finds herself having to try to find her voice as the new leader of her team. …I don't read a lot of YA novels, maybe because college was so long ago, I can hardly remember it. Reading this book made me feel wistful and long for those days of crushes and endless possibilities. Any book that evokes such emotions is one I will return to again and again. *Catching Feelings* is a wonderful sophomore effort by Ana Hartnett Reichardt. The characters are so relatable and their growth both individually and as a couple, was beautifully written. I can't wait to see what comes next from this author. Her star has only begun to rise."—*Sapphic Book Review*

"From start to finish *Catching Feelings* is such a great read. …It is full of sweet moments to delight, heart-stopping moments to thrill and steamy moments to make your temperature soar. Andrea and Maya have to navigate college, competitive sports, and people who want to get in the way of their friendship and eventual romance. This makes for a compelling read that keeps you turning the page and ends up wrapping you in a warm hug."—*Lesbian Review*

Visit us at www.boldstrokesbooks.com

By the Author

Changing Majors

Catching Feelings

Chasing Cypress

Crush

Coasting and Crashing

Coasting and Crashing

by

Ana Hartnett

2023

COASTING AND CRASHING

ISBN 13: 978-1-63679-511-9

This Trade Paperback Original Is Published By
Bold Strokes Books, Inc.
P.O. Box 249
Valley Falls, NY 12185

First Edition: December 2023

Credits
Editor: Barbara Ann Wright
Production Design: Susan Ramundo
Cover Design By Jeanine Henning

Acknowledgments

Wow. Senior year…

Wrapping up the Alder Series with Emma's story was an emotional experience to say the least. Emma is confident, sure of herself, ready. But things don't always turn out the way we think they will, and they certainly didn't for Emma Wilson. They turned out better.

No matter how established we are, or how far down a certain path we are—when we're just coasting along—life throws a wrench in our plans. Makes us swerve.

Makes us crash.

My friend Emily says there is always some breaking in the business of growth. And if love is growth, well, I reckon there's some breaking in love too.

First, I want to thank my editor, Barbara Ann Wright, for starting and finishing this series with me and for letting me keep the fun epilogue. You've been kind, patient, and ridiculously supportive. Not to mention hilarious. You continue to help me grow with every book, and I cannot thank you enough.

Thank you to Bold Strokes Books for making these books possible. Rad, Sandy, Ruth, and all the crew, thank you for your nonstop work and for giving us authors a home.

A very special thank you to Anissa McIntyre for sensitivity reading this story. Lake is such a special character, and I am beyond grateful for your work in helping me to do her justice. Also, thank you for always welcoming me with the biggest smile.

This community means everything to me. Lauren Eve, thank you for helping me hit my word counts and motivating me to be a better writer. Morgan, thank you for being the world's best friend.

Kris and Rivs, I truly couldn't imagine doing this journey without you guys. And endless gratitude to the all the amazing authors who show me continuous support. Georgia, Melissa, Aurora, Luc, and so many more. Big shout-out to Kate, Kat, and Laura for simply being amazing. You all make writing a truly beautiful experience.

Thank you to my family for always being supportive and my biggest fans.

As always, thank you to my readers, who make being an author possible.

Dedication

For anyone who's crashing right now

CHAPTER ONE

Jealousy tastes like summer-fat strawberries and fresh whipped cream. Cream I've whipped myself. Not with an electric whisk; that's cheating, and I'm very competitive. Too competitive, my younger siblings would say. I'm talking about wrist-breaking, fresh whipped cream. That is what my jealousy tastes like today.

Yesterday, it tasted like salt in a festering wound. Hard to believe, but yesterday was better. Not because I'm a heathen for infected lesions—I much prefer strawberries—but because jealousy *should* taste like a burning sore. I know when it makes me want to drive my fist through a crisp plank of drywall, I'm where I'm supposed to be with it. I'm working through it.

But when it tastes like berries and cream…I'm pretty well fucked. All stuck in the sticky sweet trap of my self-indulgent, narcissistic, goddamn fucking—

"Em." A deep breath cuts off my name as Whitney's chest heaves against mine. I know in the morning, I'll have eight little circular bruises on my butt cheeks. Four on each. Her thumbs never leave a mark. "Don't stop." She groans and digs deeper. The bruises from Wednesday are still tender, and her fingers are perfectly atop the sensitive marks. "Damn, Emma. Just fuck me. *Fuck.*"

Maybe if it was a salt-in-the-wound kind of day, I'd buck up and fuck Whitney Mahoney until all those little bruises seeped together and painted my entire ass purple. Or until she inevitably soaked through to her mattress. I *like* both of those things. But it's a strawberries-and-cream day, and the crassness that usually makes my limbs shake until sweat drips from my brow hurts my feelings. Makes me feel used up. My strap cuts into my thigh. It's too tight.

I pull out of her.

"Emma, what—"

"Whit, please." I raise my hand to keep her from begging. "Damn thing's too tight." I trace the strap to the plastic adjustable buckle and yank, but it's stuck. I hop off the bed and spin in a circle like a dumbass. "Get this cheap thing off me."

Whitney slides out of bed, her entire body red and wet and raw. I like Whit. It's not her fault I'm a shithead. It's not her fault that when she loosens the strap on my harness, and it falls unceremoniously around my feet, the silicone thudding against the hardwood, I feel like I can breathe again. I'm not fulfilling our agreement. I can't today, and she should be annoyed. For all the times I've used her to feel good, she gets to use me, too. We are equals in this arrangement for pleasure. Well, for other things, too. Relief. Avoidance. A place to put the things I don't want to deal with.

Whit doesn't care that I don't have feelings for her. It would gross her out, and she would no longer want to have sex with me. I know I'm putting our arrangement in danger by bailing right before the grand finale, but sometimes, the best thing to do is cut and run. My body hasn't caught up to my brain, and I bristle when I pull on my sports bra, and the fabric rubs against my nipples. I push my palms against my breasts and wait. Try to breathe through my racing heart and my racing thoughts like Andy taught me in high school. But now I'm thinking about *her*, and that's the whole fucking problem.

"I gotta go. Sorry, Whit." The clock on my phone says I'm going to be late to our team meeting. It's an important one, and I still have to run back to Griner Hall and shower. *Or maybe I could go straight to the Den?* No. I reek of sex. "I'm late. And we meet our new coach today." *What's her name again? Coach Jackson? Johnson?*

Whit shrugs and opens the desk drawer to fish out her vibrator. She doesn't care. It's why I keep coming back. But as I shut her door, I have a settling feeling that this is my last time with her. This little arrangement is over. Probably.

The August air is warm and thick on my skin, all cloying and suffocating as I jog across the quad. I run up the stairs to my room in Griner, a nice dorm that looks like every other building on campus, with fat ashen stone and a pointy top like a Scottish castle. And the best part: I have one of the few single rooms on campus. They're usually reserved for students who require a different living situation, but no one has needed it the last two years, and I won the dorm lottery for it.

I get lucky like that a lot. It's like a weird superpower.

All the luck in the world, but I don't have Andy. My chest tightens every time her name subconsciously lights up my brain like a neon sign. Walking to my class: *Andy.* Sit for lunch: *Andy.* Head hits the pillow: *Andy.*

Most days, I hate myself for letting her go. We had feelings for each other for six years—*six years*—and somehow, I fucked it up. For what? Because I was too scared to make a move? I'm Emma Wilson. All I do is make moves.

Rumpled clothes litter my room. Most of them are mine, but a few bits of pink stick out from the familiar navy and maroon of my shirts and hoodies. I swear girls leave clothes here on purpose. I rip off my shirt and throw a towel over my shoulder. Plug in my phone for a quick charge. It's half-past seven, and I need to be at the Lion's Den by eight. I should be leaving now. Gotta shower *fast.* I yank the bathroom door, but it's locked. *What the fuck?* I jiggle the handle and beat on the door. Piper wasn't supposed to be on campus for another week, and she never mentioned when her new roommate was moving in.

"Hello?" I call through the wood. "Kinda need to get in there, like, *right now*."

The door flies open, and a short Black woman with deep brown eyes and a magnetic energy stands in the doorway. Her brows creep up, as if she's annoyed at my interruption, and I straighten when her gaze flits down my body. Forgot I'm not wearing a shirt.

"You're not the only one on a schedule," she says. Something about her voice makes me want to listen to her all night. She looks as if she's also on her way to something, with a perfectly light face of makeup, her shiny hair in side-parted locs, hitting an inch past her shoulders, an Alder basketball tee tucked into her tight blue jeans, and a crisp white pair of Nike Blazers. *Wow.*

"Who are you? Piper never mentioned—"

"Lake Palmer. Just moved in today." She peeks over my shoulder, and I wish I'd cleaned.

I flatten my palm over my chest. "Emma Wilson. Point guard."

Something flashes in her eyes as she narrows them. "Point guard? Cool." But it doesn't sound cool when she says it like that, all bored and indifferent. It sounds like she finds me very *uncool*, and I'm not gonna lie, it stings.

I don't even know why I introduced myself that way. I'm usually smooth as butter when it comes to talking to women, but the way Lake looks at me has me off my game, which is a shame because Lake Palmer may be the hottest woman at Alder. I nod to her breasts—to her *shirt*. "You date a guy on the team or something?"

She rolls her eyes and leans against the door frame, arms crossed, and I have to force myself to act normal. To act like her sharp attitude isn't turning me on when her gaze scrapes over my skin like that. Like I repulse and intrigue her at the same time.

I catch her check out my abs before she pushes off the door and turns to leave. "You're going to be late, Emma Wilson. And Coach Jordan hates when people are late." She winks over her shoulder and closes the door to her room behind her.

I'm a wet tongue frozen to an icy pole. *How the hell can she be on the basketball team?* She's barely five feet tall. Barely five feet tall, and I've never heard of her. She's not a freshman; we met all the recruits already.

I grin. She couldn't keep her eyes off my—

Fuck, I'm late.

❖

The Den is almost the same as it was last year. Same slightly graded stadium seating, same permanently smudged whiteboard, same projector for watching film, same squishy navy and maroon seats. But it feels like a different place without Coach Carson. I'm not entirely sure why I loved that guy so much. Truth be told, he was a bad coach, and we haven't had a winning season since my freshman year. But with him, I felt safe in a way. Not a lot of stress when you can't get worse, and at least I knew what I was walking into every day.

It was easy to coast right along with Coach Carson.

The new coach glares as I stride past her. I'm five minutes late, but as we have all learned from countless punishment suicides: five minutes early is on time, and on time is late. So five minutes late is…bad. I give her an apologetic nod. Lake sits in the front row and watches me with a hint less animosity than our coach. I wave two fingers at her, still a little shocked she's on the team, and sit next to Rachel, Andy's roommate, in the row behind her.

"What's up, Em? You coming over tonight?" she asks in a hushed voice. Rachel cut her braids over the summer and now rocks a fade that's a shade lighter than her ebony skin and dapper as fuck.

I kick my bag under the table and sink into my hoodie. "Yeah. Of course." Apparently, I love going to Andy's dorm to torture myself as I watch her be so perfectly her and so far from mine. Maybe I'll be extra lucky and Maya will be there, her claws digging into Andy's thigh like a vise grip. As if she's scared I'll pounce on her girl the moment she lets go.

But I won't. Andy doesn't want me anymore. Hasn't wanted me in a long time. And because the universe loves a bad joke, it only makes me want her more. And more.

I think Rachel knows it, but she gives me the grace of pretending she doesn't because it's easier for us that way. If we ignore it, we can all still be friends and hang out. At the end of sophomore year, I think Andy knew it, too. Nothing gets past that girl. I remember how her eyes fluttered, like a loose lash was bothering her, and she turned away from me, choosing to accept my words and not what she knew was behind them: my feelings for her. And if she knows it now, she's ignoring it, too.

Coach Jordan walks to the front of the Den and obtrusively clears her throat. "Now that the entire team has arrived"—she glances at the clock I know is on the wall behind me—"seven minutes late, we'll begin. I'm Coach Jordan. As you are already aware, I came from Georgia State and am eager to build this Lion program back to its former prestige."

She takes a moment to look us over, surely matching our faces to our player profiles and photos on the roster. She lifts a hand to my new suitemate. "Lake was also at Georgia State and decided to transfer to Alder. As a Panther, she was our starting point guard and has a lot to offer this team."

I stare at the back of Lake's head. I may have been late to this meeting, but there's no way in hell she's taking my spot. There's also no way in hell she can play a different position at her height. And there's *no way in hell* I'm moving positions.

Welcome to the Lion's bench, Lake.

Coach goes on about team rules, her expectation of excellence, and every other thing I'd expect a new coach to drone on about. I shift in my seat as she very pointedly discusses her policy on being late. "Because Miss Wilson was late today, we'll be tacking on an extra hour of conditioning this week. That means one hour of individuals will now have to be an hour of open gym instead." She taps the desk with her marker. "And this will not be your standard conditioning, so please arrive fueled and hydrated."

My team shoots me side-eyes of disapproval. Guess that's the last time I show up late. My stomach churns in a funny way, and I fiddle with the sleeve of my sweatshirt. It's not that I'm apathetic. I care a lot. I want to win and be the best teammate possible. I just normally get away with this stuff. But now, I know and can adjust. It won't happen again.

"Fuck, dude," Rachel whispers.

I ignore her.

"Okay. That's about it," Coach Jordan says, her shoulder-length chestnut curls falling into her ruddy pale face and brushing over her freckles. She seems to be in her forties and has a bright look about her that balances her strict demeanor. "Classes start in a week, and

I expect you to put forth as much effort into your education as you do on the court. You'll find I don't tolerate anything less than your best." She turns to Coach Fulton, our assistant coach who has been here for at least a decade. "Anything you'd like to add, Coach?"

"Nope. Glad to have you here, Franny."

She nods. "Great. You're dismissed. See you tomorrow for conditioning."

❖

Walking through Wilder Hall fills me with a slurry of dread and excitement. Like, I know I shouldn't touch the flame, but I crave the heat. Need to burn. That's what it feels like to see Andy.

And I'm sure it feels like nothing for her to see me.

It's been a year. An entire year pining for a woman I could've had at any point during the six years prior. I would trade a decade of my life to turn back time, drive her to that little park on the Chattahoochee that we loved, and kiss her under all the constellations I don't know. A kiss she'd been hoping for, dreaming of, for years. And when she'd make love to me in my back seat, she wouldn't be thinking about anyone but us.

But that's just a distant dream that never came true.

Kissing her, being inside her, molding my body to hers in her dorm room. That was real, however brief, and it was a taste of the sweetest thing in the world. But it ended like a slap, left me shocked, wobbly, and teary-eyed.

I'm not quite over her, I guess.

"You good?" Rachel asks.

I nod. *Good enough.* She opens the door, and I follow.

"Hey, guys." Andy wraps me in a quick hug. I squeeze her tight before she pulls away and pats my shoulder. "How's the new coach? I'm dying to know everything."

Rachel flops on her bed in exasperation, her long limbs flailing in a dramatic show of agony. "Emma here got us a punishment conditioning. She was ten minutes late to the *first* team meeting."

Andy swats me. "Em," she says. And fuck, it does things to me when she scolds me like that. She's so *good.*

I remember to be normal. "Seven. Seven minutes late."

Andy tilts her head, her blond hair falling past her shoulder and blue eyes narrowing. We have the same color eyes, but somehow, on her, the blue is magic. She's normally pale as snow, but her slight summer tan makes her eyes pop. "That's just as bad, and you know it." She sits and scoots against the wall. I sit next to her like always, at least when Maya isn't here. Andy leans into my shoulder, then sways away. "Why were you late? Not much happening on campus right now."

Rachel chuckles and rubs her hands together. I want her to say exactly what I was doing so I can clock Andy's reaction. It will be nothing. She knows I've hooked up with women since the one time with her—a lot of women—but I still want to see.

"She was fucking Whitney Mahoney from the volleyball team." Rachel yanks her sweatshirt off and waves a finger. "Scratch that. She's *always* fucking Whitney Mahoney from the volleyball team."

Andy's brows scrunch together. She looks a little confused. "Why do you have to be so crass, Rach?" Then, she looks at me, and I see nothing. Nothing but a friendly friend full of friendly curiosity. *Fucking. Brutal.* "Do you like her, or is it more for fun?"

More for necessity. "Fun."

She shrugs. "Cool. Well, you probably need to set an alarm next time. Whenever Maya and I—"

"There's a transfer player from GSU. Followed Coach Jordan to Alder," I say. No way I'm listening to her tell me how she sets a million alarms when she fucks Maya before whatever thing they could be late to.

Rachel hops across the room in one leap and curls between us, stealing our closeness. I think Rachel knows exactly how I feel. *Asshole.*

"Well, hello." Andy rubs her back, and it bothers me that everyone in her world is now closer to her except for me. Rachel and Andy were never this close until now. I mean, they were close but not quite cuddle close. "What do you think of them, Rach?"

"It'll be cool to have a coach who cares. And Lake seems fine. Won't know until we see her play, but she's cute as hell."

"Short as hell," I say.

Andy laughs and reaches behind Rachel to poke me. "Is someone worried about their starting spot?"

I scoff. *Hell, no, I'm not.* "I doubt she can even see over the opposing point guard."

"And is she cute, Em?"

Lake is beyond cute. Beyond gorgeous. The only person I've met who makes me more nervous than Andy. Watching her watch me from the doorway of the bathroom was kind of hot. But she wants my position, and that's never going to happen. "Yeah. She's cute."

CHAPTER TWO

The protein bar I ate before conditioning spews against the black trash bag in a stream of yellow and white chunks. Lake watches as I pull my practice jersey from my shorts and wipe my mouth. She struggles for breath like the rest of the team, hands on knees and sweat dripping down her forehead and chest. The gym is stuffy, and I struggle to breathe between my dry heaves and, well, *wet* heaves.

This is the first time I've thrown up during practice since freshman year of high school. I don't like it. Makes me look weak. It's some sick poetic justice that I'm the reason for this hellish conditioning, and I'm the only one to vomit.

"Shit. You okay?" Nicky asks. She's the starting small forward and my favorite junior on the team. My favorite person on the team besides Rachel. She's wily and always down for an adventure.

"I'm good. I'm good."

Coach Jordan strolls over to my vomit corner of the gym, and I brace myself for whatever she's about to say or yell. "We have one more set, Emma. Take a minute, then back to the baseline."

Coach Jordan is fiery, but she also has these moments of something resembling tenderness. I nod, and Nicky hands me a water bottle after Coach leaves. "Come on. This is all your fault anyway."

I take a swig and try to catch my breath. "Fuck you, Nick. You missed an entire practice because you were boning Ben in the utility closet. You were just lucky Coach Carson was too clueless to notice."

"Girl, you better—"

The whistle pierces through the gym, and my stomach sinks. Coach Jordan is going to kill me with this conditioning before Nicky kills me for bringing up her on-again, off-again fling with Ben, our nerdy equipment manager. When we caught her last year, she tossed her braids over her shoulder and said, "What? The boy is packing."

We walk under the hoop, and I toe the baseline, trying to avoid eye contact with Lake. I hate that I'm giving her the impression I'm beatable. There isn't a chance on earth she's better than me. I just didn't hydrate properly or eat enough before this conditioning from hell.

Coach Jordan stands on the free throw line with a ball. She bounces it a few times, like she has zero cares in the world; it's not her ass on the line. I can tell from her few dribbles and the few shots I've seen her take that Coach is a true baller. She did play for Tennessee…

"One free throw. Someone needs to step up and make one free throw, then we're done for the day. If they miss, then we run it again. And again. Until someone makes it." She drops the ball and clears the line.

After a second, I take a step forward, but Lake is already halfway there. I fall back as she snags the ball with the same confidence and skill as Coach, almost like the ball is an extension of her. It pains me to watch her bounce it once, spin it in her hands, and shoot so effortlessly. We sigh in relief as it swishes through the net. But I also cringe. Lake isn't just good at basketball. She seems to have something special. *Fuck.* And I haven't even seen her play.

"Well done, Lake. All right, great work today. Y'all rest up this weekend for classes Monday." Everyone meanders to the water station, feet heavy and skin drenched with sweat. "Emma, meet me in my office after your shower."

Rachel and Nicky shoot me nervous glances. "Sure thing."

We walk together to the locker room. It may be one of my favorite places on campus, a locker room so nice, we don't deserve it with how badly we've done recently. Our names and numbers glow above our lockers, and we each have our own chair. There's a snack station along the far wall with a fridge that's always stocked with electrolyte water and protein shakes and a coffee maker that comes in handy after morning lifting. Lake is three lockers down from me on the other side of Quinn, one of our guards. I glance at her as she sorts her things.

She just met the entire team this week and has zero friends at Alder. Also, I'm the leader of this team, so approaching her is kind of my responsibility. I toss my dirty jersey in the team hamper and walk over. "Nice shot," I say.

She turns, raising an eyebrow in appraisal. "Why is it every time we speak, you don't have a shirt on?"

I glance down my torso, my sports bra soaked through with sweat and the waistband of my Nike compressions peeking out of my shorts. "Is that a problem for you?"

She pulls off her jersey and tosses it in the hamper with mine, and *holy shit*, she's hot. Her stomach is just as toned as her arms, and I want to lick the sweat from the shallow valley between her abs. "Nope. Not at all."

"I, uh, have to meet with Coach after I shower, but maybe we can grab lunch with Piper after?" This is nothing more than me fulfilling my team duties.

She stares. I think we're both dancing around each other, unsure how much of a threat the other one is. We've avoided all contact the entire week until now.

Finally, she nods. "Sure."

"Great. Can I get your number?"

I don't miss the way she sways slightly toward me. Or the way her hair is tied back, revealing her throat. "What? You're just going to remember it after hearing it once?"

I grin. "I'll remember it long enough to get it in my phone."

She recites the number, and I'm happy to hear the "404" Atlanta area code. I like Lake. For now. "Good luck remembering," she says, her smirk showing off a hint of a dimple. Just one.

"I'm usually pretty lucky," I say and head for the showers.

❖

After I towel dry my hair and eat a banana to replace some of the nutrients I ejected into the trash can, I stroll to Coach Carson's—Coach *Jordan's*—office. The door is cracked, so I knock once and push it slowly open. "Coach? You wanted to see me?"

She scrolls through something on the computer, an amber glow highlighting some of the gray in her hair. It's almost the same color as mine, but mine is a bit lighter, stuck in the middle of brown and blond, and is straighter and longer than hers. When I'm tan, like right now, my hair and skin are basically the same color.

"Emma, have a seat. I'll just be one more second."

I slink into the cushioned chair. Normally when I'm called into the office, it's for praise or Coach Carson wanting my feedback on something. It's never felt like this. Like I'm a disappointment. My dad would have my ass if he knew.

The office is similar to when Coach Carson inhabited it, except for the family photos. Now, a row of six stands atop the maroon square bookshelf on the back wall. A little girl and boy laugh and play, chasing each other from frame to frame. They look like Coach. There's a woman in a few of them with gray blond hair and a tall athletic build who I assume is Coach's partner. I like her more thinking she's queer.

After a few more taps on her keyboard, the glow from the screen disappears, and she turns to me. "Sorry about that. So, Emma, how did you find conditioning?"

Normally, when someone speaks to me—asks me a question or interacts with me in any way—I get a quick read on them. A read that tells me which direction to take our conversation and what they want from me. I think it's why I'm so successful with women, but staring at Coach, I have no idea what she wants from me or how to proceed. "Well, I haven't thrown up at practice since freshman year of high school, so I'd say it was…memorable."

The delicate crow's feet around her eyes deepen for a moment in a ghost of a smile before she narrows her eyes again. "As you can imagine, I watched countless hours of Lion game film before I accepted this job." She leans back, and it hits me that Coach Jordan kind of reminds me of me. Me if I had everything figured out, which feels less true every day. "You know what stood out to me in all that film?"

Again, I'm momentarily frozen, unsure of which direction she wants to drive us. "Um." *Shit.* I hate when I start with filler words. "A lot of Coach Carson yelling until he's as red as his shirt?"

A dimple forms in her cheek, but she clenches her jaw to keep the smile from blooming. I'll get there eventually. She leans on the desk and pushes her hair behind her ear. "I saw a lot of talent on that court. Talent that just needs more molding and guidance. It's a big reason I took this job. You ladies deserve to shine. And you, Emma, have more talent than most, but I need more from you. There's something holding you back, and I can see it plain as day when I watch your film."

"Holding me back?"

She steeples her fingers and presses them to her lips while she thinks. "Tell me, why did you choose basketball over softball? From what I've heard, you were an exceptional shortstop."

I fold over myself, elbows on knees, hating that I have no perception of this new coach. What she's getting at with all this. The point of this meeting. "I don't know. It was a long time ago. I guess I just like playing basketball more."

She nods as if she was expecting me to say that, but the answer clearly disappoints her. "We'll come back to that. Listen, you're an invaluable member of this team. And I want you to know that." She clears her throat. "I also want you to know that, in terms of positions and starters, everything is on the table."

I nod. Preseason just began. It'd be weird if she tried to blindly pick starters. I guess she's letting me know that Lake is in the running. *She's not.* But whatever. "Okay. I understand."

She stands and shoves her keys in her pocket, so I stand, too, assuming this weird little conversation is over.

"And, Emma, that is the last time you will be late. Do you understand?"

Her tone sends a jolt down my spine. Suddenly, I know exactly how to respond. “Yes, ma’am.”

She nods a dismissal, and I leave for the dining hall. Clouds a few shades darker than the stone gather over campus. Not many students have moved back for the semester, and everything is peaceful still. I like campus like this. It reminds me of freshman year, when Andy and I moved into our dorms early, me for preseason and her for me. That familiar ache in my chest returns.

The first week at Alder was the closest I’d ever come to kissing her. We’d just eaten dinner and were walking around campus, trying to memorize every little nook and cranny as the sun set.

“Oh, okay. This alley apparently does *not* connect through.” She turned to give me the smirk that she had perfected just for me, the golden light of dusk playing in her hair.

I took a few steps closer. “I could’ve sworn I walked through here the other day.”

She didn’t say anything, then. She just gave me this *look*, and I reached for her hand, pulling her into me. Only, I didn’t kiss her. Just wrapped her in a hug.

Any other girl, I would have kissed her. Taken her home.

I groan as I reach for the door to the dining hall. Biggest fucking regret of my life.

Chapter Three

Piper body slams me with a hug when she spots me browsing lunch options in the dining hall. About as short as Lake, she's a little dollop of big energy, a splash of glitter against the Alder stone. We're not as close as me and Rachel and Andy, but she makes my days better. And that's all I can really hope for from people.

"*Oof.* Hey, Pipes." I steady myself with a hand on her shoulder as she beams at me, a hint of red shading her dark brown cheeks. "When did you get back?"

She smooths her black hair and gathers Lake from behind her. "This morning while y'all were at practice." She tugs Lake by the hand. "Isn't she the best? And she's on your team. You guys are so lucky."

Lake's mouth stretches in a tight smile. Piper can be a lot.

"When's your first golf meeting?" I ask. It cracks me up that Piper is a golfer and totally straight. I thought golfing was supposed to be the gayest sport in the world.

"Not until Thursday." She grins, her gaze bouncing between me and Lake. "Are we all going to be best friends this year?"

Lake's eyes widen, and I can see the social anxiety behind them. I chuckle. "For sure. The bestest of friends."

After we buy lunch, we meet at a table near the fireplace. A summer storm brews outside, and the dark clouds dim the already cavernous dining hall. In a good way. Softer somehow, like a black-and-white photo, except for the roaring red of the fire. A rumble of thunder reverberates through the stone walls as I sit across from Lake, and Piper sits next to me.

"So, Lake, how do you like Alder so far?" Piper asks.

Lake takes a small sip of coffee and dabs the corner of her mouth with a napkin. Almost like she's stalling. So I hop in.

"Alder isn't so bad," I say. "I mean, it's a bummer you transferred all the way here just to ride the bench your senior year, but other than that—"

She barks a laugh, slapping the table and making Piper jump. Had a feeling that would liven her right up. "I didn't know you're funny, too. That's cute." She wipes her eyes. "Oh man. Good joke."

Piper chews her turkey club while she tracks me and Lake, as if she thinks we may reach over the table and fight one another. Lake stares at me, a hot challenge in her eyes, but she looks warm and inviting in her new Alder sweatshirt, blowing a gentle breath over the top of her steaming coffee. Her hair is pulled back in a bun, showing off the cut angles of her jaw and cheekbones. But there's a softness in her eyes, no matter how hard she tries to sharpen it. Something I can't quite put my finger on.

"No offense, but I've started at point for three years here," I say. My own turkey sandwich remains untouched, and I realize I'm starving. I take a huge bite.

"And I've started at point for three years under Coach Jordan."

"I guess you'll find out who's starting eventually. No use arguing about it now," Piper says.

I grin and give Lake a little kick under the table. "Yeah, Lake. I'm sure everything will work out just fine."

She tilts her head and pierces me with a raised brow. I kind of want her to cut me open. Dissect me. From my one week of knowing Lake, I get the sense that she's guarded—a bit serious—and it tickles me to push her buttons. It gives me butterflies to make her brow rise, as if she's breaking character just for me.

"So what are you studying?" Piper asks Lake, obviously trying to pivot away from our posturing.

She turns to Piper, her expression instantly lightening. "Communications. I want to be a sports broadcaster after I retire from the WNBA."

I choke on my sandwich. Wipe my mouth with the back of my hand. "The *WNBA*? The league that only has a hundred and forty-four roster spots available, and you don't even know if you're starting this year?"

She bobs her head, sucking her lips between her teeth. "You're the only one who isn't sure I'm starting." She takes another sip of coffee and makes a show of staring me down. Joke's on her, though. She doesn't know I like it. "Emotionally prepare yourself, Emma."

"Oh, broadcasting. That's super cool," Piper says, clearly trying to cut the tension. "And do you have any siblings?"

"I…" Lake shoots her a confused look, something dark flashing in her eyes. "What?"

Piper looks just as confused. I'm confused, too. "Siblings. Do you have any brothers or sisters?"

Lake hears the question loud and clear this time because she shakes her head. "No. No siblings."

"Me neither. But Emma is the oldest of four. Can you imagine?"

I shift on the bench. Something is off here, and Piper is oblivious. I hate the sudden melancholy that has clouded Lake. Her shoulders hunch, and her gaze isn't focused on anything, but scatters over the trays of food into a million little pieces.

"I'm a business major," I say. Lake doesn't look up, as if she didn't hear me. "My dad wants me to go to law school and be some hotshot merger lawyer, which sounds cool, I guess. Wouldn't mind making a shit ton of money."

"Oh yeah. I can totally see you rocking a power suit," Piper says.

My dad doesn't know this, but I'd *only* be in it for the money and power suits. Being a lawyer sounds about as riveting as a tepid bath. But, hey. It's just a job, and it will be a good one. Plus, if it gets him off my back, it will be worth it.

"Yeah, cool. Listen, I've got to run," Lake says and stands to leave. "Catch y'all later."

"Oh. Okay. Bye, Lake," Piper says.

She nods and walks away.

"I'll be right back." I jog to catch up before she makes it to the doors. "Lake, wait up."

She turns, looking annoyed that I stopped her escape. "What?"

I shake my head, unsure of what to say. Again, this never happens to me. Except for with Coach and Lake. "Just…I'm right next door."

Her brows scrunch together in a vee. "Yeah, I noticed."

"Okay. Well, I'll be there if you need anything. Contrary to what you may think, I'm actually pretty nice."

Her eyes drop to my chest, and my usual confidence surges through me. "You have a mustard stain on your sweatshirt."

I look down. A bright yellow stain on my left boob taunts me. I wipe at it like that would do anything. *Shit.* When I look up, Lake is gone.

When I get back to my room, I lie in bed and think about Lake. The door to the bathroom is shut. She's right there. I could go talk to her. *No.* She doesn't want to talk to me. Plus, she's kind of my mortal enemy. I consider calling Whitney, but I don't think I want her. I want…

I expect Andy to pop into my head like always. Instead, someone worse does.

My phone buzzes against my chest. *Dad.* I take a deep breath and answer.

"How's the new coach? Does she seem legit?" he asks, completely blowing through any and all pleasantries.

"Hello to you, too."

"Oh, come on. Don't be a smart-ass. Tell me everything."

I bristle at his intensity, as if every dark car ride after a game threatens to seep through my phone and strangle me. His disappointment. *What were you thinking, Emma? You should've taken that shot.* Sometimes, I think the only reason he doesn't care that I'm a lesbian is because in his mind, I won't be getting fucked or dominated by someone. I'll be doing the fucking and dominating, as a Wilson should. He has no grip on reality in that way; I love to be fucked.

Let's just get this over with. "She seems good."

I hear him sigh in annoyance. "Good? What's that supposed to mean?"

"You know, she seems like a good coach." I need to say more to satisfy him, but the truth is, I still don't know about Coach Jordan. Her style, her methodology, her playbook. "Very…thorough."

My dad grunts. I don't know why he's still so obsessed with my basketball career. I don't have any illusions of going to the WNBA—well, not anymore—and though I'm extremely competitive and want every second on the court I can get, I don't see why he cares. For as much as *I* care about basketball, this season won't affect my life at all. Win or lose. He's just obsessed with success.

"Let me know more once you all settle in," he says.

"Yeah. For sure."

"All set for the LSAT next month? We have to get those law school applications polished and ready."

"All set."

"Great. Call us after your first week of class and give Andy our best. Love you, Emma Bear." The familiar nickname is always like a dab of aloe on a sunburn. A reminder that my dad loves me and that I have it all. A little brother, two little sisters, and two parents who love each other and us.

I have it all.

"Okay. Love you, too."

We hang up, and I roll onto my belly, smothering my face in my pillow. That was one of the biggest lies I've ever told. And I keep telling it. And telling it. I haven't registered for the LSAT, and I don't really plan on registering for the LSAT. I don't really plan on *anything*. The sinking feeling that started after Andy made it official with Maya pushes me under. *Sinking. Sinking.* I'm nervous all the time now. The complete opposite of who I am. I'm confident and effortlessly successful. And have everything figured out. I'm Emma Wilson.

Chapter Four

Em, get over here," Professor Weber says, his tree-trunk arms spread wide for me and his belly accentuated by his favorite purple belt. The black beard that covers his big cheeks is mostly kempt, but as the semester progresses, it will become more and more scraggly. His clear brown eyes twinkle behind his Warby Parkers, the thick frames dark against his freckled pale skin.

I step into his hug and try to connect my fingers around his back, but he's too wide. "Missed you, Weber." And I did. Some people just feel like home, and Doug Weber is one of those people for me. He's been my professor for various business classes since freshman year, and we struck up a close connection. He's like the older brother I never had. I would definitely trade my little brother for him.

"We need to talk about the LSAT soon," he says as other students flow into the classroom. He must catch my vibe because he adds, "Or not," and lightly pushes me in the shoulder. "You know, the best thing about majoring in business is that it can take you just about anywhere you want to go. Mergers and acquisitions, well, that could be for the birds if you wanted. Either way, I'm here for you, kid."

I grin and shove him back. "Get off that 'kid' garbage. We have to be the same generation."

"I'm offended, and you obviously don't know how generations work. I'm pure Millennial gold."

"Whatever you say, Doug."

"That's right, Angelica."

I *hate* my middle name, and he knows it. "Dick," I mutter and sit in an open seat in the second row.

Ever since *the sinking*, let's call it, these little chips in my confidence have grown like holes in the ozone layer, and the nearing of graduation is only exacerbating everything. But not here. Not really. Sure, I lied to my dad and have no plans to take the LSAT. Sure, I have no plans *at all*. But one thing I do know is these courses are as easy as a slice of pecan pie, and I will graduate come May. No problem. I lean back in my chair and enjoy the feeling of being in control at least of that.

The rest…I don't know. It'll sort itself out, surely.

As Weber regales us with tales of his summer and tells us what this semester will bring, I think about basketball. Well, I'm always thinking about basketball. More specifically, I think about Coach Jordan and Lake Palmer. They both have this air about them. As if they *know* something. Not a secret but, like, a truth.

A pencil flies from the front of the room and bounces across the wood of my desk, startling me out of my thoughts.

"Emma, bring it back. It hurts my ego when you daze off on day one. Save it for next class. I'm not done talking about my trip to Brazil," Weber says.

I grin. "Apologies. Please, continue."

After class, I walk to the Den for my solo, and a nervous feeling brews in the pit of my stomach. This solo is with Lake. Just me and her. And Coach Fulton. But who cares about him? Part of me is curious as to why Coach Jordan doesn't want to see us run all the same drills and exercises side-by-side, but I know she'll get the report after.

"Hey, Emma. Hop on up," Suzy says. She's a year or two older than us and is our graduate assistant trainer and ankle wrapper extraordinaire. We see her before and after practice and games.

I hop onto the cushioned table and lean back while she wraps my left ankle in prewrap. I love getting wrapped by her. Kind of comforting to have someone take care of me like this. It could also be that I'm in love with every woman in my life in some way or another, and Suzy always looks so cute in her maroon Polo that stretches over her breasts and her quintessential khakis and white Nikes. "Thanks," I say and bite my lip as she leans over my leg.

Suzy can get it.

"I really like Coach Jordan," she says. "It's going to be an epic season. I can just feel it."

She rips the tape with such precision, the mere sound of it turns me on. I know, I'm an animal. "Yeah. She seems cool."

She smooths the end of a piece of tape and looks up at me with her light hazel eyes. Her left brow arches, and a sexy smirk forms on her lips. "Heard she made you throw up at conditioning."

Did I mention I love getting wrapped because I have a crush on Suzy and am so into our little training room interactions? The way she looks at me sometimes makes me want to lie her down on this table. It's soft. We could do some fun things with the athletic tape. With the ice…

I lean closer and hold her gaze. "Me? Throw up at practice? Now, come on, Suzy. You can't believe everything you hear out there." She gives me a look like she knows all my bullshit is bullshit and rips a crisp piece of tape. "I prefer 'vomited,'" I add through a grin.

"You are too much, Emma."

Then it hits me. It's senior year. Suzy is kind of fair game now. This flirting could build and build until postseason when I'm no longer part of the team, and then…*boom*.

"Too much? Or just enough?" I ask.

A flash of something I can't pinpoint heats her eyes. It's something good. She likes it. We stare at each other over my mummy foot for a beat, the quiet of the training room buzzing around us, her fingers resting on my shin. Are we about to make a fun mistake?

"Hey."

We jump away from each other at the sound of a voice. Lake's voice. She hops on the table next to me looking fresh and beautiful. The Alder colors look good on her, and I enjoy the amount of skin our practice jersey leaves exposed. Vascular arms, a hint of her sports bra, collarbone. "Hey, Lake. Getting wrapped?"

She looks at me like that was the stupidest question she's ever heard. "Yeah." Then, she looks at Suzy, who busies herself with the finishing touches on my ankle. When Lake meets my gaze again, she narrows her brows and gives me a slight shake of her head, as if she knows exactly what she walked in on.

"Be right with you, Lake," Suzy says. "Welcome, by the way. We're glad to have you and Coach Jordan."

"Thanks."

Suzy nods. "Right. I'm just going to grab another roll of prewrap, and I'll be back."

"Emma," Lake says. And I look at her again. It's hard not to look at her, really. She has a levity about her today. A hint of a smile pulls at the corner of her lips, and she peeks over her shoulder to make sure Suzy is still occupied. "I'm pretty sure you're not allowed to fuck our trainer," she whispers.

"I don't remember reading that in the team handbook. Besides, I'm not the type." I press a hand to my chest as if I'm scandalized by the idea.

Lake laughs, and I soak up every note of it. It's effervescent and gravely, like riverbank pebbles drying in the summer sun. It's the first time I've heard it, and all I want is to find the keys that hit those notes. "Something tells me you're exactly the type."

I shake my head. "You have no evidence."

"I can hear you snore. Can you imagine what else I hear?"

Okay, so I hooked up with Whitney one more time on Saturday night. Sue me. But that's—probably—the last time. I hate that Lake heard it, but it also kind of turns me on. She doesn't seem bothered by it. Just amused. "My nightly prayers?"

She bellows a laugh, and I like how I can see the veins in her neck, can see how I've made her blood rush. "Something like that."

Suzy appears with the prewrap, ending our conversation for now. "Okay. Emma, you're good to go. Your turn, Lake."

I lace my shoe and slide off the table. "Catch ya on the court."

❖

I always thought the pump fake, quick dribble, and shot was, like, my specialty. But training with Lake is making me feel like it may be hers. The way she moves with the ball is so seamless, as if it's magnetized to her. Sticks to her like a sweaty jersey.

"Good. Five more," Coach Fulton says.

I sink back into my dummy defense, and Lake fixes her gaze on mine. Her eyes are different on the court, stormy and penetrating. "Slowing down on me already?" she asks, just loud enough for me to hear.

It's early enough in the season that I'm not too stressed about our competition for point guard. Right now, it feels almost flirtatious and fun. "I want you to be able to practice your shots for when we actually scrimmage."

She pump-fakes, takes a sharp dribble to her right, and sinks a shot so effortlessly, a flare of jealousy ignites in me. "Sure about that?" The challenge in her eyes lights something else in me. Kindling low in my gut.

"Let's study together later."

The ball bounces under the hoop, and Coach Fulton tosses it back to Lake. She spins it in her palm as she contemplates my offer. I didn't even consider how silly it was until it was already out of my mouth. "Study together?"

I nod. Unfortunately, I'm a double-down-on-my-mistakes type of person. Watch me charge straight into a losing battle.

She hits another shot. Has only missed one. "It's the first day of classes. Not sure I need to study the syllabus."

I roll the ball off my fingertips, and it bounces in front of her. "You sure? Some of the phrasing can be tricky in there. Plus, are you positive you know which professors are cool with you retaking exams we miss because of games?"

She smirks. "If you think I transferred during my senior year to a new university without thoroughly researching every class and professor and teammate"—she looks pointedly at me—"then you really don't know me at all."

"I *don't* know you at all." I shove her gently in the shoulder. "Come on. Let's fix that." I shrug. "You know, for the team's sake or whatever."

She continues to stare at me with that mysterious look.

"Hang out with me," I say softly.

"Ladies," Coach Fulton calls. "Let's keep at it. We don't have all day." I forget to squat into a defensive position as Lake runs through the drill again. *Swish.* "Emma, come on. Give her a defender. Okay, let's take a water break."

He passes the ball back to Lake, and she holds it on her hip, examining me. "Do you always have to beg for it?"

I feel blush rolling through my cheeks like a storm front. A rarity for me. Typically, I'm the one making women blush. But the way her eyes roam over me is utterly agitating. "Only with you."

She shoves the ball into me with unnecessary force, and a puff of breath escapes my mouth. "You're cute when you beg, Emma."

I know she just stole some literal breath from me with the ball, but as I watch her stride to the water station, it's clear something else is keeping me from breathing. Her flirtatious words, her hips as she moves, her everything. I like Lake very much. "Was that a yes?" I call after her.

"Yes."

❖

Rachel: *How was your solo with Lake? You didn't kill each other, did you?*

I eat a burrito alone on a bench outside of Lipsey Hall, where my business classes are, balancing my phone in my clean hand and trying to avoid burrito juice dripping onto my legs with the other. It's still warm out, so I wear a light gray tee and navy shorts. I look good in these shorts.

Me: *We did not kill each other. Don't worry.*

Rachel: *Come over and hang.*

As I read her invitation, it hits me that I haven't thought about Andy all afternoon until now. And yeah, the sharp arrow of her pierces my chest again, but it's progress. Half of me wants to see her, but I have someone else I'm looking forward to seeing, too.

Me: *Nah. I'm good. I'll catch you tomorrow.*

Rachel: *Maya won't be here.*

Me: *It's not about that.*

Rachel: *It's always about that.*

Me: *Don't be a dick.*

Rachel: *Don't be a lovesick puppy over someone who's been in a relationship for over a year with someone else.*

Me: *Dick.*

I push my phone into my pocket and wrap the rest of my burrito, wiping my hands on my already dirty napkin. Rachel rarely calls me out on that shit. *Fuck.* I hate being so obviously pitiful. And I hate that Rachel seems annoyed with me. I sigh and try to rub the back bar of the bench under my shoulder blade. That one spot I just can't get. There's a knot that's been driving me—

Lake appears out of literal nowhere and sits next to me.

"Shit," I say, hand pressed to my chest. "Scared me."

"My bad. Just saw you over here rubbing your back like a bear. Need a hand?"

I stare into her eyes for a moment too long before I remember to answer. "That'd be great. Thanks."

She guides me into her by my hips, then digs her thumb into the exact spot I need it. As she works on me, completely encompassing me with her hands, the skin of her inner thigh against my hip, and her gentle breath on my neck, I groan in obvious pleasure. "You're like a rag doll. Stay still," she commands, bringing her other arm over my chest like a bar on a roller coaster, so I stop flopping forward with every rub.

"*Argh.*" I groan again. When I accidentally brace myself with a hand on her bare leg, she releases me.

"Well," she starts, sounding a little breathless. "Hope that helped." She slides away, putting a foot of distance between us.

I rub my neck and face her. She wears an Alder tee and cute jean cutoffs. But my favorite thing is the peach-colored plastic glasses. "You came out of nowhere."

She grins and pushes a loc behind her ear. "If Lipsey Hall is nowhere, then yeah."

"Why were you there?"

"Talking to one of my communications professors."

"Ah, okay."

We sit in quiet for a moment, looking at each other. It doesn't feel awkward; it feels like sinking into a hot tub. Her gaze moves from mine, to my ear, to my neck, then back to my eyes, a curious expression spread over her face. "So. Where did you want to 'study'?"

I nod. "Right. Let's 'study,' um"—I think about where I want to hang out with her the most—"in my room."

She arches her brow as she considers my offer, then she shrugs. "Okay."

Chapter Five

I glance around my room, pleased at the lack of clothes, specifically Whitney's clothes, strewn about. "I cleaned," I say with a bit of pride.

Lake steps carefully into my room as if on alert for booby traps or the real reason I asked her to "study" with me. I don't even know the reason, really. Her presence is low-key intoxicating, but her presence *on the team* scares me. Both of those things make me want to keep her close.

She runs her fingers over my desk and chuckles. "We could say *tidied*. You tidied."

I sit on the edge of my bed and watch her, enjoying the little gaps that form between her waistband and body every time she moves. She shoots me the look I'm beginning to associate with her the most. The one that says she sees straight through my bullshit and is, at least, mildly entertained by me.

I shrug. "Okay. *Tidied.* I'll take whatever you want to give me." A surge of heat swells in my gut when I see my words are like a whetstone sharpening her gaze. She smirks and sits next to me, our bare thighs pressing together, an oddly innocent site for where all my blood seems to be rushing.

"As if you could handle that," she says slowly, as if she wants me to memorize her words.

Dead. *I'm dead.* For a moment, I consider if I could, in fact, handle that. Something about it intimidates me, so I pivot. "Where are you from?"

She takes a second to adjust. "Atlanta."

I grin, though I already knew from her area code. "Same. Favorite food?"

She clamps both hands on her knees as she thinks. She smells fresh and sweet. Like orange zest and honey. "Hmm. I love pretty much all food, but the thing I get most excited to eat is probably mushroom risotto."

"Mushroom risotto?" I don't know why this surprises me. Probably because I've never had risotto.

"Yeah. My family makes it on special occasions." She considers me. "What? Do you not like mushrooms?"

I shake my head. "I love mushrooms. There's not a food in the world I wouldn't eat. Just have never had risotto."

Her jaw drops. Drops so hard, I can see the glistening wet of her tongue. "How can you have never had risotto? It's like"—she makes a show of her head exploding—"the most warming, savory meal ever. It's my delicious."

Something about the way she says that last bit... "Your *delicious*?"

"Yeah." Her face brightens for a second, then falls. "My delicious." She rubs her knee and shakes her head. "It's from this old book, *The Search for Delicious*. About this boy who has to poll the entire kingdom to find what is delicious, and obviously, everyone thinks something different." She pauses, seemingly debating her next words, and meets my gaze. "My older brother would read it to me when I couldn't sleep."

"I thought you said you don't—"

She nudges me, cutting me off. "But really, Emma. How have you not had risotto?"

I shrug. "I don't know. I'm one of four, and we all play sports and have these wild schedules, so big family dinners are a bit of a rarity. We do lots of spaghetti, meat loaf, and turkey sandwiches. The easier the meal, the better for my mom."

"Well, we'll get you some risotto one day. Don't you worry." She seems to relax and leans back on her elbows in a sexy lounge. I wonder if I should do the same. *Of course.* I lean back on one elbow, facing her. It's quiet for a moment as we adjust to our new positions.

We aren't touching, but something about it feels intimate. Like maybe we shouldn't be doing it. Then, Lake looks at me. Looks *down* me. "What's your delicious, Emma?" she almost whispers.

I feel delicious all over. Fuzzy and sweet. An ache gathers between my thighs as I watch her watching me. I swallow. "I…don't know. Maybe I haven't found it yet." But looking at her lips makes me feel like they're the place to start.

She shrugs. "I think when you taste it, you'll know."

I wonder what she would do if she knew what I was thinking as my gaze slips to her mouth. Something about her confidence makes me want to be strong. Something about the way she looks at me makes me want to be vulnerable. Every time she catches my eye, she pulls something from me, threading us together somehow. When our conversation slows and our gazes linger, I decide it's best to keep talking. Otherwise, something may happen. Something already is. Lake feels inevitable.

"I really like biscuits," I sputter. She grins and covers her mouth with her hand as if trying not to offend me. It gives me butterflies. "Not the dry kind that stick in your throat," I assure her. "The savory kind with bits of cheese and sausage and garlic. Maybe that's my delicious."

"Maybe." She squeezes my arm, and I feel her touch everywhere. "But I have a feeling there's something else out there for you. And when you taste it, your mind will be completely blown." She smiles. "I want to be there when it happens." Her hand drops to the mattress, and I instantly miss it.

I grin. "Oh yeah? I guess you have to join me for every meal now. Don't want to miss the big moment."

She laughs and lies on her back. I inch closer, my fingers so close to her waist. "I have a feeling it's not going to happen in the dining hall."

"You don't know that," I say. I take a deep breath and finger the thick fabric of her belt loop. She probably can't even feel me touching her, but I'm engulfed by flames. "I'm very easy to please."

Her hand slides off her stomach on top of mine, and the entire world stops. My room is hazy in my peripheral as I stare at her, my hand frozen under hers. Her thumb brushes slowly and gently over my knuckles, a centimeter at a time, and I've never felt so alive. My entire existence at her fingertips.

"Are you?" she asks. Her voice is quiet, and I get the feeling that we're not talking about food anymore. I wiggle my finger through her belt loop and give it a soft tug, wanting to be sure she feels me there. On her hip. Under her fingers.

"Yeah. But I'm not looking for easy. I'm looking for someone to blow my mind."

Her lips pluck apart, and she drags in a slow breath. "*Someone*, huh?" She strokes my fingers as I stare at her.

"Someone." My entire body buzzes like radio waves. "Someone who makes me feel like I'm going to pass out just from her hand on mine." I lick my lips. "Or from tugging her belt loop."

A knock on the door startles me into a sitting position. I yell for whoever it is to come in. Lake straightens, too, fixing her hair and adjusting her glasses. Our moment vanishes, and I mourn it.

My door creaks open, and—

"Andy." I shoot off the bed to wrap her in a hug, faintly registering the pitch at which I basically yell her name and how that must look to an outsider like Lake.

"Hey, Em." She hugs me back, and I'm momentarily absorbed by her familiar warmth, my feelings for her racing back to me like it's all muscle memory. I briefly wonder if I'll ever be able to forget her.

A bit of clarity settles over me, and I take a step back, remembering Lake is watching all this. My face burns. "Um. This is Lake, my new teammate." I turn to introduce them. "Lake, this is Andy, my…friend."

Lake's brows rise as she nods and pushes off my bed. "Hi Andy. It's nice to meet you." They shake hands, and Lake reaches for the door. "I was just going, anyways. I'll leave y'all to it."

"You don't have to," I start. But then I realize Andy and I are about to hang out in my room alone. Lake pauses at the door. "Well, okay. But I'll catch you soon. Obviously." *What the actual fuck am I doing?* Everything feels wrong.

She sucks in her lips and takes one more look at us before she leaves, and all my focus is back on Andy.

I take her by the elbow and guide her to my bed where Lake was just sitting. "What's up? I didn't know you were coming over."

Her blue eyes scan my room, a sweet smile on her lips. "I texted you, silly. Where's your phone?"

I was so absorbed by Lake, I have no idea where my phone is. Something tugs my gut. *Lake.* "I don't know. It doesn't matter." I wave dismissively at the room. "Anyway. What are you doing here?"

She squeezes my shoulder. "Just popping in to say hi and to see how your practices have been going."

"Fine. Yeah, they're fine." I don't know why I don't want to elaborate or why I feel like a want to keep Lake from Andy and Andy from Lake.

She gently pushes against my shoulder. It lacks the bit of fire from when Lake did the same thing. "She's cute," she says.

And, *ugh*, I hate it. I still fucking hate it. She sounds like she's trying to pawn me off on someone so she doesn't have to be bothered by my emotions, which I *never* bother her with. I'm perfectly quiet and self-loathing on the matter, not bothering anyone—except rarely Rachel—with my giant broken heart.

"Yeah. Want me to give you her number?"

She chuckles. A sound that normally warms me and makes me feel at home but hits me like a slap of condescension. "You know what I mean. She's cute for you."

"Andy." I say her name a little too sharply, and she looks at me with a nervous glance. "I'm fine. I've always been fine." We're quiet for a couple seconds.

"Are you?" she asks so softly, it almost doesn't hurt.

I stare at her. At the face I've known for ten years. The face I've dreamt of for six. Her blond waves are wind-tousled and free, and her knobby knees are pinched together. A couple of circular bruises dot her thighs. She always did bruise easily, but it makes me nauseated because I know why she's littered with them now: Maya's fingers digging into her. "What do you want me to say, Andy?"

"It's been a year."

I straighten. "I am very aware of that." She stays quiet, staring at me. And it really starts to piss me all the way off. "Do you want me to just sit here and tell you how much pain I've been in? Is that what you want?"

"Emma—"

"Every damn day has felt like a year without you. Without the possibility of you. You happy now?" A flash of hurt passes over her face, and I look away. Can't take it. "Why are you doing this now? I don't bother you and Maya. I keep my mouth shut. And I definitely don't burden—"

"Hey." Her fingers curl around my wrist. "Don't do that." I take a deep breath and look at her, waiting for her to say something that makes sense. "You don't have to yell at me or Maya or storm out of a party or make a scene for me to know how you feel. I know you. I've known you forever. And I've given you time and space to heal from this, but I'm concerned. I don't want to be cruel to you if you're not…" She looks around my room as if looking for words. "Over me."

I hear the shower, and I know it's Lake. I wonder if she heard any of this. Not that she needs to hear anything to know something weird is going on with me and Andy. I'm sure she could sense it right when Andy walked in. I realize I miss her, Lake.

I roll out my shoulders and try my best to let this go. To let Andy go. I know I can't completely. Not yet. But I'm trying. "Look. You're right, okay? But I'm not willing to stop being friends. I don't need you to nurse me through this, I just need you to be my friend. It's not your fault, and you're not being cruel by hanging out with me. I'm fine. I'm going to be fine."

It's basically the same conversation we had at the end of sophomore year, so I don't know if anything has changed, but she nods. "I'm sorry. I didn't mean to upset you. I just want to be a good friend to you."

"You are." I take her hand and squeeze. "But I kind of really hate this conversation and am ready for it to be over."

"Yeah. I hate it, too."

"How's your dad?"

She drops her head back and laughs. "Wow, you really know how to lighten a conversation, Em."

I grimace. "I'm sorry. Not my best move."

She slides her hand casually out of mine. "It's bad."

"I'm always here for you," I say. Because what else do you say to something like that? It's only a matter of months before Andy's father passes away. We all know this.

Andy pats my knee and smiles. "And I'm always here for you."

"I love you and all. And yeah, you broke my heart or whatever. But you kind of interrupted something."

"Oh?" She scrunches her brows and thinks about what I'm saying. "*Oh.* I knew it." She shoves my shoulder. "Bring your A game, Emma Wilson. That one just may be out of your league."

She stands to leave. "Impossible," I say, but I know she's right.

"We'll see." She winks and disappears into the hallway.

I spy my phone on my desk and grab it. Lake's initials in my phone are encapsulated in a red circle. I hit the message button.

Hey. Sorry about the interruption. It doesn't feel like we got to finish our studying, and that's my bad. Do you want to pop back over?

I stare at the ceiling, trying to untangle my feelings. For Andy and for Lake. My feelings for Andy are a jumbled mess of everything. But my feelings for Lake are sharp and clear. I have a huge crush on her.

My phone buzzes on my chest, and I rush to open the message.

Nah, I'm good. Good night, Emma.

I groan as I reread the words next to her name. I close our conversation and text Whit.

CHAPTER SIX

The squeak and screech of basketball shoes on freshly waxed wood fills the gym. I backpedal down the court after taking Lake to the hoop and scoring. She fouled me, but Coach didn't call it. For our scrimmage, the teams are split evenly and in a way that makes it hard to tell if one team is made of potential starters and one isn't. But Rachel and Nicky are on my team, so I'm feeling pretty good.

It's been three weeks since Lake came to my room to "study" with me, and I've thought about her sitting next to me on my bed, her hand on mine, every day. Since Andy interrupted us, it's like Lake has done a one-eighty on me. She's not mean, but in every interaction, her entire being screams *disinterested.* Unless we're on the court scrimmaging or going head-to-head in drills, then it screams *get the fuck out of my way.*

Coach Jordan still has not mentioned starters and hasn't pulled me aside for another meeting, yet. Though she has been at more of our solos. And for the last few weeks—

My back hits the court, and every ounce of air in my lungs vanishes. I roll over to my hands and knees and gasp for breath.

"Shit, Lake," Rachel says as she kneels next to me and puts a hand on my back.

I try to capture some kind of oxygen as Coach Jordan blows her whistle and joins us at the top of the key. I'm fine. Lake just knocked the wind out of me.

"Foul," I manage to eke out with a few labored chuckles. Leave it to me to crack jokes on all fours in front of my new coach.

Lake scoffs. "Your feet were moving."

"Lake," Coach Jordan says. Her tone makes it sound almost like a scolding.

"Her feet were moving, Coach."

Everyone stops milling around to focus on this interaction. We all think Lake is the golden player and Coach's pet, so this little conversation is intriguing. I extend a hand to Rachel, and she pulls me off the ground. I smooth my jersey and join my team in listening.

"There's playing hard, then there's whatever you just did."

"Coach, she—"

"See me after practice." Lake nods. "Emma, you good?" I nod. "Okay, let's go."

The next play, I take the ball down the court with my eye on Rachel. She's been battling in the paint, and it's time to feed her. She hooks a leg in front of Molly and gives me a target, but when I cross the ball over, Lake steals it. I chase her down before she can score an easy layup and get a fistful of her jersey. No, this is not legal. Yes, it's completely against the rules. I tug her backward, bringing her to a halt, and wrap my arms around her waist. Then, because I'm brilliant, I pick her up from behind while she squirms and protests and curses me and place her out-of-bounds. With the ball in her hands.

The shrill whistle sounds. "Emma. Dare I ask what that was?" Coach Jordan calls, her voice sounding tired and annoyed.

Lake glowers at me. "What the hell?"

I look at her feet and the ball in her hands. "Looks like you've run out-of-bounds. Our ball." I extend my hand.

The horrified look on her face makes my little charade completely worth it. Lake may be a beautiful player. Lake may care more than anyone. Lake may be Coach's favorite. But Lake isn't me. She plays with so much grit and seriousness, I wonder sometimes if she remembers to have fun. To let it hang loose.

She stares at me with her mouth hanging slightly open. Then at Coach.

"Lake, take it from the top of the key," Coach Jordan says. She claps. "Let's go. Let's go."

❖

The rest of the scrimmage was a bit tense. Lake glares at me occasionally from her locker as I slip on my sweatshirt and towel dry my hair. She looks incredible today—every day, really—with tight dark jeans, white Nikes, and a light gray Alder tee snug around her breasts. A goddamn college dream girl. She catches me staring and walks over. I pretend to busy myself in my locker.

"You fouled me," she says, as if she didn't knock the shit out of me the play before.

I pull my head out of my locker like I'm surprised to see her. "Oh, Lake. Hi."

She sighs and rolls her eyes. Her cheeks are a touch rosy from the shower, and I still love those glasses. "What? You just couldn't stand being beat, so you had to ruin the play like a five-year-old?"

I look her up and down in obvious consideration. "Really? I doubt a five-year-old could pick you up. Even if you are very, very small." I pinch my fingers in front of her face.

She gives me a light shove in the shoulder. "You're so annoying," she says. But she says it in a low voice that does something to me. Makes me feel like she doesn't mind being annoyed by me. I grin and flick her wrist, and she swats me. I'm the oldest of four; my flicks hurt like hell. "Emma," she scolds as she rubs her wrist. The sound of her saying my name like that goes straight to my core.

"That's for knocking the wind out of me. And for shoving me just now. Oh, and for bailing on our study session."

She scoffs and takes a step backward. "You bailed on me. I want to stay as far away as possible from whatever's going on between you and that girl."

"There's nothing going on between me and Andy."

She arches her brow, and it peeks at me over her plastic frames. "You're a bad liar. And it's none of my business, but when she walked through that door"—her eyes widen as she shakes her head and takes another step back—"let's just say your priorities are crystal clear. And that's cool, but I don't want to be involved."

I hurt her. I'm momentarily speechless as that fact soaks in. I invited a friend over and basically asked them to leave fifteen minutes later so I could hang out with someone else. Yeah, that tracks. "Walk back with me," I say.

"No."

"Please."

"I have to talk to Coach because of your bullshit." She pushes her glasses up her nose and pins me with a look of disdain.

I tilt my head back and forth, debating if I'm going to say what I want to say, but we all know I'm gonna say it. I shrug. "I think you have to talk to Coach because of *your* bullshit."

Rachel appears to my right and slaps my shoulder. "Let's go eat. I'm starving."

Lake continues to stare like I'm her worst nightmare. And because I'm kind of an asshole, I wink. "Have a nice chat with Coach."

I walk away as she shakes her head.

❖

"Okay, so," Rachel starts. Her mouth is full of pizza, and her words are gummy and wet. "You hate her."

I shake my head. "No. She hates me. I think I…" I tilt my head to look at the ceiling as I consider my next words. "I think I like her."

Rachel stares at me. "Care to elaborate?"

"I like her," I say again. "She's got a lot of feelings in there, I think. Or emotions or something." I shrug. "I don't know. The girl is deep, and she's a baller." I shake my head. "And, like, *so* hot. What's not to like?" And she sets me on fire when she touches me.

Rachel drops a pizza crust. "Oh, I don't know. Maybe the fact that she tried to flatten you into the earth today." It's cute that Rachel is protective of me. Makes me feel all loved and shit.

"She's got a lot going on. Can you imagine transferring your senior year and not knowing anyone?"

She shrugs. "That was her decision."

I take a bite of pepperoni pizza, and the hot tomato sauce sticks to the roof of my mouth, burning me. "Ah, shit." I fan my mouth and take a sip of water. "Just give her a chance and let it go. Okay?"

"Fine." She rolls her eyes. "Andy told me she dropped in on you two a couple weeks ago."

"You make it sound like she walked in on us doing something."

She raises a brow and stares at me over her pizza. "Were you?"

"Really? You think I got Lake to hook up with me within her first week here? When you know damn well we can't hook up with teammates—I think—*and* she's gunning for my position?"

Rachel shrugs. "Yeah."

I chuckle. I guess it does kind of sound like me. "Well, I didn't. But, yeah, Andy dropped by for a chat."

"And?"

"And it was great." I shake my head. "I mean, it was brutal at first. She was worried she was being cruel because it's become clear that I'm not over her. It's nothing new, really. But I told her I wanted to be her friend, and everything would be okay. Progress."

Rachel stares for longer than I'd like. "She really fucked you up, huh?"

I drop my head back and sigh. "I deserve it."

"No, you don't. Sometimes you have your head, like, really far up your ass. But in general, you're a solid person."

"A *solid* person?

She nods. "Solid."

I chuckle into my napkin. "I'm pretty sure that's the worst compliment I've ever received. The last thing I'd want on my gravestone. Emma Wilson, she was a solid person."

"I'd take it if I were you. I know some women who wouldn't be so generous in their description of you."

"Right back at ya."

❖

The rest of the week passes slowly. I think it feels so slow because Lake still refuses to interact with me beyond accidental touching at practice. I love guarding her. Love when our sweaty arms brush against each other and when she puts a hand on my back to keep track of me. She plays a little dirty like me, tugging my jersey and backing her ass into me with enough force to make me stumble.

And Coach Jordan continues to be hard on me. I'm not sure why, since I haven't been late since our first team meeting, and from my vantage point, Lake is the one with the problem. But I can just feel it. She's always slightly disappointed in me. With the real season just around the corner and real practices starting in two weeks, I still have a lot of opportunities to prove myself. To prove I'm the best pick for the job.

"*Oof.* A little tight, yeah?"

Suzy looks up from my ankle as if I just asked her to take her pants off. "Can't handle it?" she asks in a whisper.

And there it is. *She's mine.* I glance at her breasts pushing against that damn Polo and wonder if we could get away with something. There's always her office.

This is the thing that always happens to me. I can't turn it off, and I honestly don't want to. As Suzy stares at me, her fingers resting on the bare skin of my calf, I decide I want to make a mistake with her. Whether that mistake happens today or next month, I don't care.

Sometimes, I can hear a voice in my head warning me, but I have the uncanny ability to ignore it, and I've been ignoring it a lot lately. I think it's because I don't have much to look forward to. I'm lying to my father about taking the LSAT, Andy is gone, and I may not even start this year. Then what? I graduate into nothing. An emptiness I've never known fills me a little more each day. But when women want me the way Suzy does—out of nowhere and for no reason—it makes me feel…*something*. At least one thing about me has to be good if so many women are attracted to me.

So yeah, I want to fuck Suzy on her desk while she wears that nerdy Polo. I want to unzip those khakis and push my hand into her panties. Just the thought makes me feel alive again.

I lean forward so our heads are only a foot apart. "There's not much I can't handle. But this"—I push her hand to the tip of her tape job, to the last strip she placed, and make her finger the taught edge of it—"is very tight."

If I didn't know I could have her already, the look she gives me—with her teeth scraping over her lip and a fire in her eyes—solidifies it.

"I see," she says, her voice a little throaty. If practice weren't about to start in fifteen minutes, I'd already have her on her back in the office. It'll have to wait until after. "And you don't like it tight?"

I squeeze her fingers until her plump bottom lip plucks away from her top. "I very much like it tight. But not the tape." I release her and lean back, enjoying the blush that flows down her cheeks. I bet her breasts are pink, too. Utterly fuckable.

A thick swallow sinks down the column of her throat as she cuts the last piece of tape off my ankle. I shift on the cushioned table, a little hot and bothered myself, but keep my distance. I know Lake hasn't been in to get wrapped yet, and she'll be coming any second.

And if she comes in now…

Suzy finishes wrapping my ankle with care, making sure it's a little looser this time, and lets her hand rest on my knee. "Good luck out there. I know you don't need it."

What she doesn't know is that I definitely do need it. All my luck is faded.

I wink and hop off the table. "Thanks for the wrap. Maybe you'll stick around later than usual today?" She stills, seemingly letting my words sink in. Once she apparently finds the meaning in them, she nods slowly. "Right on. Maybe I will, too." I leave her with a wink.

Lake brushes by me in a hurry as I walk out of the training room but does a double take when she sees my face. "Um, why are you bright red?"

I guess I was blushing, too. "What are you talking about?"

She crosses her arms. "Oh my God. Did you just hook up with Suzy?"

"No," I say defensively. Then I shrug. "Not yet."

She shakes her head. "Wow. I didn't know your type was so basic."

"Why are you concerned about it anyway? So what if I hook up with Suzy?"

"Emma." Her gaze falls hard on me, and she takes a small step forward. "I want to be very clear with you. I couldn't care less." She may as well have clapped with each syllable.

Sure, I want to hook up with Suzy. And I know something about that agitates Lake. Which is funny because if she knew what I wanted to do to her, she'd have nothing to be jealous of. But the thought that she may be sends a surge of heat through me. Makes me want Suzy even more.

Our scrimmage is less heated, though I still take every opportunity to annoy Lake. I don't know why, but I feel called to push her buttons, especially on the court. Like, by bothering her with silly shit, I lighten her somehow. Though really, I agitate her. Distract her. But hey, it only helps me in terms of fighting for my position.

Coach Jordan walks across the locker room straight to me as I pull on my T-shirt. Lake and Nicky watch from the corner of their eyes.

"Come chat, Emma," she says and walks toward her office.

"Fuck, dude," Nicky says.

I swivel to watch Coach leave, then turn back to Nicky. "You don't know if it's bad or not."

She shakes her head and laughs. "Girl, how many times did you get yelled at today? Like, five times? It's bad."

"Yeah, well you…" I start, but I really don't have anything on her. I mean, I do. But nothing relevant.

"That's what I thought." She points to my head. "Fix your hair before you go. Your cowlick's all fucked-up."

I run my hand over my wet cowlick and smooth it down. "Careful, I might just fall for you with all that sweet talk." I sling my bag over my shoulder and walk to the door.

Lake has remained on the periphery of our team dynamics, struggling to really engage with anyone beyond practices and meetings. It's not that the team doesn't like her. She's just all business when she's here, and they don't know her. *I* barely know her.

"You can close the door," Coach Jordan says when I walk in. Not the best start.

I close it and sit across from her. "What's up, Coach?"

She sighs and leans on her desk. I hope this doesn't take too long because there's a horny athletic trainer I need to attend to. "Emma, I know you're a good player." *Good* isn't really the raving review I'm used to receiving. "And your attitude is generally positive." Again, not the best compliment I've ever received, but whatever, I'll take it. "What I don't understand is why you have to constantly torment Lake."

I fidget with the drawstring of my shorts. "One could argue, Coach, that—"

She holds up a hand to cut me off. "I see you, Emma Wilson." I stay quiet because I honestly have no idea what she's talking about, and I also have no idea how to respond. But her tone makes the hairs on my neck stand up. "Life is easy for you, right?"

I'd typically agree. But now, I'm not so sure, so I shrug. "Sometimes."

"Listen, I get it. You're the comic relief on the team, and let me tell you, that is a valuable role. It's important to have fun and bring a lightness to things. What I don't think you understand is that you and Lake are *both* leaders on this team, and you have all the respect of your teammates. You have all the power." She clicks her pen a few times. "With all that sway, how will you make this team better? Lake is part of this team. How will you help to make *her* better?"

I stay quiet, still a little confused by what Coach actually wants from me or if I'm in trouble or not.

"She needs you. And you need her. You're not as subtle as you think when you push her buttons on the court," she says, her brow slightly raised. "I mean, picking her up and placing her out-of-bounds?"

I chuckle, but she just stares at me. "So let me get this straight. You want me to *stop* messing with Lake?"

Coach Jordan chuckles. As it turns out, she doesn't seem to hate me. In fact, I think she likes me. "Yes. Like, yesterday." I can't help but smile. "You're a great player. Keep working hard, okay? And we'll talk about positions after we start real practices."

I nod. "Okay. Yeah."

"And, Emma, if you ever want to talk about anything, I'm here. The university pays me to listen." She points to the ceiling and grins.

It kind of feels like she knows something. "Thanks, Coach. Anything else?"

"That's all."

Great. Time to find Suzy.

Chapter Seven

Coach's little meeting was the perfect delay. My teammates have all left to study or whatever they do on Wednesday nights after practice, and all the coaches have gone home. I had to linger, sure. But now, from what I can tell, it's just me and Suzy. I knock on the training room door, and she opens it after a second.

Her blush either hasn't faded or just bloomed again from my knock. "Hi," she says, holding the door for me. There's a bit of red in her brown hair that reflects the light in a pretty way, and her eyes are the brightest hazel. Almost gold. I've always been attracted to her. Love her curves and the sweetness she treats us with. She reminds me of flirting with my friends' moms in high school.

"Hi." I stroll into the empty training room. I hear her shallow breath as she walks in front of me. I can tell Suzy has never done anything like this before, hooked up with someone in any place that wasn't a bed. I peg her for the "makes love" type. It only makes me want to spread her on her desk even more.

She stands quietly next to me. It's clear she needs me to lead, and I'm more than happy to.

"Thanks for waiting for me," I say and brush my fingertips down her forearm. She shivers at my touch, and it turns me on in a big way. I pull her toward one of the padded training tables and sit, slouching against the back of it as if I'm getting my ankle wrapped. "I've been having this bit of pain down my leg. Shin splints, I'm guessing. Do you think you can help me out?"

A spark flashes in her eyes, and I know I have her now. "I'll get an ice cup." She leaves for a moment and returns with one of the blue plastic cups of ice. Her gaze falls on my bare legs, and she licks her lips.

She lowers the ice to my shin, and I gasp a little when it hits my skin. Wet and cold. I've been iced a million times, and it's never felt like this. Like liquid fire. Suzy's small smile tells me she enjoys my reaction. She lets her other hand run up the inside of my leg. Being touched feels so fucking good.

"How's this?" she whispers as she glides the ice up the inside of my thigh. It's erotic as fuck, and I appreciate her sexy form of continuing consent.

I lean back and pull off my shirt, running a hand down my abs. I'm still tan, and I look good. "All of this hurts, too."

Suzy meets my gaze, and I swear the hazel in her eyes has all but been swallowed by the black of her pupils. She keeps one hand planted on my thigh as she brings the melting ice cup to my stomach and rubs it over my abs. I shudder.

She glides the ice over my skin to the base of my sports bra. "Good?"

I sigh. "You've made a wet mess of me."

Her grip tightens on my thigh. "Isn't payback a bitch?"

There's a moment before sex where my brain flips on the lights—or maybe off—and everything else fades or becomes more clear or whatever bullshit. It's the feeling I search for. The thing I'm after. That moment is now. And I'm soaked.

"Lick it off," I command. She lowers her mouth to my stomach, and all I care about in the world is how wet and soft her tongue feels as it laps up the ice melt on my skin. Like a cool silk ribbon brushing against me. "Fuck." I groan and grip the back of her neck, burying my fingers in her hair. She abandons the ice cup and continues to lick and suck like I'm fresh water, and she's been thirsty for days.

I slide out from under her, my legs a little wobbly, and pull her toward the office. It's my turn to do the touching. With just the light from the training room, the small room is dim. Dark enough for a bit of privacy but light enough to be able to see. And I like to see *everything*. She closes the door behind us, and I pile the contents of the desk onto the chair. I want space.

She wraps her arms around me from behind, but I tug her in front, pinning her against the desk. Her breasts look like they could burst right through her Polo, and I'm overcome with the primal urge to rip it off and watch her tits bounce free. I know, I'm an animal. "Do you have a lot of these?" I whisper as I finger the hem of her shirt. A *polite* animal.

"Like, ten. Why?" Her voice is breathy and full of want.

I kiss her, and her mouth is hot and wet and as eager as it was on my abs. I part the V-neck of her Polo, and she groans into my mouth at the same time I rip open her shirt.

She gasps and pulls back in shock, and *fuck*, that felt amazing. Her tits look edible, bulging from her black lacy bra and heaving with each of her deep breaths. I know she wore this for me. "Suzy?"

She pulls my hips into her. "Hmm?" She's all sex hazed, and I've barely touched her. But I did just destroy her shirt, so it's time to check in.

"You good?" I drop my mouth to her neck and scrape my teeth over her hot skin. "Fair warning, if you say yes, I'm going to fuck you on your desk."

"Yes."

❖

"Knock, knock," I say, even though I hate when people say that. The door to Lake's room is cracked, and whatever, I panicked.

She looks up from her book and pushes her glasses up her nose. The scene is like a Sunday morning with her sweatshirt and steaming mug, but it's Friday night. I sit at her feet without invitation. "What are you reading?"

She straightens and dog-ears the page, sliding the book on her desk. "I *was* reading *Pretty Girls*, by Karin Slaughter."

I glance at the cover. "What is it?"

She stares at me, seemingly unamused by my small talk. "A thriller."

"Does someone get *slaughtered*?" I grin.

"Wow." She rolls her eyes. "No one has ever made that joke before. Congrats, Emma."

I pull a leg under myself and angle toward her. "What are you doing tonight? It's Friday, you know."

She raises a brow. "Are you shaming me for staying in to read on a Friday night?"

I shake my head. "Nope. Not at all. I wondered if maybe you'd want to keep me company? You know, so I stay out of trouble."

"Can anyone keep you out of trouble?"

I try to give her a sincere smile. "I'm not actual trouble, you know? I get good grades, I mostly show up to things on time, and am, in general, a solid person."

"A solid person?"

I chuckle. "Yeah, that's what Rachel says, and she never exaggerates."

She scoffs and leans forward. "Why do you feel the constant need to mess with me, then? Every scrimmage, every practice, you have some little torment up your sleeve. Are you scared? Is it just one of your stupid defense mechanisms?" Her tone is sharp, and I lean away, a little shocked.

"What do I have to be scared of?" I ask.

"I don't know, but you're constantly hiding. So you tell me."

I shake my head. "Hiding? I literally just walked in your room to hang out. I'd hardly call that hiding. Besides, you're the one with all the intensity." I point at her, a little horrified at my behavior. "You know, you'd definitely get the starting job if you played with some heart. But you're like a robot on the court. What is *that*? Some kind of stupid defense mechanism, so you're not crushed when you have to ride the bench?" Her face shifts through a range of emotions all the way to the end: apathetic. I can't stop. "Do you even like basketball?"

She closes her eyes and takes a deep breath. Why am I doing this? Why do I all of a sudden feel angry? I'm being straight-up mean. I stand and grab her book from the desk, noticing a small photo tucked behind her laptop. It's a high school photo of some guy on the basketball team. Not in a frame, just lying on her desk. I hand her the book. "Is that your boyfriend?" I eye the photo that looks like it was meant to be hidden, a ribbon of jealousy curling through me. And I thought Lake liked me. "What's his name. *Pond*?" I chuckle.

"Look at me." She tugs my wrist until I'm standing over her, her eyes dark and focused on mine. She doesn't blink, and her intensity makes me want to squirm out of her grip and run. "That's my dead brother. And his name was River." She shrugs. "I guess you were close with Pond."

I freeze. The blood drains from my face, and I worry I'll pass out on her. Instead, I lower myself onto the edge of her mattress. "I'm so sorry."

"No one asked you to be."

She looks impenetrable, like she's been through the darkest shit, and this—me—is the smallest annoyance. "No one needed to," I say.

After a minute of silence, she rolls her eyes and sighs, slouching against her pillow and releasing my wrist. And because I have no words, I squeeze her sock-clad ankle. She shakes her head and stares across the room at Piper's empty bed. I just sit and rub my thumb over her.

"Sorry I'm not, like, overflowing with joy every second of the day," she says.

I slide my hand up to her calf and squeeze. I'm not coming on to her, just getting her attention. She looks at me, and I can tell all the anger between us has dissipated. Gone as quickly as it came. "No one asked you to be."

The smallest grin flickers on her lips. "No one needed to."

I wince. "I'm sorry. I've been…" What have I been? Annoying, childish, oblivious.

"An asshole."

I chuckle as I rub her muscle a little harder. She doesn't bat me away or move her leg. "Yeah. That."

Her gaze drops to where I'm touching her. "Feels good," she whispers.

"Sometimes, when I don't understand someone, I think I like to shake them up to see how they explode. Like, that will help me assess them in some way." I tap her other leg, and she shifts to give it to me.

"So that's what this is all about? All your annoying little jabs on the court are to learn more about me?" She gives me a skeptical look, her skin soft under my fingers.

"Yes. But I also have a massive crush on you. And I'm basically a schoolboy, so…"

She rolls her eyes. "You do not."

"How would you know?" I ask in mock offense. I let my hand slide to the top of her calf and drop my voice. "I couldn't have been the only one feeling something that day in my room."

Her gaze falls to her lap. "You seem to go after every woman you meet. So even if you did have a crush on me, would it be much different than say, Suzy?" She looks at me when she says her name.

There's a teasing arch in her brow. "Damn, Lake. You're putting me on blast." She shrugs. "And for the record, I don't have a crush on Suzy."

"You just want to bed her." I can feel my cheeks heat. *Shit.* "Oh," she says, her voice higher. "You already did, didn't you?"

I bite my lip. Probably shouldn't admit to this. Instead, I shrug.

Her mouth drops. "Oh my God. Is there anyone you haven't slept with?"

The way she says it is light, not accusing. I look at her expectantly. "Well, yeah. Haven't slept with you."

She bursts out laughing. "Not that I'm aware of, no."

I already know the answer, but I ask, "Are you into women?" She nods, and I stop massaging. Run my fingertips up and down her skin as the moment becomes heated. "Are you into me?"

"Not a chance, Emma Wilson." She winks, and it sinks straight to my core.

"Never say never."

"I didn't."

I clear my throat and try to chase away the feeling of being out of control. There's a thin line between us. One that I could so easily cross. One I think she *wants* me to cross. But I feel like I have something to prove first. Probably that I'm worthy or something.

"I'm sorry, Lake."

"Make it up to me." She stands and smooths her shorts. "Come on. Let's go somewhere fun."

She slips on her Nikes and stares at me as I race through all the places I want to take Lake. I don't know many good ones. But I know one great one. "Okay. But you have to promise not to kiss me."

She laughs and slides her lion card in her pocket. "I can guarantee you that won't happen."

I walk past her, brushing her shoulder, and hold open the door. "We'll see."

Walking through the dark campus with Lake feels like a date. I know it isn't, but all I want to do is hold her hand. Well, I want to do so much more, but I have to go slow. The breeze has developed a slight chill as summer slips into fall, and we huddle in our basketball sweatshirts to keep warm, our shoulders brushing every so often. Normally on Friday night, I'm with Whitney. But I didn't call her, so I have no plans tonight except to hang out with Lake Palmer.

And since Piper is at an overnight golf camp, I'm pretty sure I'm the only one on Lake's agenda, too. The thought of spending the entire evening together fills me with an electric energy, like the start of a basketball game.

I walk to the stairwell in the library that is completely deserted. "This way." I open the door and wait for her.

"Are you, like, going to kill me in here?" She peers around the piss-stained stairwell, eyes wide.

"You've been reading too many thrillers." The lights flicker before resuming their ominous glow. I shrug. "The lighting is a bit murdery, huh?"

She chuckles. "And it smells like a million frat boys have peed in here."

"Oh, they have. Do you not like our date?"

She shoves me gently in the shoulder. "This is the farthest thing in the world from a date."

I roll my eyes, continuing to hold the door. "The farthest thing in the world?" She nods, smiling with her bottom lip trapped between her teeth. "Getting a colonoscopy would be closer to being a date, then?"

She tilts her head in consideration. "Perhaps."

I sigh. "Come on. I'll race you to the top. Winner can decide just how close to a date this is. Deal?"

"Deal."

She's halfway up the first flight before I even start chasing her. The soles of our shoes slapping against the stairs and our heaving breath is the only sounds pinging off the metal and echoing in the stairwell. Lake has me beat most of the way up the five flights until we hit the landing of the fourth floor, and I get a fistful of her sweatshirt. Just like at practice, I pull her backward, stopping her momentum.

Her back thuds into my chest, and she spins in my arms, trying to push away. But my grip is tight. We wrestle, pushing and pulling in a dance for dominance, before she breaks free. But she doesn't take off, she steps into my arms again and crooks a finger at me. I lower my head, expecting her to whisper something, but she presses her lips to my cheek and vanishes.

I stand with my hand flat over my face where her mouth was.

"Emma," she calls from the top. "I beat you." I look up the empty stairs, unsure I can even walk after that. "Don't tell me you got murdered or something."

"Not murdered," I call back. I grip the rail that looks like it should be sticky but thankfully isn't and walk slowly up the steps, seriously concerned about tripping and eating shit with the way my limbs are feeling boneless.

"I win," Lake says when I reach the fifth floor.

I tug on her sweatshirt as I walk to the opposite side of the small corridor. "This isn't the top. Come on."

There's a skinny ladder attached to the cinderblock wall that leads to what looks like a trapdoor in the ceiling. Lake eyes it warily. "Where are you actually taking me, Emma?"

"Just trust me, okay?" She considers my words for a moment, then nods. I climb the ladder and unhitch the lever. "They never lock this thing." I push open the door and climb onto the roof of the library. When Lake emerges, I lend her a hand and pull her next to me.

"Wow." She walks to the edge of the roof and leans against the railing, looking at the night sky.

"Yeah. It's so beautiful." I step behind her, and because she literally just kissed me on the cheek, I reach for the railing on either side of her, enveloping her. She pushes against me, not to free herself but to feel me. And I feel her. I don't trust myself to behave. But I stay behind her and dip my face to her neck. It's warm and fresh, and I'm absolutely dying to taste her. Anywhere I can. Dying to earn an inch more intimacy.

She spins and gives me a little shove in the chest, a grin spreading over her lips. "I won the race, and this isn't a date."

I tilt my head back and forth. "*Mm.* I'm pretty sure you just kissed me on the cheek in the stairwell."

She laughs. "I kiss my dog on the cheek all the time. Doesn't mean I want to date him." She grabs my hand and pulls me into her again. "But it's cold up here, so come back, please."

I do what she asks. Instead of reaching for the railing, I wrap my arms around her waist and press into her back. I don't really know what's happening, or how I got on the roof of the library with Lake, my arms around her, and her head falling back against my chest. We literally don't even know each other. In fact, she may kind of hate me.

But it's like I'm called to be close to her.

"River was two years older than me," she says.

Every thought about the strangeness of our proximity evaporates. Who cares about the reasons? I'm where I'm supposed to be. I tighten her against me, the warmth between us turning to heat. I nod against her neck, silently asking her to tell me.

"I was a sophomore, and he was a senior. He was driving home after an away game on a Friday night. Some drunk guy swerved into his lane and killed him." She snaps, and the sound is so achingly hollow, I shudder against her. "Just like that."

I don't speak. I hold her. I'm sure she's had enough condolences to fill a goddamn Hallmark section in the hospital gift shop. I'm here to listen.

"He had everything ahead of him. A basketball scholarship to Furman, a passion for kids and teaching, his whole life. And my parents…" She shakes her head. "I don't know how they survived."

"Lake, I literally can't imagine," I whisper.

"I just want to be enough. To make them happy and proud, the way they were of River. And I will." She squeezes my arms around herself. "They're going to be able to watch me play in the WNBA one day, and not even you can stand in the way of that."

I chuckle against her skin. "I'm not going to let you have my position just because you have a sob story."

She laughs that warm, gravely laugh. "This is why I like you. Sometimes, you're not entirely full of shit."

I step back, and she spins to face me, a look of question on her face. I just wanted her to turn. "I wasn't lying in your room. I like you, too." I take her hand and close the space between us, leaving just a few inches between our mouths. "Something about you just gets me."

"Emma," she whispers. "We really shouldn't do this."

I interlace our fingers. "I'm so numb. I can't feel anything or anyone, but I can feel you, Lake. And that has to mean something big. I don't know why this is happening, but I don't care. Who cares?"

She releases my hand and flattens hers under my collarbone, but she doesn't push. Just leaves it there over my heart. "I care. The season hasn't even started."

"I have nothing to lose," I say. It's true. I have nothing to lose. I'm nobody, doing nothing, with no one. But Lake is this shining light, pulling me in, and I want so much more than this kiss. So much more than to have sex with her.

I want *her*.

"And I have everything to lose," she says, but she keeps looking up at me like she's willing to risk it. And I'm just reckless and selfish enough…

My phone rings in my pocket, startling me. Startling us. It's always on vibrate. Must've have knocked the little switch or something. "Sorry," I mutter. I pull it out of my pocket and decline the call. It was just Rachel, anyway.

"It's okay." She runs her hand down my arm, giving me hope that we could pick up where we left off.

It rings again. "What the fuck, Rach?" I pull it out and decline it again, but right when it stops, she calls again. "I'm sorry."

She nods for me to answer.

"Rach, I'm kind of in the middle—"

"Listen, Em." Her voice is strained, and I already know what she's about to say. "Andy's dad just passed away."

I blow out a deep breath, my heart completely shattering in my chest. Little sharp pains reverberate through me with every breath. I'm so sad for Mr. Foster. But it's her pain—Andy's pain—that makes me feel like I'm about to cry. "Okay. Okay, I'll be there in fifteen."

I hang up. Lake watches me with a concerned look on her face. "What's wrong?"

"That was Rachel. Andy's dad has been sick for a while, and he passed away tonight."

She worries her lip. "Shit."

"Yeah." I take a deep, achy breath. "I need to go over there, but I'll walk you back first."

Something flashes across her face, but she recovers quickly. "Don't worry about me. I'm going to enjoy this a bit longer. I'll see you later."

"Are you sure?"

She smiles. "Positive."

"Okay. I'll text you."

I walk away feeling weirdly bad. Lake wasn't angry, but still. On my way to Wilder Hall, I call my mom to let her know.

CHAPTER EIGHT

I open the door to Andy and Rachel's room without knocking. Maya and Rachel sit on the edge of Andy's bed, their arms draped over her back like a blanket. When she looks up, her eyes are red-rimmed and raw. I've seen her like this a handful of times, all related to her father's health and her lack of control in the matter. Her inability to help.

"Andy," is all I say. She's in my arms in an instant, and I squeeze her as tight as I can without hurting her. She presses her face into the crook of my neck, and it's warm and wet and intimate, but the only thing I feel is an overwhelming need to be her best friend. I look over her shoulder and catch Maya's eye. She gives me a sad smile and a nod, as if to say she's glad I'm here. So I keep my arms around Andy.

She pulls back to catch her breath. "I knew it would be soon, I just"—she hiccups a breath—"why am I in shock?" She fans her face and stares at me.

"Of course you're in shock." I rub her shoulder. "When are you going home?"

She cries quietly, so Maya answers for her. "We're driving down tonight. Just taking a moment to process and pack a bag, then we're off to be with her mom."

I nod. "Andy," I say, gently bringing her back to the conversation. "I talked to my mom, and my folks are on their way to your house to be with your mom until you get there. They're going to help her with all the little stuff she shouldn't have to deal with right now, okay?" She collapses against my chest and nods. "And I'm sure my mom will keep everyone fed."

This earns a chuckle. If my mom is a rock star at anything, it's feeding people. I may have the most traditional gender-role-fulfilling parents in the world, but I swear she loves it, cooking for an army of constantly hungry teens. She was socialized to love it, but still. Even if we rarely got to eat dinner as a family, and our meals were, let's say basic, her cooking still felt like home. Hot spaghetti, store-bought garlic bread, and precut Pillsbury sugar cookies.

"Thank you," she whispers.

"I didn't do anything." I release her only because I get the sudden feeling that I should and look at Maya. "Anything y'all need me to take care of here?"

She shakes her head. "I think we're good. Got everything sorted with Coach Clayton and classes. We should be back on Wednesday."

"Wednesday," I repeat for no reason. "Okay."

"Do you want to come?" Andy asks. "Come."

I meet Maya's gaze, and she shrugs like she doesn't mind. But I can't come. For, like, a million reasons, no. "Andy, I...I can't. I'm sorry."

She shakes her head. "Yeah, no. I know."

"It's just, I have basketball and..." *You have Maya.* And maybe I have Lake. I definitely don't have Lake, but I have something. Maybe.

"I know. I know," she says. "I'm sorry."

"Stop. Don't say that. *I'm* sorry. So very sorry."

She hugs me one more time. "I love you," she says, her words wet with tears.

"I love you, too."

❖

I give Lake space the rest of the weekend. Don't really know why, other than something in my gut tells me to back off. It could be Andy, sure. My feelings for her have never stopped me from letting my hands wander all over Whit's body or Suzy's body or whichever woman of the week's body. But they're sure as shit making me second-guess what I'm doing with Lake. Or what I *was* doing with her.

Because I care for Lake.

In some unfamiliar way that excites and terrifies me. And what I definitely don't want to do is hurt her. I don't know if I'm capable of not. I hurt Andy and every other woman who's ever cared about me. So why would I trust myself to not hurt Lake? I wouldn't even know how to do it right, so why do it at all?

I've been in almost constant contact with my folks, checking in on the Fosters from a distance. Things are straightforward. I guess when you've known you're going to die for years ahead of time, you make arrangements. Make things as easy as possible for the ones you love. That's what Mr. Foster did. He was always such a generous, loving guy.

A twinge of pain cuts my chest, and I feel this one just for him.

"Emma, what can I do for you?" Coach Jordan leans back in her chair and watches me fidget in the doorway. It's an entire hour before practice starts, and she seems confused to see me here so early. When I don't respond, she says, "Come on. Come sit."

"Sorry I'm so…" *Incompetent. Avoidant.* These words rocket through my brain like cannonballs. I casually brace myself on the door frame, unsteady from the unintentional slap I just gave myself. I never do this. Typically, I see myself as goddamn glimmering ocean under the sunrise, completely ignoring whatever is lingering in the deep. Where the light can't reach. "Early," I finally say.

"Better than late." She gestures to the chair again.

A wave of guilt hits me from remembering our first meeting. Seven minutes late because I couldn't keep it in my fucking pants. A long sigh coasts from my mouth. "Yeah." I sit across from her, and she watches me with curiosity.

"What's bothering you?" she asks.

Nothing. Everything. I shake my head. "I just wanted to talk to you about a couple things." I scratch at my sweats. "My friend's dad passed away and—"

"I'm very sorry to hear that." Her eyes are narrowed in sincerity.

"Um. Thanks. Her family is close to mine, and I want to go to his service. It's next week. I'd miss practice on Friday."

"If it's important to you, of course you should go."

I nod. "Thank you." She waits me out, seemingly knowing I'm going to eventually spill whatever else I want to say.

I don't know why almost kissing Lake and Andy's dad has me so fucked-up, but I'm starting to question myself at every turn. I don't trust myself. Kissing Lake would have been a giant mistake. I need to focus on me, not fucking with—or just fucking—my teammate.

I clear my throat. "What do I have to do to win the starting position?"

"I assume we're talking about point guard?"

I feel instant guilt, gunning for Lake's—for my—position. But it's the right thing to do for me. Besides, if Lake can't beat me, she's never going to make it in the WNBA. I'm doing her a favor, really. "Yeah. Point guard."

"And why not shooting guard?" she asks.

I shrug. "I mean, you're the coach. I'll play where you put me, but I know I'm the best point guard on this team, and it's arguably the most important position. My impact will be greater at point."

"If you are the best for the job, then I agree." She swivels gently in her chair, thinking. "I don't know who will start. Lake knew when she decided to transfer that it would be a risk, but she seems just as stubborn as you." She grins. The mention of Lake's name makes my gut sink, like I've already fucked her over somehow. "You need to develop your leadership skills. I know you're a natural leader, but it's not enough. Look for ways to elevate your teammates."

It stings, but I nod. "Okay. I will."

"And don't get lazy on defense."

"I don't—"

"*Don't* get lazy on defense. I don't want that on my team. I want a complete player who gives it all on every play. That's what I'm looking for in my starting point guard."

I nod. "I can do that."

"Okay, then." She slaps the desk. "Go show me."

❖

"Nicky, you're rolling off the pick the wrong way," I say. We've been running through our playbook in a casual scrimmage for almost an hour. But there's nothing casual about me. Not right now. I'm out for blood.

"No she's not," Lake says. She's orbited around me today, as if she knows something is different between us. Before practice, I'm sure she thought the difference was I'm not into her anymore, the opposite of the truth. And now, during practice, she probably thinks I'm trying to insert myself into the starting position, and that is *definitely* the truth.

The coaches watch me and Lake hash it out at the top of the key. I know I'm right.

"She is," I say and tug Nicky by her jersey. "Listen, when Rachel is pulling the defense out of the paint, it's clear for you to roll inside. Take it every time. If they want to collapse on you in the key, they'll probably foul you."

She nods. "Yeah. Makes sense."

Lake gently pushes my arm, her fingers slipping in my sweat. "It would make sense, sure. But only if the defense falls back into either a different zone or is in man, but right now, you need to roll off the edge of the key. This way." She pretends to set a pick on the shoulder of the key and rolls the opposite direction.

I blow out a breath, trying not to get too frustrated. I am supposed to be elevating my teammates, after all. "It doesn't matter. If Nicky pulls a defender, that means an easy dump to Rachel. It still results in an open shot."

Lake shakes her head and stares. "What are you doing?" She asks it in a hushed voice meant just for me. And it doesn't feel like she's asking about this practice but asking about everything. *Why are you being weird? Are you avoiding me? Am I wrong to think we have something?*

I shrug. "I just know how to run our motion."

"It's our motion," she says, as if she and Coach Jordan are on a team separate from the rest of us. And it really kind of pisses me off.

"That's so weird. I thought your jersey said *Alder U*, not *GSU*." She rolls her eyes, but she's the one being a dick. "Come here. Let me just"—I pull at the hem of her jersey so it's taut and easy to read—"oh, yup. I was right." She scoffs and swats my hands. "Hey, look, it also says to stop being a bad teammate."

Her jaw drops as she steps back, and I let her go. "Fuck you, Emma."

I'm vaguely aware of the coaches watching, but no one has stepped in to stop us yet. "Listen, Lake. It's not you and Coach Jordan versus us. It's only us. Get that through your head. If you're not here to be a part of our team, then why are you here at all?"

She shakes her head, momentarily speechless.

"Dude," Rachel says as she tugs my elbow. "That's probably enough."

Her eyes water for a split second, and it's clear I've made my point. Put the distance between us that we need. "I didn't mean it like that, and you know it," she says quietly. Then, she looks at the rest of our team. "I meant that this is a play I've already run for three years under Coach Jordan. For Alder, this is a new variation of the motion you're used to. But the options and the flow are just a bit different than you'd think. And that's what makes it such a great play."

She tugs Nicky, our poor pawn, to the shoulder. "Pivot this way and roll out," Lake says, mimicking what she wants her do. "Cool?" Nicky shoots me a look, but I don't say anything. "Just try it. This is our motion, and it works really well when we run it properly."

"Cool," Nicky says.

"Okay," Lake says with finality. "Let's run it again."

As Lake bounces me the ball at the top of the key, she stares me down, narrowing her eyes and shaking her head. "I don't know what your problem is, Emma, but let's just make it through this practice, okay?" she whispers.

"I don't have a problem."

I pass it to Quinn. Nicky hits the shoulder and sets the pick on Lake, then rolls out down the outside of the paint instead of the inside. I get the ball back, and even though I really don't want to, I pass it to Nicky because she's wide open.

"Okay," Nicky says. "Lake's right. Roll out, not in."

I swallow. "Yeah," I say. "Roll out, not in." Nothing looks worse than not conceding, but damn, it makes me itch. To try, to put it out there, and to be wrong? Fuck, I hate it.

We all walk to the water station and take a breather. Coach Jordan strolls over and stands next to me on the edge of the group. "While I appreciate the effort, that's not exactly what I meant by be a leader."

I wipe my chin with the back of my hand and stare at the empty court. "Yeah. That felt like shit."

I can feel her look down at me. "That's 'cause it was shit. There was nothing elevating about whatever it was you did out there."

I meet her gaze. "I'm going to fix it."

She shrugs. "Seems like Lake already did." I look away. Coach squeezes my shoulder, and it feels like a consolation prize. "Let's run it again."

❖

I linger in the locker room, wasting time until I see Lake leave. I'm avoiding her, of course. Sure, I was the one who ended up being the asshole today, but I still don't agree with her sentiment. I know she meant it when she said "our play." It's not just a—

"Emma?"

I jump and find her waiting for me outside the Den. "You scared the shit out of me."

Her jaw is set tight, and she's not wearing her glasses, so there's no barrier between me and the hurt in her eyes. "What just happened in there?"

"The play—"

"Stop." She crosses her arms. "I think we both know it's not about the play. Friday night…" She shakes her head, dropping her gaze to her shoes.

"Friday night shouldn't have happened, and that's my bad."

She snaps her attention to me. "Are you serious right now?"

I don't know what I am. It's kind of starting to feel like I'm nobody. With no one. I could've not shown up to the funeral on Friday, and no one would've missed me. No one needed me. Not Andy. And not Lake. I'm sure she'll realize it soon. "Yes, I'm serious. Come here." I touch her arm, and she shirks away but follows. I take a couple steps to a walkway that cuts through a small patch of trees and stop by a bench. "Look, if Friday night continued, where would we be, huh?"

She recoils as if appalled. "I don't know. But probably not here. And honestly, anywhere but here, like this, would be better."

"Really? If we weren't interrupted on the roof, I would've had you against the railing with my hand down your fucking shorts. Then what? Huh?"

Her eyes water like they did on the court, but I can't stop. I have to be clear. Be strong. It's the only thing I can give her. The best thing I can give her. Fucking run away from me as far as you can, Lake.

"Then you'd just be another girl I've hooked up with. A good time. And you'd probably be all weird about it and hurt, and it would mess up everything with basketball. And not to mention, Lake, I just don't like you like that. I don't like anyone like that." It's a lie, a complete lie that shocks even me. I just can't be what she needs. I'm not capable of being everything to someone when really, I'm no one.

She nods slowly, her lip looking painfully trapped between her teeth, until she releases it and sighs. We both turn at the woosh of a bird flying past, then focus back on each other. "I would hate you if I believed you," she says. "But I see you, and I know you're full of shit."

"You have no idea—"

"Bet you didn't give Suzy this spiel. Am I right?"

"What does that have anything to do with anything?"

"You're an idiot, Emma." She shoves me in the shoulder. "If you felt nothing, you wouldn't care. You'd fuck me the way you fuck every other woman and move on with your life. Instead, you're standing here like an asshole, hoping I can't tell you're trying to push me away. The only thing I don't understand is why."

I can feel my mouth dry. We haven't even kissed, and it's already shit. All of it. So I lean in to kiss her. Why not? I'm already paying the price, may as well reap the benefit. And she's got me so fucked-up…

She dodges, shoving me hard in the chest. "Are you serious right now?" Her eyes are wide, dark and stormy with rage. "Literally, go fuck yourself. You're a mess, and I want nothing to do with you." She brushes by me, and I stay rooted where I am.

On Friday, Lake looked into my eyes like, if only I would kiss her, she'd be the happiest woman in the world. If only my phone didn't ring, and I pushed my hips into hers, and her back hit the railing, then she'd be…I don't know. Mine or something. But today, I blew it up. I looked down to find a book of matches in my hand, shrugged, and torched us.

The thing is, as I stand here in my shock, I don't even remember why. Because I'm Emma, and she's Lake? And Lake needs to be with anyone but me? I think that was it, yes. Also, I need to figure myself out before everything I thought I wanted slips through my fingers. I need to start at point. It's what I do. I need to be a lawyer. It's what I should do.

Chapter Nine

The rest of the week is difficult. I'm late to Weber's class, not that he'll care. I mean, he may care. I kind of feel like he has a limit to my bullshit, and one day, I'll hit it out of nowhere, and boom, I'll lose him. But hey, I'm a senior. Gonna lose him soon anyway. Regardless, I take the steps two at a time in case today is the day I hit his bullshit threshold.

I push through the door in a hurry. "Weber. Sorry, man. I know I'm…" I look around the mostly empty room. Two students casually lounge in their seats, shuffling through their folders and notebooks. "Late."

"Late? Sure, if twenty minutes early is late." He cocks his head. "You're not huffing markers or putting Tide Pods up your butt or some weird TikTok thing, are ya?" My stomach sinks. How did I mess up the time? I can be a little scattered, sure, but something about this seriously freaks me out. "Emma?"

"What? No. Don't be gross, Weber." I tighten the straps of my backpack.

He smirks, his chunky green sweater with the folded collar and huge brown buttons making him look even larger than usual. I like it. Matches his big love for life. "Or is it some basketball mentality from the new coach? Must be an hour early or you're late, type of thing?"

I can't play right now. "Can we talk about the LSAT?"

"Oh." He straightens, fiddling with a pen as if that was the most uncomfortable question I could have asked him. "Yeah. I mean *yes*.

Of course." I stare, gripping my straps so hard I know my knuckles are white. "Now?"

"Well, yeah. We have time, right?"

He glances at the clock on the back wall and to the other students whose names I don't even know. But the one girl is pretty hot. Then he nods. "Yeah. What do you want to talk about? Did you change your mind about taking it?"

"I know I'm past the deadline, but is there any way I can still register and take it in the spring? I really need to get rolling on my law school apps. Avoided it for too long."

He looks at me for a moment, his soft eyes narrow. "No," he says simply. "No, you can't still register. This is the LSAT we're talking about, not some 5k fun run to support Trip, the three-legged dog."

"Jesus, Weber. Relax. I'll figure it out."

He sighs as if he's exhausted by me. The thing is, it's not, like, an exaggerated sigh. He's actually bothered. I can feel the other students watching. "Emma, I told you weeks ago it was time to register."

I shift my weight to the other leg. "Damn, dude. You're acting like this affects *you* somehow." I pull my backpack tighter against me like a hug. "Everything is fine. I'll just push it back and find an internship or something. Or are you too pissed to help me with that, too?"

He crosses his arms, and other students begin to walk in. "Emma." It's like my name melts him. His shoulders drop, and he rolls out his neck before looking at me. "Clearly, I care about you. I'm pissed because I want you to succeed in whatever way is right for you. When I brought it up last time, you had me convinced that you didn't want to go to law school, and I'm frustrated because I could have helped you get a leg up on everything."

I must be a little raw from Lake and the funeral on Friday because Weber is making me want to cry. I gnaw my lip and wait for the strange feeling to pass. "I wasn't ready then. I'm ready now." He levels me with a skeptical look. "I'm sorry. I'm done fucking around, okay?" He nods. "Still willing to help me?"

He huffs a dramatic breath. "I suppose, since it's my job."

I grin. We're back.

"Go sit before I change my mind."

I sit and stretch my legs so far in front of me, I almost get a cramp in my right calf. As the rest of the students file in, the pretty girl who was here before me turns in her seat to wave her friend over. I catch her eye, and she gives me a shy smile. Normally, that would be hook, line, and sinker. I'd slip her a note and ask her out. Instead, I avoid catching her eye again and absentmindedly scroll my phone.

The service for Andy's dad on Friday was nice. Nice and…gut-wrenching. Every part of it was completely brutal. My father, though helpful to Mrs. Foster, was a grade A asshole to me. He always kind of is, though, and I did well at brushing off his disappointment. Then, there was my mom, who seemed to have an annoyingly big crush on Maya. "Maya seems nice," she said in the car ride home.

When I didn't respond, I think she got the hint and quieted about it but not before my dad jumped on the bandwagon. "Maya is great. But it's such a shame. I always thought you and Andy would end up together."

Rip my heart out.

Maybe I'm a terrible person, but the service was painful because of her. Watching Andy cry quietly, her shoulders shaking in her black dress, cheeks red, and the watch her mom gave her for graduation hanging from her wrist, was pure agony. I couldn't do anything for her, so I watched as Maya did, her arm around Andy's waist, steadying her throughout the day. I was glad Andy had her. Glad she has her. I guess it was the first big life event where I wasn't that person for her, and it shook me.

Class passes in a blur. I pack my notebook that I took zero notes in, plan another meeting with Weber to discuss the next LSAT registration and finding summer internships, then I'm out of there.

I have a bit of a break before practice, so I walk back to my room for a snack and to drop my backpack. It's chilly today. The beginning of October means the beginning of full team practices, the end of solos, and a ratchet up in basketball intensity. It also means I've known Lake Palmer for almost two entire months. Two months, and I've already ruined not only my shot with her but my friendship with her, too.

And it really bothers me.

Ugh. Of, like, the entire human race, I'd say I feel less shame than most. Whitney, no regrets. Suzy, no regrets. But when I think of talking to Lake on the path after practice, think of the disgust on her face after I tried to kiss her like a fucking idiot, I feel so much shame. Overwhelming regret.

Lake is on my mind all the time. The only recent time Andy has been centerstage was Friday.

"Oh shit." I stutter-step awkwardly in the threshold of the bathroom as Lake finishes washing her hands. "Sorry," I say and begin to close the door.

She wipes her hands in a towel. "Relax. It's not like I'm naked." Her words are all exhales, breathy and annoyed. I stand frozen with the door cracked, and she glowers at me. "What? Scared you're going to try to kiss me again in the most inappropriate moment?"

I shake my head and try not to look her up and down. She's devastating as ever. "No. It won't happen again." I try to sound as sincere as possible. I *am* sincere. Never again will I be such an asshole to her.

She must take me at my word because she doesn't say anything else. Just nods.

"See you at practice," I say as she leaves the bathroom.

"Emma," Coach shouts.

I jog to the bench, already knowing what she's going to say. Today's scrimmage has been a mess; no one is on the same page, our communication is shit, and as if we weren't disappointing Coach enough, Lake is visibly avoiding me. "What's up?"

She looks pissed. As pissed as I've ever seen her, at least. The dimples that I normally associate with her small smiles deepen with what I'm pretty sure is pure rage. Directed all at me for some reason. "Y'all look like you've never met before, much less played basketball together." Her voice is strained, as if she wants to keep her cool, but she can't.

"I know. I'm sorry. It's not our best—"

"I'm afraid you think being a leader on this team solely means beating Lake." She puts her hands on her hips and stares.

I shake my head. "That's not—"

"Does the team get together for activity nights? Anything?"

"I..." I wipe my hand down my shorts. It's soaked from me literally dripping sweat. "No."

"You want to start at point? Listen to me, Emma, because I'm only going to say it once. If you can't look out for your team, you're not starting. If you can't pull everyone together and help them achieve, you're not starting. If you can't turn your selfishness into true leadership, you're not starting."

Shit. I know the entire team is watching us. They probably can't hear Coach's whisper-yell, but her body language is crystal clear. I don't know how to respond, so I nod.

She sighs. "You starting at point isn't about Lake. It's about you. Do you understand?"

Again, I nod.

"The three of us are going to have a little chat after practice."

She dismisses me, and I stroll back to center court, feeling scattered as I let everything she said settle in me. What have I done to make my team better? To bring us together? Season starts in a month, and our performance today was worse than all of last year with Coach Carson. It's not that we don't know the plays or that we're not in shape. We're just lost. Distant from each other. Completely devoid of chemistry.

After practice, Lake and I meet with Coach in her office. It's awkward. Especially since I insisted on walking in together but didn't tell Lake that. Instead, I watched her at her locker until she left and caught up with her in the hallway. She turned when I called her name and leveled me with one of those annoyed and disinterested looks she's perfected.

When my back is against the wall, I have two modes: lean hard into my blind confidence or crumble. And it's rare I crumble. I squeezed her shoulder and said, "You smell so good. Orange zest and honey." I nodded to the office door and smiled. "Ready?"

And here we are. I stand straight while Lake shoots me glances, and Coach's gaze bounces between us.

"Sit, please." We sit as Coach leans back in her chair and considers us. "There are a couple things I want to talk about with you both. First of all, I will not be deciding who starts at point guard this year."

Lake leans forward, elbows on knees like she's about to sub in a game. "What? What do you mean you're not choosing the starters?"

Coach grins as if this is already going exactly to plan, whatever *this* is. "Oh, I'm choosing starters. Just not point."

I stay quiet and try to digest this information. Of course Coach has an end goal, I'm just not sure what it is. Maybe she actually prefers I start but doesn't want to be the one to pull Lake's dreams out from under her. I don't mind. I'll do it. I'll take the LSAT. I'll ruin the dreams of the girl I like. I can be a no-nonsense Emma.

Lake closes her eyes and shakes her head, seemingly struggling to compute the meaning of this, too.

"Just to be clear, who will make the decision?" I ask.

"You," Coach says, looking at me. Then, she directs her gaze to Lake. "And you. Together. It obviously has to be unanimous, meaning you both have to agree. The season starts in one month, and I want your decision by"—she tilts her head back and forth—"let's say the twentieth."

"Less than three weeks?" Lake asks, seemingly horrified.

"Eighteen days," I say.

She cuts me a sharp look. "Less than three weeks. That's what I said." She leans back, shaking her head. I think she's shocked. I'm shocked, too.

"Okay," I say. "We can handle that. There was something else you wanted to talk about?"

"Yes. Today was extremely disappointing. In an effort to build team chemistry, we're going on a little weekend trip. We leave Saturday morning and get back Sunday afternoon."

"What trip? Where are we going?" Lake asks.

"We're going camping in Tennessee."

"Coach. What? I don't camp. I don't have a tent. None of us have any gear—"

Coach raises a hand to stop her. "Lake, please. All you need to bring is an overnight bag. We're staying at a campground with yurts. No gear necessary. Position players will share lodging. That means you two will share a yurt." She looks pointedly between us as if expecting protest. When we stay silent, she continues. "There's a lake that will be cold, plenty of trails, and we'll have a fire at the end of the night." She grins. "I'll let the rest of the team know. I think it's just what we need."

Well, shit. This doesn't really fit well with my *keep a distance from Lake, she deserves better than me, and I don't have the capacity to fuck with her anyway* mode of operation. And it's certainly a wrench in my *Lake only deserves to start if she's better than me, which I don't believe is true* outlook. Now, her dreams are in my hands. And now, we'll be forced to share a yurt in the woods when we can barely pass each other in the hallway without being weird.

Oh, the messes I've made.

CHAPTER TEN

Bright and early on Saturday morning, we pile onto the team bus in a sleepy heap. I nod to the driver and walk down the aisle. Lake sits near the front of the bus with her bag in her lap, an open seat next to her. She wears her glasses and the navy pair of our team sweats. I pause momentarily, considering how warm her skin must be under all that cotton and how effortlessly sexy she always looks. When she meets my gaze, I flash her a grin and keep walking.

Maybe I should've sat with her, but we'll be together all weekend, and I'm not sure forcing her to sit with me on a bus for two hours is the best way to start this trip. There's a lot between us right now, and I piled most of it up, laid an impressive foundation of shit for us. Invited her to be vulnerable, made it clear I wanted her, and *boom*, ripped it all up and torched it in front of her face.

Then leaned in for a kiss. Classic.

If that weren't enough, now we have to decide which of us is going to start. So yeah, gonna give her some space while I can. Instead, I sit next to Rachel.

"Hey, loser," she says.

I slide my bag under the seat in front of me. "Hey."

She raises her brow and turns in her seat. "What's wrong with you?"

"Nothing." I sigh and dig my skull into the headrest. "I don't know. Things feel a little complicated all of a sudden."

"Complicated? That's not normally something you mess with."

While she's totally right, and part of me wants to tell her how I complicated everything with Lake, I only tell her the part that isn't in my control. "Trust me, I know. Promise not to tell anyone? I don't think the rest of the team is supposed to know."

She nods and plucks out her solo AirPod. "Yeah. You know I got you."

"Coach wants me and Lake to decide who's going to start at point guard. She's not going to choose."

"I'm sorry. What the fuck?"

I groan. "I know. And, like, I feel this guilt because I'm not trying to play after college, but Lake is." I rub my chest, feeling the creep of anxiety. It used to be a foreign feeling. "But if I'm the better player, I should start on principle. If she can't beat me, there's no way she can go toe-to-toe with the Diana Taurasi's of the league."

Rach blows out a breath.

"What?" I ask.

"You're not wrong, but friends keep it one hundred, right?"

My stomach sinks. "Right..."

"Lake is good. Like, *good* good. She's so good that when you're on the sidelines watching her play, you get this look on your face, like you're in awe. Your mouth is weirdly open, and I swear to baby Jesus you drool a little."

I lean away from her. "Fuck you, dude."

"But the thing is, you don't even look mad about it. You honestly look a little happy."

"Bullshit."

She shrugs. "Whatever. I just call it how I see it."

I slink down and put my headphones in. "Get your eyes checked," I say and turn up my music.

I'm not mad. Just a little surprised. I'm not denying she's good. Not denying she's got something most people don't: this weird natural connection to the ball and the court and the hoop. But that doesn't mean she's better than me.

"Doesn't mean she's better than me," I mumble.

"It doesn't," Rachel says.

I close my eyes and melt into my music, filtering through my go-to daydreams. I could replay fucking Suzy on her desk. Ripping her Polo off her tits is one of my particular favorites. Or maybe I spend this song with Andy, her fingertips dragging over my palm. *No.* Instead, I fall into the one daydream, the one memory, that I really shouldn't. On the roof of the library with my arms around Lake, my mouth against her neck. Only in this daydream, Rachel never calls.

❖

Red Dawn Lake is *iffy*, its water murky and ominous. If there isn't a dead body at the bottom waiting for vengeance, then there's sure as shit flesh-eating bacteria waiting to crawl through my ear canal and feast on my brain. Plus, it's probably ice cold. I guess I'm not the most outdoorsy person. We grew up playing sports, not camping.

"Gross." Nicky bumps my shoulder. "I'll give you fifty bucks to jump in."

I peer into the still black water. "No. Fucking. Way."

"Come on, y'all. Coach is assigning cabins and giving us the spiel," Rachel calls from the top of the ledge we climbed down.

"They're yurts," I say.

Rachel looks at me in utter disgust. "Whatever the hell they are, they're being assigned. So let's *go*."

Nicky and I climb after her and join the team around the giant firepit in the middle of a ring of yurts. The lake may give me the creeps, but the campsite is gorgeous. It's cold, but the sun finds its way through the green vegetation to warm our faces. There are ten yurts in total and a giant rack of firewood by the canoes that I pray Coach won't make us use. Lake catches my eye and looks away just as quickly.

"Okay, everyone. Here's the deal." Coach Jordan's words pepper the air in white puffs. "We're going to spend our time at Red Dawn Lake getting to know each other a little better. There's no ropes course, no trust falls, no scavenger hunts. Just us and this lovely place. You can spend your days doing whatever you want. But please, be careful, I don't want anyone twisting an ankle in the trails. We will meet back here at five. I've selected with whom I want you to room, and there is no debating. I have my reasons."

She flips through her Moleskin notebook that always peeks out of her back pocket, and I look at Lake before Coach even says our names. She stands alone a couple feet from Quinn. It's clear she hasn't formed any real connections with our teammates, but it's also clear that it's because of her. As if she's trying to keep her distance, get in and out. Except for me. She wanted to build a connection with me.

She catches me staring and raises her brows, shaking her head a little, as if to say *what*? I momentarily forget what my game plan is with her. Distance? I think it was distance, but not only is that being taken away from us this weekend, it doesn't seem to be helping our team figure out how to build chemistry again. And we certainly need to be in each other's space to figure out who's starting.

"Lake and Emma, yurt three."

We walk together to snag the keys from Coach. I stutter and fall back, letting Lake grab them. "Thanks," we both say and walk to our new digs.

The yurt is cozy. Basic but nice. In our little circular cabin, there's a dresser, a bunk bed with a twin on top and a full-on bottom, and fairy lights lining the ceiling. I drop my bag on the desk and spin in a circle while Lake pulls open the top drawer.

"It's nice," I say, casting my first line.

She shrugs and places her few items of clothing neatly in the drawer. "Are you going to unpack?"

I plug in my charger and connect my phone. "Not sure I see the point for one night."

"My mom always says you haven't really arrived until you unpack." She closes the drawer and tucks her bag away.

"Um. Okay." I grab my bag and walk over to the dresser, pulling open the bottom drawer.

"You don't have to."

I try to take as much care with my things as Lake did with hers, but it looks as sloppy in the drawer as it did in my bag. But whatever. It's for solidarity. "I know. But I want to *be here*." I close the drawer and look at her. "There, I have officially arrived."

A hint of a smile pulls at the corner of her mouth.

"Lake, I know I—"

"I'm going to go look around. Maybe take one of the trails." She tucks her phone in her pocket and grabs her water from the dresser. Reaches for the door.

"Wait," I say.

She turns and grimaces. It's not a put-on look, manicured to make me feel a certain way or to hurt me. It's sincere and achy. "Emma, please."

I've never heard someone say my name like that. So exhausted and sad. "Lake…"

"I can't. I don't *want* to. I'm here for one season, then I'm gone." She looks me up and down. "And whatever roller coaster you'd be in my life, I don't want to go on it. I'm sure the highs would be great, you're clearly a fun girl, Emma. But I know lows, and I don't want to do them anymore. All I want to do is enjoy a walk. By myself. Please."

She closes the door behind her, and I lower myself onto the mattress. Bury my face in my hands. For the first time in my life, I wonder if I'm a bad person, and it scares the living shit out of me.

Suzy flashes through my mind. She was so eager the weeks after we hooked up, dropping flirtatious bombs in front of my teammates and letting her gaze linger on me for too long. As she should. I've been knuckle-deep inside her, made her come while I sucked her tits, whispered how fucking sexy she was as I bent her over the desk. And now I can barely look at her because she wants more than I can give. Than I'm *willing* to give.

And all Lake wants from me is to not do the same to her. To leave her unscathed. And I'll do my best. I'll be a good teammate, a force to be reckoned with on the court, and a friend if she'll have me.

❖

Lake uses her free time to be anywhere I'm not. Which is mostly anywhere that isn't around the firepit. As I mentioned, I'm not outdoorsy. I'm *not* going hiking on my day off. Rachel and I laugh at something Quinn says and demolish a bag of Sun Chips as we stand around the nonexistent fire. This is my idea of relaxing.

Quinn knocks Nicky in the shoulder. "Brian was looking like a snack last practice in his tight little shirt. You still hitting that?"

Nicky flashes a sharp smile. "He's fair game, but I keep him pretty busy, so good luck."

We erupt into chuckles because we all know Nicky is the hottest, smartest, chillest girl Brian could ever get. He's a lucky son of a bitch.

I look around at everyone just chilling and vibing and realize I miss this. Guilt hits me because it was my responsibility to bring us together. To make things like this happen. Team activity nights will be reinstated as soon as we're home.

Lake appears at the mouth of one of the trails in the distance, and I watch her stroll toward the firepit.

"What about you, Em?"

She looks so defeated. I wonder if she feels like transferring was a mistake. She had one more—

"Emma," Nicky says.

I turn to her. "Hmm?"

"Had any fun conquests lately?" She gives me a slight nod as if she already knows what stories I have.

Lake opens the cooler and grabs a Propel. She glances at me before peeling a banana and sitting in the chair farthest from us. I don't normally kiss and tell. And there's no way in hell I'm telling them about Suzy while Lake is in earshot, even if Lake pretty much already knows.

I look into my cup of water, a little horrified to see dirt floating in it, and toss it out. "Nope. Just trying not to die every day at practice. That's my conquest."

Quinn slaps me in the arm. "Come on, Em. We all know you fucked Suzy."

"Dude. Don't be so fucking crass." Rachel pops her, and she stumbles back a foot. "Just because you want Suzy doesn't mean everyone else does."

She rubs her shoulder. "Oh, come on. You've seen her around Emma. I don't think the girl could blush any harder."

I watch Lake, who fiddles with the peel, obviously listening as Quinn continues with her bullshit.

"She practically strokes your leg when she tapes you, and don't get me started on the looks she gives you. Like she knows exactly what it's like to be fucked by Emma Wil—"

"Stop. Can you please just stop," I say. Not only is this conversation gross, but Lake is literally right there. "There's nothing going on between me and Suzy. She's all yours, Quinn."

Quinn and Nicky shuffle about while Rachel squeezes my shoulder because she knows I did, in fact, fuck Suzy.

"So you couldn't seal the deal?" Nicky asks.

I throw my empty cup at her. "Screw you guys."

The day slips easily by until five, when we need to meet at the firepit. As the sun continues to fall, it grows colder and colder, and I walk to the yurt to add some layers before we begin whatever Coach has in mind for tonight. Lake lies on her back on the bed and gives me a small wave when I walk in.

"How were the trails?" I ask. I peel off my sweatshirt and T-shirt. Me in no shirt is a scene Lake is very familiar with at this point, but I still feel her eyes on my skin. I pick a long-sleeve shirt and tug it over my head.

"They were gorgeous," she says softly, as if she doesn't want to concede her joy but can't help it.

I quickly switch my sweats for jeans, wondering if her eyes are still on me, then sit on the edge of the bed to tug on my boots. "It's so beautiful here," I say.

She pushes onto an elbow and reaches for me. I freeze. We haven't touched or been so close since I tried to kiss her, except for on the court, and I have no idea where her hand is about to land.

"Your shirt is caught." She runs her finger along the elastic of my sports bra, her knuckles brushing over my back ribs and freeing the tail of my shirt from itself. Her touch makes me shiver. Makes my stomach drop. She lies down again. "I know. It's so cold today."

"Freezing," I say.

"You did hook up with Suzy."

I don't look at her. I don't normally have an issue with lying. Not sure why everyone freaks out about it so much. All of life is one big cost-benefit analysis, and if lying benefits me…it's just a tool in the toolbox, really. I'd deny hooking up with Suzy to Quinn until my last breath. Cross my heart, hope to die. Cheat on a test. No shame.

But I don't want to lie to Lake.

I stare at the wood wall behind the desk. "Yeah, I did."

She straightens, sitting next to me, and squeezes my shoulder once. "Do you mind leaving? I need to change, too."

I'm wildly confused. She looks at me with sincerity, not anger, not judgment. Her eyes are soft. And she touched me. *Twice.* "You're not angry?"

She shrugs. "Why would I be? I mean, you're Emma Wilson. You're single. You can do whatever you want." She shakes her head. "Or whomever you want. Besides, I already knew."

"I don't want Suzy."

We stare at each other for a moment, and she nods. "I know you don't."

Something is thawing between us. Even if it's just a little warmer, I'll take it. "Okay. I'll give you some privacy. See you out there?"

"Right behind ya."

CHAPTER ELEVEN

The fire is roaring, which is a feat because Coach Jordan made us build it. And she swore there would be no team-building activities. But given we're a team of fifteen college-age girls, none of whom grew up camping, building the fire was a challenge.

There was lots of yelling. "Give it air," or "More sticks. We need more sticks," and "Blow harder." But after an hour, we figured it out, and I think we're all very proud of ourselves. I chuckle as I look around at my smiling team. If we ever crash on a deserted island, we would all die on day one.

We pass around Coach Jordan's phone that is hooked up to the Bluetooth speaker. Everyone adds two songs to the playlist, and we put it on shuffle.

"Did everyone enjoy the day?" Coach asks as the phone makes it back to her. We respond in a smattering of yeses. "Good. Good. As I said, there's no assignment for the evening."

"Except the fire," Nicky calls, and we all burst into laughter.

Coach chuckles. "Well, that was an unintended team-building activity. I can't believe not a single one of you knows how to build a fire." She shakes her head in obvious amusement. "Anyway, tonight is just for enjoying each other's company. There's more pizza than you could possibly eat, salad, and, like, ten pies. Go wild. We'll leave at around noon tomorrow."

We spend the evening laughing and indulging in pizza and pie and each other's company. Lake doesn't avoid me, but our interactions are short. I know she doesn't hate me. Maybe she feels more chill because she knows she dodged a bullet.

Me. I'm the bullet. The thought that she's emotionally let me go is kind of devastating. I drink my Diet Coke and wish it was beer as I watch my team dance around and be silly. It hits me that we haven't been silly together in a while. It's nice. Light.

"You should talk to her," Rachel says.

Lake smiles softly at something Justine, a freshman guard, said and tucks her hair behind her ear. She looks so good in her tight jeans, Timbs, and plaid wool coat. She catches me looking and grins, pushes her glasses up her nose, and focuses on Justine.

"What would I even say?"

"Just be honest."

I take another sip, the carbonation tickling my lips. "I don't even know how I feel."

"I think you do."

The night carries on in this nice little world away from Alder and stress and basketball. As I continue to catch Lake's eye and she continues to hold my gaze, I wonder if getting away from campus and the Den is the reset we needed. And something about me admitting to getting with Suzy helped, too. Not sure why.

Lake fist-bumps Justine and says something to Coach, then walks to our yurt. Excitement bubbles in my chest, followed by stress. I've been looking forward to and dreading this moment all day. Lake and I alone. We can talk, I can make things right, and we can move on from this once and for all. Right before the season starts.

I wait a few minutes so I don't look like a creep chasing her. Then I say, "Okay. Wish me luck."

"You've never needed luck," Rachel says.

I drain what's left of my drink and toss the cup in the trash. "I do now. See ya tomorrow."

"Good luck."

I walk by the coaches. "Night, Coach Jordan."

She gives me a pointed look, one brow raised. "Good night, Emma."

I nod. "Coach Fulton."

When I get to our yurt, I take a deep breath and knock. Lake yells, "Come in."

I crack open the door like I'm worried a wild boar may be lurking inside, ready to pounce. Or charge. Or whatever offensive move wild boars make. Lake sits on the bed, scrolling her phone. "Hey," I say. *Fucking brilliant.*

"Hi." She looks at me with a faint smile on her lips. So different from this morning.

I kick off my boots and hang my coat over the chair back on top of Lake's. It feels intimate. I quickly change into my pajamas to match her. "Can I join you?" I look at the space next to her.

"Sure."

I sit and have zero idea of what to say. Our team is rowdy outside, and I can hear the rumbling of laughter and the beat of the music, but it's quiet in here. Peaceful and dark.

"So how was it?" Lake asks.

"How was what?"

"Suzy."

I groan. "Come on. You don't want to know about that. Can we talk about literally anything else?"

She presses against my shoulder, and the proximity gives me butterflies. "C'mon. Did she tape you up?" She laughs, and it sounds so bright. I missed it. The few times I experienced it.

I can't help but laugh, too. "She did not tape me up."

"All that tape and ice and no foreplay? Maybe I overestimated you."

"I didn't say there was no ice."

She bites her lip and stares. And shit, she's devastating. I may be completely off, but it feels like this is turning her on, talking about Suzy. And I'm all about it. Even though literally hours ago, I swore to be good. But let's be real, I'm *bad*. "She iced you? Were you in pain?" she asks.

I swallow, hot and bothered. I was in pain. From not being able to have Lake. "She did."

"Where?"

I lift my shirt and run my hand over my abs. I can basically feel the cold ice dripping down my stomach. "Here."

She watches me without shame. "Sounds hot."

I drop my shirt and grin. "It was actually very cold."

She shakes her head and laughs. "Thanks for being honest with me. I don't care who you sleep with. We're just friends."

It kind of sounds like she's trying to convince herself of that, but I nod. "Yeah." Even though "just friends" is the last thing I want to be with Lake Palmer. And the thing I really need to be with her. "I know you don't want to hear it again, but I'm so sorry."

She stays quiet for a moment, watching me. "Are you? I kind of feel like you'd do it again."

"Do what again, exactly?"

She stares at her hands in her lap. "Give me so much and rip it all away. Then try to kiss me as if it wouldn't feel like a knife in my gut. And try to pretend you care at the same time."

Fuck.

She looks at me. "Whatever this is, can we just stop with the bullshit? We're clearly attracted to each other, but you have shit you haven't dealt with and, like, zero self-control. No offense. And I can't mess with that. I just can't. Like I said, I'm here for one season, one year, then I have no idea where I'll be. Either way, I'm going to lose everything I gain here. You and the team. So I'd like to keep things easy. Chill." She drops her hand on my shoulder. "I forgive you. Now, can we just get on with it and be friendly teammates?"

I let her words sink in. She doesn't want to lose people, so she doesn't want to invest in us. "You can't just skate on by and not connect with any of us. That definitely won't help us on the court."

"I'm not trying to skate on by."

"You never hang out after practice, and you're always standing away from everyone else. Coach is right. We need to build back our team chemistry, and you are a leader on this team. Whether you want to or not, you have to build connections here."

She's quiet, fiddling with a ring on her middle finger. I take the opportunity to move past this moment and go on building *our* connection. "River was a baller, huh?" I ask gently.

"The best," she says, looking at her lap again.

"Did he—"

She shoots me a look. "I'm not talking about this with you. Not when you haven't told me anything about yourself that isn't menial." Her words don't sound harsh, but they're demanding. "I don't know you."

"And you want to? Even though that'd be something to lose when you're gone?"

She shrugs. "At this point, I feel like I already lost you. So why not?"

I grab her knee, and the connection feels like a live wire. "Clearly, I have no idea what I'm doing when it comes to you. You haven't lost me. I just fucked everything up because I don't know what's right. You're the coolest, most beautiful girl I've ever met, so naturally, I self-sabotaged. Plus, you're trying to steal my spot on the team, and now we have to decide who gets to start." I shake my head and squeeze. "It's such a mess. I've been such a mess."

She looks at my hand and covers it with hers. "We have time to figure out who starts." She takes a deep breath. "Let's just…rewind. Okay?"

I feel her hand on mine all the way down to my toes. "Rewind?"

She nods. "Start over. Before we messed things up by going too fast." She takes her hand back and shifts away from me as if she just became aware of the intimacy. "We can be friends and teammates. We can have a winning season. We can do this."

I nod. *I can do this.* It feels important to not let her down. "Yeah. Okay. We can rewind."

"Great." She lies down and pats the space next to her. I lie beside her, and we both stare at the bed above. "So have you thought more about what your delicious is?"

I smile, instantly transported to my room with her telling me about her family's risotto. Before I ruined everything. "Still haven't found it yet. I'll keep you posted."

"Promise?"

"I promise."

"So in the spirit of getting to know each other better, can I ask you a question?" she asks.

A nervous crunch squeezes my stomach. "Yeah."

"You have this easy confidence about you. So why are you so terrified all the time?"

In the quiet, I think about her wanting to know me. And how I don't feel like a lot of people do. Andy knows me. Rachel mostly knows me. And that's it. *I can do this.* "I drive an old Subaru Crosstrek. My dad picked it out for me when I got my license. I had to pay for half of it and promise to drive my siblings to everything that I could if I wasn't in season for softball or basketball. But it was a manual, and I didn't know how to drive a stick."

She turns on her side and rests her head in her palm. "Go on."

"So me and my dad go buy this car, and he takes us to an abandoned lot to teach me how to drive a stick. He could tell I was nervous, but he told me to not worry, that it would come naturally to me since I was an athlete." I scratch my forehead. "I wasn't nervous about driving a stick. I was nervous to disappoint him. And, man, did I disappoint him."

"What happened?"

"Oh, I stalled out, like, a million times. It was terrible. I couldn't take the pressure of my dad in the passenger seat, getting more and more frustrated with every stall. I would've been way better off alone with a YouTube video. Finally, he turned to me and yelled, 'What the fuck is wrong with you?' And I straight up cried."

"That's so intense, Emma." Her fingers graze my arm. In a friendly way.

She's watching me with such gentle sincerity, it makes me want to tell her everything that has ever happened to me. Good and bad. And I want to know everything that's ever happened to her. "It gets better. Or worse, I guess. I'll never forget how he looked at me with such disgust and said, 'I guess I'll drive us home, then. Since you can't.'"

"Fucking brutal," she whispers.

"I'm not even finished." I laugh and take a moment to indulge in her touch. Funny how this is such a faded, normal memory to me, but telling Lake makes it sound so terrible. It *was* terrible. Every second of it. "We switched seats, and right when he was about to drive us home, he got a business call. He talked for half an hour while I cried quietly next to him. When he finally hung up, he said, 'We should go.' And that's how I learned how to drive a stick."

She strokes me slowly. Up and down. "But not really. How did you actually learn?"

I chuckle. "My mom taught me. And YouTube."

"And I imagine this wasn't a onetime type of thing."

I shake my head. I could tell her stories like this all night and still have a thousand more. "It's so much easier to try to please him—to try to please everyone—then to let the boat capsize. Guess I got pretty good at bailing water."

"Sounds like a lot."

"It is. But he also loves me so much, you know? Like, when we got home that day, he hugged me and apologized. Told me he loved me. It can be confusing, having a parent who's so quick to anger but quick to love, too. I don't know. You asked why I'm so confident and so terrified. I think I'm good at reading people and being what they want me to be because I have a lot of practice with him."

"So this is why you're so prolific with the ladies?"

I turn to her, a little shocked at how much I've already shared. "Yes. I'm a cocky, confident, insecure mess, and the women seem to love it."

She rolls onto her back again. "Your looks don't hurt, either."

"Sorry, what was that?" I shift to my side and hold my head in my palm like she just did. "I couldn't quite hear you with all the music and laughter outside."

She laughs and covers her eyes with her arm. "You heard me."

"We just established that I'm insecure and need *so much* validation. My dad was *so hard* on me, remember?" I whine and peel her arm away from her eyes so I can look at her.

"Fine. You're, like, stupid hot. It's not even fair, and you never have a shirt on." She shakes her head. "I'm pretty sure you do it on purpose."

My entire body is on fire. "Sometimes," I admit. "Lake, my stomach, like, twists in this super fuzzy weird way when I see you. You're stunning. Literally. And when I watch you play basketball, it's breathtaking. Everything about you is breathtaking."

She meets my gaze for a brief second and looks away. "Thank you."

I want so badly to kiss her, but I can't. Not only is the timing not right, but it's not what she wants. Not what we should do. We're starting over and have the opportunity to be good teammates who find each other super attractive. To be…friends.

"You already know this, but I didn't mean a single word I said to you on the trail," I admit.

"I know. But it still fucking hurt. You were trying to throw me away."

I wince, the shame barreling into me. "I was trying to save us. Save myself from fucking you up. And you from me."

"I'm a big girl, Emma. Don't make my decisions for me, okay? If I want to take a risk on you, that's what I'm going to do. If you didn't want me, that'd be one thing. But don't *Air Bud* me."

I grin at her movie reference. "I'm an idiot."

"Yeah. Sometimes. But I know you mean well."

I sigh, ready to move past this. "I told you something about myself. If you want to share with me, I'd like to hear more about River."

"Okay." She takes a moment, scratching the fabric of her pajama pants. "He was sunshine. Could walk into any room and all eyes would find him. People were just attracted to his energy. You remind me of him in that way. Though it may have been born of some pain for you, it still feels effortless." As she tells me about her brother, I lay my arm over her, letting it rest on her stomach. Only touching her as much as she touched me. "Anyway, he was the best brother I could have ever hoped for. It used to piss me off that he was better at basketball, but he'd play with me in the driveway every night before dinner until our mom called us in to eat. He was patient like that."

"What was his delicious?"

"Oh." She laughs, and I can feel it deep in her belly. A true, good laugh. "Not risotto. That boy's delicious was cinnamon sugar Pop-Tarts. He had a wicked sweet tooth."

Listening to her talk about River makes me feel close to her. She smiles in a way I've never seen her smile before. "Okay." I chuckle. "So he loved basketball, cinnamon sugar Pop-Tarts, and…"

"Playing *Madden* in the basement with his friends, chasing pretty girls from school, driving me to games. He loved to swim, too. Probably could've swam in college if he didn't choose basketball."

"Did he get along with your folks?"

"Too well." She grins. "It used to bother the shit out of me, actually. They were thick as thieves, and even when he got caught trying to sneak a girl out of his room in the middle of the night, they'd let it slide. Because he was such a good, nice guy."

"Do you get along with your parents?" My thumb twitches against the hem of her shirt.

"Um, yeah. I mean, things are so different now that he's gone. It's all a little muted, like the bottom of a pool. We're closer than ever but also further apart than ever. It's so weird."

I swear it's an accident, but my thumb slips and brushes against her skin. She takes a shaky breath. "Can you tell me more?"

"There's just too much grief for any of us to truly reach each other anymore. All I want is to cut through it and make them happy again. To give them this contentment they haven't had since River. I want to see them in the stands at my first WNBA game. I dream of seeing their smiles—their real smiles—in that moment." She shakes her head and sighs. "I want it so badly."

I stay quiet. I want it so badly for her, too. But it's on her if she achieves that dream or not. Not on me. At least, that's what I tell myself. I'm not going to hand her the starting position. Doesn't benefit anyone.

"Can I ask you something now?" she asks.

"Of course."

"You and Andy…"

"Ugh." I roll onto my back again, feeling weird about touching Lake while I talk about her. "You sure you don't want to keep talking about my dad?"

"I mean, I do. But not right now. Andy really fucked you up, huh?"

What do I tell her? Yes, but I fucked her up first. It's probably all my fault that things never worked out between us, and I've spent an entire year heartbroken over it. Do I tell her that Andy was there for half the things with my dad? That she was standing a foot away from me when he backhanded me for not wearing sunscreen? So close, we could've been brushing fingers when it happened. That I loved her and she loved me.

But for the first time, I feel like I can breathe again, and it's because of Lake. For the first time, I think Andy and I weren't meant for each other.

"Yeah. She did. But I'm okay now."

"How long did you two date?"

"That's the thing. We never dated." I chuckle and wipe my hands down my face. "We were friends growing up and were both too scared to make a move. Then, Andy found Maya, and I found out I was in love with Andy. And, yeah, it sucked. A lot." When she doesn't respond, I turn to her. "Listen—"

"I know you don't owe me anything when it comes to this stuff," she says, her voice sounding tired. She looks sad again.

"Lake?" She meets my eyes, and I let my fingers rest on her hip. "I don't have feelings for Andy in that way anymore, and I'm asking you to believe me. Sometimes, I lie. But I think you know I've never lied to you."

"Mostly," she says.

I flash back to the path. To me telling her I don't want her. "Yeah. Mostly."

She takes off her glasses and rubs her eyes. "It's getting pretty late, Em."

I just now notice the sounds outside have almost completely dissipated. She stretches to slide her glasses on the side table, and I begin to crawl off the bed to leave her alone, but she snags my arm.

"Don't make it weird," she says and pulls me down so I'm holding her big-spoon style. And she's holding me, too. By the arm at least.

I focus on how her stomach presses against my palm with every breath she takes. This must be what it feels like to meditate. To be hyper-focused and calm. I close my eyes and pull her tighter against me, bending my knees to match the exact angle of hers, erasing all the space between us. She tugs my hand up to her chest, interlacing her fingers over mine. And now I feel her breaths there, too.

Nothing about the way I feel is familiar. Like I have a fever but no pain. Like I've been dipped in aloe but don't have a burn. When I had Andy's body against mine, my hands exploring her skin, I felt hot and needy. Wet and excited. But right now, I feel home. I push my mouth against her neck, overwhelmed with the sensation of her warm skin against my lips, and I kiss her. Can feel her swallow in surprise.

"Emma—"

"Don't make it weird," I whisper against her pulse.

❖

I wake sometime in the early morning, I assume. It's still dark in the yurt, but I sense a brightness shouldering its way in. Lake's body is coiled around me like a corkscrew, her leg twisted with mine and her head on my chest. She groans and squeezes me tightly for a brief second before falling back into whatever dream she's having, her hand tucked under my shirt. The unfortunate thing is that I have to pee. It's not a casual get-to-it-when-I-can sensation; it's an emergency.

Lake's breathing is heavy and slow, but her hand pushes higher up my shirt. She's just shifting in her sleep. And now *this* is an emergency, feeling her hand on my bare skin, so close to my chest. How can I leave now?

Fuck, I gotta pee so bad.

She stirs again and slides her hand down, her fingertips dipping into my sweats. And now I'm wet.

Fuck, I want her so bad.

"Hey," Lake mumbles against my shirt. She pulls her hand from my waistband and tucks it against her chest. "Shit. Sorry, Emma." As she becomes aware of her entire body claiming mine, she peels her limbs from me and puts some space between us. "I can be a cuddly sleeper."

My bladder is going to burst. "I liked it," I say as I scramble over her and run outside to pee. The cold air feels incredible as I jog to the bathrooms. I can still feel Lake's entire body against mine, her hands on my skin. I splash some water on my face when I'm done washing my hands, and I'm a little shocked to see how red my cheeks are. I have it so bad for this girl.

No one else is up yet, and I walk back to the yurt. I knock once as I open the door. "Hey," I say.

"Hey." She sits up in bed, back against the small headboard. I kick off my shoes and crawl to sit next to her. She pats my knee but doesn't linger. "Sorry again for being so touchy last night."

"You're going to make me say it again?"

She grins. "Say what again?"

"I liked it, Lake."

She nods, her lips sucked under her teeth. "Yeah. I did, too."

"But you don't want to touch each other anymore?" I ask. I'm honestly a little confused about where we're leaving things. We rewound, sure. Rewound right back to that night we almost kissed. And now what?

"Of course I want to touch you," she whispers, and I feel her words all over my body like the brush of her knuckles. I'm still wet. "I'm a cuddly sleeper, sure. But I've never woken up with my hand in someone's waistband." She shakes her head. "Clearly, my subconscious very much wants to touch you. But this is, like, the farthest thing from a good idea."

I pick at the cuticle on my thumb. "I thought you trusted me when I said I was over her." I sound hurt. I guess I am.

"I think I do. It's not about that." She squeezes my hand and drops it. "It's literally everything else. We don't even know where we're going to go after we graduate."

"So what? No one can predict the future, and people still get together all the time. Just because it may not work out isn't a reason not to try."

"It is for me." She turns her entire body and crosses her legs, picking at her wool socks. "Of course it is for me. You think I want to fall for you? We're going to get back to Alder, then we still have to figure out who's starting, and who knows what that will be like? Then, we'll almost definitely go to different cities after we graduate. And you may be over Andy, but do you even want to be with anyone? I thought casual was you MO. I mean, are you even capable of a real relationship?"

I bristle at her words, had hoped she'd seen more in me. Was convinced she did. After last night, talking for so long and sharing myself with her, everything she just said feels like an actual fever. A tender burn. "Probably not," I say. "Guess I'm only capable of a good time."

"Hey, I didn't mean—"

"It's chill. You're right, anyway. This would probably never work." I dodge her hand reaching for mine and crawl out of bed before she can see my eyes water. "I'm going to see if Coach has some breakfast."

Chapter Twelve

So what if I avoid Lake for an entire week? It's completely fine. Everything is fine. I'm a professional about it. I've even perfected my casual *don't give a fuck* smile. There's not much left to say or do when it comes to us. My life is slowly falling apart, and she has a lot to do with that. What she said in the yurt wormed its way into my brain, and I can't claw it out. I almost believe her. Can I do anything other than casual? I don't know. Never tried.

But, fuck, it hurts.

So, yeah, I've been keeping my distance. Every time I see her face, I get this sick buzzing feeling in my stomach because I like her. A lot. Then I remember spilling my guts to her and her not taking me seriously. Well, I am serious. Practice has gone way smoother this week after our team building, and I'm working on planning another activity soon.

We have a week to decide who starts at point guard. One week.

I lie in bed, sore and exhausted from practice, and shoot a text to Whitney. I don't have any energy—my body is spent—but I'm hoping maybe she can fuck me into oblivion.

The door to the bathroom opens, and Piper pokes her head in my room. "Hey," she says all chipper and bright. I've never hated her more.

"Hey, Pipes. What's up?"

She takes a full step inside my room and fiddles with the purple drawstrings of her hoodie. "Just haven't seen you much in the last week or two. Wanna get dinner?"

Absolutely not.

"Oh, man. I was just about to head over to Rachel's. Rain check?"

"Yeah, okay. Rain check." She leaves me with a big smile and closes the door.

I feel a little guilty, but I just don't have the capacity for her right now. My phone buzzes against my stomach. It's Whitney. *My roommate is here tonight. I'll be there at nine.* I slide my phone in my pocket and tug on my hoodie. Turns out I don't want to lie to Piper, either, so I walk to Wilder.

❖

"What's up, Em?" Rachel asks. She slides to the head of her bed, making space for me.

"Hey, y'all." I sit by Rachel's feet and give Maya and Andy a little wave. They lounge together on Andy's bed, Andy's head on Maya's shoulder, and she straightens when my gaze falls on them. But the thing is, I feel nothing.

"What's been going on, Emma?" Maya asks. Things have never really felt natural between us, and her words are still heavy with effort. But I respect that she tries for Andy.

"Yeah, Rachel said the team had a good time at the lake. Did you enjoy it?"

I rub my thumb down my tight quad, thinking about the lake. Thinking about *Lake*. Rachel nudges me. I look up. "Yeah. The lake was nice, and correct me if I'm wrong, Rach, but we've been playing really well this week."

Rachel raises a finger. "We have."

"And have you picked a starter?" Andy asks.

I chuckle at the mess that is my life right now. Not only have we not picked a starter, we haven't even discussed how we're going to pick a starter. There's no good ending. Either way the chips fall, someone is going to lose. And at this point, basketball feels like the only thing I have left to hold on to. Who would I be if not Emma Wilson, starting point guard of the Alder Lions? I'm not willing to lose the one thing that tethers me.

"No." I expect myself to say more, and I can feel the awkward silence in my bones, but I can't. Normally, I could give an hour-long bullshit soliloquy about literally anything and at least earn a smile or two. But I can't seem to find my magic.

And I can't even find five more words to make my friends less uncomfortable.

Maya leans forward. "You want the spot?"

"Yes."

"Then fucking take it, Emma." Everyone glances at one another except for Maya, who stares at me. Andy lays a hand on her thigh, seemingly asking her to tone it down. "It's cool," Maya says to her and focuses back on me. "I normally think you're a cocky asshole whose ego can't possibly get any larger."

"Maya," Andy scolds.

But Maya smiles a sharp smile that only she could perfect, and I grin back. "Just like you," I say.

"Exactly. Because we're the best at what we do. I've seen you play more times than I can count, and there's no way this girl is better than you." She bites her lip with her sharp canine. "Much as it pains me to admit. So buck up, yeah? It weirds me out when you're all soft and insecure."

I can feel Andy and Rachel staring at me, waiting for some kind of reaction, but I've never felt closer to Maya in my life. It's what I needed to hear. This position is mine. I've held it for three years, and just because Lake wants it doesn't mean she's going to get it. Doesn't mean she deserves it. It's fucking mine. Emma Wilson, starting point guard for the Alder Lions, prelaw, and just may steal your girl.

"Asshole," I say. Everyone erupts into chuckles, and an ease falls over the four of us. An ease that has never existed before. It's like Maya just thawed my goddamn heart for her. A huge grin stretches over Andy's lips as she wraps an arm around her shoulders.

If she can make Andy smile like that after what she's been through recently, then maybe Maya's actually okay.

"At your service," she says with a wink.

"How's softball world?" I ask.

They both shrug. "Softball world is chill. We're going to have our best season yet. It's the Alder Queer Fellowship that's completely wild right now."

After the softball team joined forces for AQF's Fall Fest last year, Andy gradually became more involved with the organization that lobbies the university for protections for LGBTQ+ students and faculty. Its biggest goal is to get the university to officially recognize it as a school club.

"What's been going on?" I ask.

"Well, you know how Maggie Hyde got suspended for this semester?" I nod. "Jesse, the guy who was harassing her and her brother, Aiden, still has had zero consequences. Zero. Bailey is scrambling with the other officers to get something big planned for when she and Olivia get back. Like, maybe a walkout that would be coordinated with other private universities in the Southeast."

"Wow," I say.

"Yeah. I mean, think about it. Being recognized by the school is their big goal, and they're all about to graduate," Rachel says.

"I didn't really think about it that way." To be fair, I haven't thought much about AQF at all, though I've always liked the whole crew. Bailey seems awesome, and her girlfriend, Noelle, is sweet and gorgeous.

"Well, start thinking about it that way. We need everyone behind us," Andy says with that new ferocity that suits her so well.

"Okay," I say. "I will."

❖

"Harder. Like you want to hurt me," I say, panting against her damp shoulder. Her sweat on my lips is sweet and salty and familiar. I sink my teeth into her, and she groans as she drives into me, the wet thudding between my thighs chasing everything else out of my brain until all I can feel is Whit fucking me literally senseless. She grips a fistful of my hair and tugs hard, the sharp pain purging any other remnants of my consciousness. "Yes." I groan. "Fuck me like you hate me."

She strokes my clit with her thumb until I come. Fast and hard and not at all satiating. She pulls out of me, hot liquid trickling down my thighs, and I feel instantly empty.

Chapter Thirteen

Suzy has gotten the picture. She avoids eye contact as she wraps me for practice. Lake sits on the table to my left, and I want to die from discomfort. Maybe if someone didn't know about me and Suzy, they wouldn't assume something was majorly off right now. But Lake can surely sense the tension, and I'm thankful for her discretion.

"Oof," I say as Suzy rips the tape. "I'm sorry. That's really tight."

She whips her gaze up to meet mine for the first time and raises her brows, daring me to say it again. She wraps one more piece along the top even tighter and rips the tape. "You're done. Have a good practice."

"Fuck," I mutter under my breath. But I slide off the table and nod at Lake as I walk out of the training room. She nods back. I can barely look at her. Lately, she's represented every damn thing in my life that stresses me out. And everything about myself that I hate. Looking at her makes me sick. And to make it all worse, I have to meet with Weber after practice to go over my law school apps before I call my dad.

What a great fucking day.

❖

Practice is brutal. My legs are cement blocks dragging along the court, and my head is fuzzy. I keep just barely missing my shots, missing my open teammates, and missing the play calls because I can't hear anything over the white noise of chaos in my brain. Coach Jordan watches me closely the entire practice. I can feel her eyes on me. But she must find me pitiful or something because she doesn't say anything.

Sweat drips down my temple, down my arms and legs, as I walk back to the locker room after practice.

"You good?" Nicky asks.

"Yeah. Just an off day."

She shrugs and grabs a towel for the shower. Lake appears behind her, but I peer into my locker as if I don't see her standing a foot away from me trying to catch my eye.

"Emma?" Her voice is tentative as she takes a step closer. She's pretty unavoidable now.

"What's up?" I throw my towel on my chair and stare at her, trying to not give away any emotions. Useless, given she just saw how practice went for me.

"Sorry to bother you. It's just...we're running out of time to give Coach our decision and—"

"I want to start. This is my team, and I've held this position since I was a freshman. If you think I'm just going to hand it to you, you're dead wrong, Lake."

Her mouth drops an inch, and her eyes widen before she wipes her expression and straightens. She's sweaty, too. The beads gather on her chest and drip between her breasts. Even when she's hurt me, even when she's my enemy, I still want her. "I wasn't expecting you to just step aside, but what do you propose we do? We have to figure this out, like, ASAP."

I peel off my jersey and throw it in the hamper. It's like my power move. Makes me feel strong and in control, even if she doesn't let her gaze drop from my eyes this time. "One-on-one."

"One-on-one?"

"I mean, yeah. Makes the most sense, right? The best player should have the job, so let's play for it."

She scoffs. "I'd hardly call one-on-one an accurate depiction of a point guard's skills, given we don't have a team to command."

I shrug. "Sounds like you're scared to lose."

"You're ridiculous," she says.

"That's the consensus. Yes." I press a hand to my chest. "May not be capable of much, but I can guarantee, I'm capable of beating you."

She shakes her head. "I didn't mean it like that now, and I didn't mean it like that in the yurt. Can you please stop?"

"Stop?" I chuckle, her words from the yurt on loop in my brain. She meant every goddamn one. "I couldn't stop if I tried." I walk away, then call over my shoulder. "We'll play tomorrow after practice."

❖

Weber lounges in his office with a cup of coffee and a newspaper. The small room is dimly lit and warm; not sure how he doesn't fall asleep in here. I sit and pull a notebook from my bag and nod to his paper. "Didn't know those things still existed."

He chuckles and takes a sip. "I'm shocked you even know what this is." He flaps the pages and spreads it wide in front of his face as if to show off how dignified and old he is.

"I guess you are kind of old," I say.

He winks from behind his thick black glasses and folds the paper. "Listen, someone is joining us today from UGA. A law school recruiter to walk you through next steps and talk to you about the law program in Athens. She's a friend of mine."

"What?" I shake my head. "It was only supposed to be us."

"Are you not okay with that?" He cocks his head as he studies me.

My heart rate quickens under his gaze, my palms itchy and damp. "I…I wasn't ready to take this step. I'm not ready to meet her."

"You asked for my help, Emma. You either want to do this or you don't. You can't keep going back and forth and expect me to—"

"Shit." I throw my notebook in my bag and stand. My entire face is on fire. My cheeks, my forehead, my ears burn. I'm going to run. Out of this office and away from the person in my life who wants to help me the most. My blood prickles with adrenaline.

Weber raises his hand and pushes it gently down. "Emma, please. Sit down."

I shake my head. "I'm not ready."

"She shouldn't be here for another ten minutes. We can sit and talk about—"

"I'm sorry, okay?" I hike my bag up my shoulder and walk to the door. I'm a quitter. A runner. Lake was right; I can't handle serious. I can't handle *it*. He calls after me one more time before I'm too far down the hallway to hear him anymore. I push open the door and sidestep a striking woman with streaked gray hair and a messenger bag. She has a pin on her lapel.

Tracy Wriggs

Recruiter

UGA Law

"Excuse me," she says through a smile.

"Yeah, sure. Sorry," I sputter and jog to the concourse where it's safe. Where students flow past me and around me. Through me. I take deep breaths, but nothing helps the self-loathing that coils around my gut. I literally ran away. *And what're you going to do now? Coward.*

My phone rings in my pocket, and I don't need to pull it out to know it's my dad, eager for updates on my life. Eager to hear how his eldest is crushing it. I silence it and walk slowly back to Griner as if a death sentence is waiting for me there. Drag my feet. This must be what it feels like to drown, heavy and sinking.

When I get to my room, I lock the door to the bathroom and collapse on my bed. I close my eyes and imagine Whitney on top of me, spreading my thighs and filling me. Fucking me so hard that maybe I could disappear into the mattress. I can feel the weight of her body settling on me. I open my phone, not sure if I'm going to call her or my dad.

I call my dad.

"Emma, how's it going?"

He sounds soft and jovial, like he's in a good mood. I have no idea what I'm going to say to him when I open my mouth. "Yeah. It's going."

"Basketball season is just around the corner. Feeling good and prepared?"

"Yeah. Yep. Good and prepared." I cringe because I know what question is coming next: the LSAT I supposedly registered for is coming up.

"Great. That's great. And you feel like you've prepared enough for the LSAT? I emailed you those resources. Alder has study groups and mentors—"

"I have a mentor, and, yes, I feel prepared. Actually met with a UGA Law recruiter today. She says I'm on track for the fall." I squeeze my eyes shut. *Delusional*. So fucking delusional.

"Fantastic, Emma Bear. Absolutely fantastic. I'm so proud of you."

I'm not much of a crier. Not that I don't feel my emotions deeply; it's just the tears never seem to form. But when my dad tells me he's proud of me, it feels like he's knocking on the door of a home I don't live in anymore. I don't know who I am anymore. A tear gathers at the corner of my eye. I'm not taking the LSAT on Friday, and after what I just pulled on Weber, I'm not sure I'm going to law school at all. And after tomorrow, after Lake and I play for keeps, I may not even be a starter. I've *never* not started. "Thank you," I eke out.

He doesn't hear the crack in my words, and I don't blame him. It's too soft, as if I'm too cowardly to even stand by my shaky voice. I hear him talking to someone in the background.

"Grace wants to say hi. You have time?"

I wipe at the tear and straighten, a zap of energy surging through me. "Of course. Put her on."

"Dad sounds happy with you," she says. I can practically hear her eye roll.

"Gracie. Gracie, Gracie, Gracie. I miss you."

She is the youngest, clocking in at twelve-years-old, five feet tall, and probably a higher IQ than all of us put together. She's sarcastic and loving and refuses to bend to what anyone thinks she should be or do. She's, like, my hero and definitely my favorite sibling.

"You know I miss you, too. Why do you think I'm wasting my time talking to you when I could be watching *SpongeBob*?"

I chuckle. "Tell me everything."

She sighs an exaggerated sigh that only a middle schooler is capable of. "Sean failed his geography test"—she drops her voice—"and Dad is *pissed*."

"Really? He sounded so chill."

"Only because he got to talk to Emma Bear, the golden child," she says with a sarcastic lilt.

"There's nothing golden about me, Gracie."

She scoffs and chews something crunchy. "I've known you since I was born. You're as golden as they come. Just like me. Don't you forget it."

"Hmm." I smile against my phone. "If any boys touch you, I'll fucking kill them. Don't *you* forget it."

"Ugh, you're so ritualistic and basic."

I chuckle at her witty sass. "It's just a warning."

"Not to mention, sexist. I'm pretty sure a girl is just as capable of hurting me as a boy."

"If not more." I scoff. "Whatever, okay? Just don't date. You're not allowed to date until..."

"Emma?"

"Hmm?"

"I love you."

I fall back onto my mattress and exhale, the tears threatening to gather again. "I love you so much, Gracie."

"Whatever's going on over there, I know you can do it," she says quietly. I wonder if it's so my dad doesn't hear.

"How do you know what—"

"A lawyer?" I can hear another eye roll, and it makes me smile. "Come on, Em. I'm not stupid. I have met you before, you know."

"Nothing to worry about over here. I promise."

She stays quiet for a moment, surely debating whether to call me on my bullshit or not. Thankfully, Gracie is, indeed, graceful. "Okay, I'm bored of you. I'm going to go watch *SpongeBob*."

"Love you, too, Gracie."

The line dies, and I drop the phone on my stomach. *Well that was a whirlwind.* It's early, but I brush my teeth and crawl into bed. Sometimes, you just have to put the day away and move on. I close my eyes and try to push everything out of my mind. Not even Whitney is allowed to stay. Instead, I imagine a flame. A single flame. No wood crackling underneath or wax dripping down a candle. Just the quiet whirring of one flame, consuming my thoughts, my worries, my stresses. Consuming me.

CHAPTER FOURTEEN

The clanking of weights rings in my ears as I struggle to finish my reps of tricep extensions. I won't see Weber again until tomorrow, and I haven't been able to stop thinking about how I ran out on him yesterday.

Focus on taking deep breaths with every rep.

The only other thing I can think about is how today is the day Lake and I settle who's starting. The hairs on my neck stand straight at the thought. What if I lose? What if *she* loses?

I dread both.

By the way Lake walks around the weight room, determined and confident, it would appear that she's not all that worried. As if she knows she'll beat me.

I push through my last reps and drop the weight on the rack. Rachel walks by and gives me a fist bump. "You good, dude?"

"Yeah," I say and take another deep breath. My shirt sticks to my back as I shake out my arms.

"You're, like, super sweaty. Here." She hands me a water bottle, her lip curled in disgust.

I squirt the cool liquid into my mouth and wipe my lips with the back of my hand. "Why you gotta be such an asshole?"

"I'm just keeping—"

"Keeping it one hundred. I know, I know."

She nods. "Exactly." She holds out her hand, and I give her back the water. "You're probably better than her. Don't sweat it, okay?"

I nod, and she walks back to her station. But the thing is, I'm not sure if I'm better than Lake. Going into our game tonight feels like a coin toss. I have no idea what will happen.

❖

The gym is empty. I flip on the lights and tuck my keys in my bag as the big fluorescent bulbs zap to life. There's something vast and important feeling when I'm alone on the court. It's just so much empty space, every step I take is dramatic and echoey. I sit on the bench and trade my slides for basketball shoes. Lace them up the same way I've been lacing them since sixth grade. I shuffle my feet to make sure my shoes aren't too tight or my soles too dusty, then pick a ball from the rack and dribble to the key.

I meant to be this early. Wanted a half hour to sort out my mind and warm up before Lake gets here. Make five from the block, five from the shoulder, and five threes. I can't start anything until I make my fives. It's ritual. Then, I drop the ball and take a couple laps to get my blood warm and pumping.

The crack of the double doors sends a nervous shiver down my spine, and I can hear Lake walking to the bench. I turn the corner, and there she is in her sleeveless, black Nike Dri-FIT, a pair of navy practice shorts, and her all-white basketball shoes and crew socks. She rolls her waistband so her shorts hit higher up her thigh. It's not fair how beautiful she is.

She nods. "Hey."

"Hey." I grab the ball and walk over to meet her. "So how do you want to do this?"

She shrugs and pulls her hair back with an elastic. "How everyone does it."

"To eleven? Win by two?" I confirm.

"How else?" She rolls out her neck and runs through a brief stretching routine. "I'm going to take a couple laps and warm up. Then you ready to roll?"

I pass the ball between my fingertips. "Yep. Let's get this over with."

After Lake warms up, we meet at the top of the three-point line to shoot for possession. Whoever misses first is on defense. Nothing is really on the line yet, but when I step up to shoot, a quick flash of nerves blurs my vision. I take a deep breath and shake my eyes straight. *Swish.*

"Good luck," I say.

Lake steps to the line and sinks her shot. No preamble. No deep breath. Nerves of steel. "Thanks," she says and jogs to retrieve her ball.

We go back and forth, shot for shot, swish for swish, until Lake shoots a brick, and it's settled: my ball. I check it, and she gives it right back, lowering into her defensive stance, her eyes lasers on mine until they lower and focus on my core. Since I'm already on fire, I take one hard dribble at her to back her off, then step back and sink a three, which in one-on-one counts as two. Two to zero. A solid start.

I retrieve the ball and meet her at the top of the key. "Coach Fulton's drills seem to be paying off. Nice shot," she says.

I don't respond. Too focused. Sure, I'm up, but I'm up against Lake Palmer. I bounce the ball to her, and she pulls up. I jump to block the shit out of her shot—an obnoxious block, where I slap the ball into the bleachers and tower over her after—but she pump-fakes and drives to the hoop for an easy layup. Two to one.

I play to win the game. Always. But when Lake brushes against me, the heat of her skin against mine, I don't even know if I *want* to win. She pushes the ball into me and grins, and something about it bothers the shit out of me. Her words in the yurt burn in my chest. Lake doesn't want me. Lake doesn't take me seriously. And Lake doesn't care.

I shove her away with my shoulder, and she stutters back with an *oomph.* I sink another three like it's nothing. Like I can't miss.

"The hell was that?" she asks, her brows pulled tight over her eyes, hands on hips.

"That's four to one. Try to keep up." I throw her the ball hard. Too hard.

She flinches as she catches it, and I feel a prickle of guilt. "In what world would whatever you just did be considered checking the ball? That doesn't count."

"You giving it to me at the top of the key is the literal definition of checking the ball. You touched the ball and gave it to me, signaling you're ready," I explain. These rules are universal.

"That's some shady shit, and you know it. You shoved me." She curls her lip, and I feel her disapproval deep in my chest. Just like my father's and Weber's and Coach's. But it feels like a slap in the face coming from her. Well, fuck everyone, and fuck her, too. She thinks I'm a shitty mess of a person, and she's right. I am.

So come at me, Lake Palmer. I've got nothing to lose.

I drop my head back and laugh. "You want some pity points, Lake? Take them. I'll hit that shot all night long, and you know it. Two to one, then. Or do you want to just make it zero to one so you have a chance at winning?"

She shakes her head as she glares at me, eyes narrowed. It could be my imagination, but it looks like they're watering. "Fuck you, Emma."

"You're more than welcome to." I spread my arms. "Don't you want to know what you're missing out on? I'd bet Suzy would give me five stars." Her mouth falls open as she watches me implode. "But you don't want to be with me because I'm a mess. Well, guess what, Lake? You're a mess, too."

A single chuckle of disbelief puffs from her mouth. "*I'm* a mess? Is that right?"

I nod emphatically. "Yes. Yes, it is. I may be drowning, but you have such fucked-up attachment issues, you couldn't even let Coach Jordan leave you. You followed her to a failing basketball program in the middle of nowhere North Georgia for your last season of college ball just because you have a fear of abandonment from your brother dying. And you say you're going to the WNBA? Fat fucking chance coming out of Alder." My yelling reverberates through the gym, echoing in the rafters and amplifying. The louder it gets, and the farther that tear falls down her cheek, the more I lose control. "And with me. You're scared to take a step with me because you don't want to lose me, either. You'd rather have nothing and no one than lose anything again."

It's dead quiet until she brushes the tear from her cheek. "Take a step with you? With *you*?" She lets the ball fall, and it bounces to the sideline. "I *hate* you, Emma." She turns, grabs her bag, and leaves me alone on the court, the doors slamming behind her.

After all my yelling, it feels so quiet. There's a buzzing in my ears. I look around the gym, a bit shocked. It's chill. I'm chill. Everything is fine.

❖

I've skipped a lot of classes in college. In high school, too. But I've never skipped Weber's class. Until today. I just can't face him. Can't face myself or all that I've done. Haven't done. Will do.

Instead, I meet up with Andy at the library between her classes for a cup of coffee. Well, coffee for her—that shit's gross—and a smoothie for me. We find a table in the corner tucked away from the anxious studying of the other students. My smoothie is not good: flavorless and chunky enough to make sucking it through my straw an Olympic sport. Andy tells me about this big gala AQF is planning before graduation in the atrium of the forestry department building. I stand mid-sentence and slam my smoothie in a nearby trashcan, pink splattering against the plastic lid. I didn't mean to be so aggressive, but when I sit across from Andy again, she grimaces.

"Emma." She says my name quietly and with such affection, it cuts through everything. Through all of our history and all of my anger, right down to the core of us. To our friendship. She'll always be my best friend. She reaches over the table and holds my hand. A speck of pink smoothie clings to my wrist, and she wipes it away with her thumb.

"I know," I whisper. "I know."

She squeezes my hand and doesn't let go. I know all her mindfulness tricks; she's anchoring me. "Take a deep breath."

"Andy, it's fine. I—"

"I've known you for ten years. We have been *through it* together. I stood next to you when your dad slapped you, when you broke your foot in eighth grade, and I thought you'd lose your mind from not being able to play, and you were with me through everything, too. The roller coaster of my dad's health. Everything. And through all that, over all those years, your light never dimmed. You never stopped being Emma Wilson. The person who could walk into any room and instantly *fit* because people are drawn to your ease and confidence." She loosens her grip on me. "Now take a deep breath and hold it for five. No arguing."

I close my eyes and take a deep breath, hold it for five, then release in a long, slow exhale. When I open my eyes, Andy is looking at me like I've just broken her heart.

"Until now," she says. "Emma, I hardly recognize you. Your energy is so, so dark. There's nothing light about you. And there doesn't have to be. There's no pressure to be any certain way, and people change. But I'm worried about you." She shakes her head as if she's willing away tears. Seems like all I do is make people cry nowadays. "You can tell me anything or nothing at all. Just know that I'm here, and I see you *drowning*. I see you, and you're not alone. Okay?"

I squeeze her hand, realizing I never lost Andy at all. "I don't know how to do anything anymore," I whisper. It's horrifying to hear myself sound so desperate.

She leans closer over the table. "I know it can feel that way sometimes. When things get dark, and you feel like all you ever do is fall, remember, living is muscle memory. Who you are in all of your confident, beautiful glory, is all still in you. It's all muscle memory, and it *will* come back to you. I promise."

"Yeah." I chuckle. "Sooner rather than later would be great. At this rate, I will have ruined my entire life by Tuesday."

"Good thing today isn't Tuesday." She winks. "Let's start with trying to figure out one thing together, and maybe things will start to follow suit. What's something you feel like you can't handle right now?"

The tornado that is my life swirls through my head. "Lake and I were supposed to pick a starter by Friday. We played one-on-one last night. Winner was supposed to start, but we didn't finish the game because…" I trail off. The memory of yelling at Lake about her dead brother as a tear falls down her cheek threatens to push me over the thin ledge of my sanity.

"What happened?"

I shake my head. "I was horrible to her. To Lake. I made her cry."

"Okay. Let me ask you something. Do you actually care if you start? Or does it feel more like an identity thing? Because I know you to be strong. And there's strength in both outcomes here, in winning a starting position and in stepping back. Letting go can be empowering. Sometimes, it's the strong thing to do. But only if it's right for you."

"My dad would—"

"Fuck your dad, Em. What would make *you* happy?"

Hah. What would make me happy? Feeling the way I used to feel. Knowing exactly who I am and what I want and always knowing how to get it. I don't actually care if I start or if I get the most playing time. It just feels like what I should want and should be. What I actually want is for Lake to look at me how she did on the roof of this building again. For her to forgive me. And I don't want to be a lawyer. I'd rather be literally anything else.

"Taking a step back. I think that would be a good place to start," I say.

Chapter Fifteen

Two days have passed since my one-on-one with Lake. One day has passed since I ditched Weber's class. Lake can't even look at me, I'm guessing. The truth is, I can't look at her, either. When we're forced opposite each other on the court, and I have to see her, smell her sweet sweat, I can't handle it. I black out. I black out this entire week. The entire year, really.

"Okay, y'all. To reiterate, for Tuesday's game against Pine Grove, we'll have three main focuses. Shut down Felicity Harmon, control the pace on offense, and feed Rachel in the post. Any other observations or questions from film?"

We sit quietly in the Den. We've been discussing film for hours. No one has any questions left.

"Great. Enjoy your day off, and I'll see you all on Monday," Coach Jordan says.

Rachel nudges me. "We should do a team activity. You said you'd reinstate them, remember?"

"Yeah. Yeah, sure." I sling my bag over my shoulder and nod. "Listen, I'll catch up with you later."

She narrows her eyes, then shrugs. "Whatever, dude."

I spot Lake from the corner of my eye as I skip down the stairs to catch Coach Jordan before she leaves. Today was supposed to be decision day for me and Lake, and I wonder if Lake told her about our failure to decide.

"Coach Jordan," I call.

She stops in the hallway, and I catch up to her. "What's up, Emma? Do you have a decision for me?"

"Um, yeah."

She stares at me as my teammates walk past us to leave. Coach steps to the side, out of the way, and I follow. "Do you have a car?"

"What? Yeah, I have a car."

"Come over for an early dinner tomorrow. My wife makes the most delicious rib roast in the entire world. Four o'clock. I'll text you the address."

"Oh. Okay."

Coach lives in the country. I mean, there's nowhere else to live out here besides the country, but I'm still shocked by her long, winding driveway and lack of neighbors. I park next to a Honda Odyssey and take a moment to gather myself. I'm typically good in these situations—meeting the family or being a good guest or whatever—but I haven't been good at anything in a long time.

I take my phone out of the holder and close my map. Against my better judgment, or with lack of any judgement, I text Lake.

My behavior on Wednesday was completely inexcusable. I'm sorry for hurting you. For wanting to hurt you. I wanted to make you feel how I feel. And it makes me sick. I hope we can talk soon.

I send it without rereading it or thinking twice about it. Rely on muscle memory for that one.

I tuck my phone in my pocket and take a deep breath, hoping this isn't going to be as awkward as I think it is. I run a hand through my hair and check my teeth in the mirror. *Good enough.* Wore my nice clothes: an acid-washed pair of Levi's with a tight, black, ribbed sweater and my tan coat. I grab the bottle of wine I panic bought and walk to the front door.

The house is gorgeous, a wooden cabin with green shutters and a basketball hoop above the garage, of course. The backyard looks to be a big, rolling green field with a view of the mountains peeking over the tops of the trees.

"Nice spot," I whisper as I knock on the door.

Coach Jordan answers with what I guess to be a five-year-old boy glued to her hip and a girl around twelve standing next to them. "Emma, you made it all right?" Her tone is lighter than I've ever heard it. Something I'm not expecting, given my poor behavior lately. But she probably doesn't even know about that.

"Yeah. It was an easy drive," I say.

She steps aside and pulls her daughter out of the way. "Come in. Come in. This is Jessa." She squeezes the little girl's shoulder. "And this is Benny."

"It's nice to meet y'all," I say. And it's true. I feel lighter. More myself. I guess being the oldest of four, having little kids around is kind of my comfort zone. A world I know and love. "Oh, is that Ranger Z?" I point to Benny's shirt, and his entire face lights up.

"You know Ranger Z?"

I flatten a palm to my chest. "The baddest zombie alien hunter in all of the galaxy? *Of course.*"

He peels away from Coach and grabs my hand, pulling me into what looks like the playroom. "Have you seen the new gear pack? There's this thingy that shoots up a building, and it has this hook thing on the end to help you climb. And—"

"After dinner, Benny," Coach calls from the entryway. "Can you please bring Emma to the kitchen?"

He sighs and calls back, "Fine." He pushes his toy gear pack to the corner and takes my hand again.

"A grappling hook," I whisper. He looks up at me with curiosity. "The thing that shoots the hook. It's called a grappling hook."

"Grappling hook." He grins.

The kitchen is straight out of an article of *Southern Living*, with an expansive white marble island, stainless appliances, deep blue cabinets, and bronze fixtures. It's beautiful.

The woman chopping onions with such finesse I almost forget to say hi, puts down the knife and smiles at me. "You must be Emma. I'm Julie. Franny has told me so much about you."

"Thank you for having me. I brought this to pair with dinner." I smile and hold up the bottle of. "Not sure if it's any good, but the guy at the shop assured me it would pair well with the roast."

Coach and Julie exchange a look, and Julie walks around the island to take the wine and wraps me in a big hug. "That is the sweetest. Thank you."

"It's nothing."

Coach watches me with a grin. "You know, Jessa's outside shooting hoops if you want to join her for a bit while we finish up here."

I chuckle. "Oh yeah? I'm kind of scared she's going to whoop me."

Coach crosses her arms and leans against the counter. "You should be. She's a little baller. Been trying to perfect her reverse layup. Maybe you can give her some pointers."

"Yeah." I shrug. "I'd love to."

"I'm coming," Benny shouts as he follows me down the hall to the front door.

I hold it open for him. "Are you a baller like your sister, Benny?"

He runs outside, tripping over a stick on the walkway but steadying himself before he falls. "Yeah. I have a hoop, too."

Jessa sinks a shot off the backboard. "He hates basketball," she says.

"That's not true," he whines. He scurries away, seemingly looking for his toy basketball in the bushes by his little plastic hoop.

The sun dips lower in the sky, and dusk begins to soften the edges of everything. The sound of the ball bouncing on concrete and knowing dinner is on the stove fills me with a warm feeling of home and innocence. *Shooting hoops before dinner...*

"Wanna play to five?" I ask.

She tosses me the ball, and I squat, shooting underhand from between my legs, granny-style. It doesn't even hit the rim, but it makes Jessa laugh. "What's so funny? This is how your mom taught me to shoot."

"Mm-hmm. Play to five. Make it, take it."

"Make it, take it?" I shake my head. "Your house rules are ruthless."

She shrugs, dribbling to the top of the driveway. "If you're too scared, you can play against Benny instead."

"Oh, shit." I shoot a hand to my mouth, looking for him in the bushes. "I mean…*oh, shoot*. Where's Benny?"

She laughs. "My moms say shit a hundred times a day. It's fine. And he ran inside to find his ball."

Jessa checks me the ball, and I pass it back. "Don't say shit."

She dribbles to the left so assuredly, I assume it's her dominant hand. Until she fakes me out with a sweet little spin move and drives to the hoop with her right, sinking a layup.

"Damn, Jessa. You got some moves, kid."

"Don't say damn. And don't call me kid."

I can't help but laugh as she retrieves the ball and struts to the top of the driveway. I almost forgot we were playing make it, take it. I may be having all sorts of life crises, but I should really not lose to Coach's daughter.

She drives to her right this time, and I steal the ball from her sloppy crossover, give her a gentle push out of my way—totally clean, I swear—and nail a beautiful reverse layup.

"How do you do it like that?" she asks.

I bend with a sigh to pick up the ball, the denim of my pants a bit more constrictive than I'm used to. "To be fair, it made me nervous with the closed garage door right there. Kind of felt like I was going to smash into it."

"I know. I feel the same way."

"Can you open it?"

Jessa grins and runs inside. The big white door creeks open, and Jessa jogs back out. "Show me again," she says.

"Okay." I go slower this time and dribble under the hoop, spinning the ball over my shoulder and sinking the reverse layup. "Just like a regular layup. Hit the same spot on the backboard and release it the same way. Off your fingertips with a little spin, especially if your body isn't angled quite right."

"Like this?" She walks under the hoop and shoots an imaginary shot.

I nod. "Yep. Exactly."

I pass her the ball, and she takes a deep breath, then completely flails under the hoop, limbs flapping in the exact opposite of what I just told her to do. I laugh hard, hands on my knees, wiping my eyes.

"Shut up," she says.

I wave in front of my face. "I'm sorry. I'm sorry. That was just terrible." The last of my chuckles escape, and I put my hand on her shoulder. "Listen, you're clearly a baller and super talented, just like your mom. But you're never going to achieve your best when you play all rigid like a robot. You gotta loosen up. Just *play*."

"Just play? What is that even supposed to mean?"

I grin and slap the ball out of her grip, score a quick shot, and sprint for the ball.

"What the—" She sprints after me, sensing that all rules are now off the table. I beat her to it, but she hip checks me out of the way and snags it, taking it to the hoop for a basket.

I chuckle. "Well played."

She grabs the ball and drives to the hoop again. And here it is: the perfect moment for her reverse layup. I cut off her angle and force her under the hoop, so her only option is to bail on her drive completely or go for the reverse.

And she fucking *nails* it.

"Yes," she shouts into the air, flexing her guns, all proud and accomplished.

And, holy shit, I feel amazing. Twenty minutes out here playing backyard basketball with Coach's daughter, and I feel happier and more myself than I have for two entire years. "Wow. That was beautiful. And guess what?" I pass her the ball.

"What?"

"Now that you've done it, it's muscle memory, and you'll be able to nail it every time." I nod to the hoop.

She grins and jogs under the hoop, hitting another reverse layup.

"Well done, Jessa. That was beautiful," Coach Jordan says. She leans against the door frame and claps.

"Did you see my first one against Emma? She couldn't even block it," Jessa says, a little breathless.

"I did." Coach wraps her in a hug. "I saw it all." She pulls up and smiles at me. "You girls ready for dinner?"

"I'm starving," I say, and Jessa nods.

"Dinner is on the back patio. You know the rules," Coach calls after Jessa, who runs inside.

I meet Coach by the front door. "What are the rules?"

"Just to wash your hands before dinner. Kids are gross." I chuckle, and she squeezes my shoulder. "You were fantastic with her, Emma. I'm really impressed."

"Me? She was the impressive one."

Coach smiles and nods for me to go inside. "Bathroom's on the left."

Chapter Sixteen

After dinner, Coach Jordan turns on a movie for Benny and Jessa in the living room, then returns to the covered patio with another bottle of wine and a bowl of kettle corn. The night hums around us as we digest our delicious meal and snack on something sweet. I sip on the same glass of wine I had during dinner, not wanting to overindulge in front of Coach. Also, wine is gross.

"Not a big wine drinker?" Julie asks, nodding to my half-full glass.

I shrug. "It's not my go-to, but this is really nice."

"One second," Coach says and disappears into the kitchen again, returning with an IPA from one of the best Atlanta breweries. "More your speed?" She pops the tab before I can finish nodding.

"Thanks," I say and accept the beer.

A quiet settles over us, and I begin to feel awkward. There's a reason Coach wanted me to come for dinner, and now's the time to talk about it. Dinner is over, the kids are occupied, and it's just the three of us.

"Look, I obviously wanted to talk to you about a few things," Coach starts. I must have a terrified look on my face because she says, "You're not in trouble. Don't worry."

"Okay." I take a small sip of beer. Julie watches me with this look on her face, like I'm her kid, and she has to break some sad news to me.

Coach clears her throat. "Professor Weber—Doug—stopped by my office yesterday."

"Oh," I say, pressing the cool can to my lip. It feels good.

She leans back in her chair and sighs. "Do you want to tell me about what happened with the UGA law recruiter?"

I squirm in my chair and stare the glow of the TV through the window. *Completely stuck.* I'm completely stuck here with no way out. That fuckup isn't supposed to bleed into this fuckup. "Weber kind of sprung it on me. I guess you could say I panicked." I shrug like me running out his office was a totally normal thing to do under the circumstances.

Coach steeples her fingers like she always does and nods. "Do you remember what I asked you the first time we spoke in my office?"

I try to remember our initial conversation after the conditioning from hell. She said a lot of stuff about the team's potential and *blah, blah, blah.* "I don't know," I say. "Kind of feels like forever ago at this point."

She chuckles. "It really does, doesn't it?"

"I honestly can't believe we just moved here in July," Julie chimes in.

"Yeah. Feels like we've lived here for years," Coach says. She turns back to me. "I asked you why you didn't play softball in college. Why you chose basketball."

The memory comes rushing back to me. The weird twisting I felt in my gut. I can feel it now. "I love basketball." I shrug. "I'm really good at it."

"Clearly. But you were an all-state shortstop your senior year, correct?" I nod. "And would've gotten a full ride to Alder had you accepted the offer from Coach Clayton?" I nod. "Yet, you chose to take a lesser scholarship to play for a losing team and a bad coach. No offense to Coach Carson."

Hearing it out loud makes me feel sick. No one knows about the offer from Coach Clayton. Not Andy. Not my father. Not a soul. Except for Coach Jordan and Julie, apparently. "How did you know?"

"Coach Clayton and I are close. We have shared interests and goals for Alder." I run a hand through my hair and break eye contact. "Accepting a scholarship to play for a successful program is very scary. Trust me, I know. I was offered a scholarship from a Tennessee coaching legend, and you know what I did?"

I shake my head.

"I threw up. It's a lot of pressure. Choosing basketball—choosing a coach who didn't care as much as Coach Clayton—I bet that felt safer, right?"

"The pressure is constant," I say. But I didn't know I was going to say it. My plan was to stay quiet. Stay still. Until this whole night is over. "It's constant." I double down.

"I know," Julie says softly, her hand on my back.

Coach Jordan leans on the table. "Emma, dear, these moments that take from us, demanding things from us we don't want to give, they don't stop. Do you hear me?" I nod. "Life throws its first punch, and it doesn't stop. You need to learn when to hit back and when to cover your face."

"What do you mean?"

"I know how your father can be. He emails me." She cringes. "Aggressively. It's very off-putting."

I straighten, completely appalled. "What?"

"I know." She shakes her head as if trying to shake my father's words from her mind. "So it isn't hard for me to imagine what kind of pressure you've felt from him or the pressure you've felt to be a lawyer or maybe the pressure you feel from me."

"Do I throw a punch or cower?" I whisper against my beer.

Coach scoffs. "Who said anything about cowering? To shield yourself and let your opponent throw useless punches is just as much an offensive move as throwing one yourself. Muhammad Ali built his career off this technique. Fight like hell for what you want, Emma. Knock 'em right in the fucking teeth. And be wise enough—brave enough—to know when to say no and protect yourself."

I let her words settle in my chest.

"You have a natural gift with kids. Watching you out there with Jessa…it was something special. Besides, I've never met a lawyer who actually likes their job. Coaches, on the other hand. Well, I can tell you from personal experience, it's the joy of my life. Working with kids, teaching and coaching them. Maybe that's something you should consider when you begin to think about what you want to do after you graduate."

I nod, staring at my beer. Coach is right; it feels natural and good to consider teaching and coaching as an alternative to being a lawyer. But that good-vibes feeling is quickly replaced by a suffocating dread of telling my father I've been lying to him for months.

"And Emma?" I hold Coach's gaze again. "It's okay to try hard at something, to give it your absolute best, and still come up short."

I shake my head. "What do you mean?"

"Choosing basketball was less pressure, I get that. But I want you to understand that putting less effort into something because you're scared you won't be good enough, or it won't work out, doesn't keep you safe. It keeps you sad."

Julie squeezes my arm. "You know that feeling you get when you win in overtime?" I nod. "How it's sweeter than a regular win?"

"Yeah."

"It's because you were so close to losing. And you had to give it every ounce of effort to *try* to win. You had to leave it on the court, risk it all."

Coach claps and startles me. "Okay. Enough of that," she says, but all of her thoughts and observations pinch at me to remember them. To come back to them. "You and Lake are going to switch off starting. I want to see how you both do in a game situation."

"I thought—"

"I just wanted you two to figure your stuff out before the season starts. Chances were there was going to be a blowup between you two, and I wanted it to happen before the season started. And it seems like it did." She tilts her head from side to side. "Or maybe still is."

I wince. "Still is."

Coach sips her wine. "Try to sort it out, okay?"

"Yeah. I will." I push the aluminum tab back and forth until it snaps off my can. "Has, uh, Lake been to one of these dinners?"

Coach and Julie exchange a smile. "Lake has been to many a dinner," Julie says.

It's suddenly not so hard for me to understand why Lake would follow Coach Jordan to Alder. After tonight, I feel like I would follow her, too. "Is she going to make it to the WNBA?"

"She could, yes. It's a very real possibility, and she has a good relationship with one of the recruiters."

I nod. "Can I step outside for a moment? I'll be right back, I promise."

"Of course," Coach says.

I walk out front and lean against my car, taking a moment to enjoy the fresh air and the feeling that's gathering in my chest. I feel calm, almost at peace when I pull out my phone and call her. She answers on the second ring.

"Hello?" She sounds surprised since she knows I'm at Coach's for dinner.

"Andy. Hey. Listen—"

"Is everything okay?" Now she sounds worried. *Whoops.* I guess I've become that friend to her.

"Yes." I look to the sky, and my gaze stops on a particularly bright star. "I know we've been over it a million times…" As I gear up to say what I need to say, the truth of it falls heavy on me. Not in suffocating way, in an encompassing way, like a weighted blanket. Knowing makes me stronger.

"Been over what, Em?" Gentle as always.

"I'm the reason we didn't work out. And—"

"Emma—"

"No, no. Just listen. I know it doesn't matter anymore, and I'm not saying it for you, though you deserve to hear it. I'm saying it for me." I take a deep breath of the fresh mountain air. "Not trying your best at something you want doesn't keep you safe. It keeps you sad. You were something I wanted, but I couldn't bear to make myself vulnerable enough to give to you. I was so scared to lose. And…"

The next part feels harder to say because Andy knows about us, but she doesn't know this.

"It's okay. You can tell me," she says.

"Coach Clayton offered me a full ride for shortstop, and I said no." The line is quiet for a moment. An owl hoots in the distance, and it strikes me that I've never heard an owl hoot before. It's pretty.

"Because the basketball team wasn't as good, and it felt safer. Right?" I nod against my phone. "It's not too late for you, Emma."

"It's not?"

"Not at all. Lake sounds pretty wonderful, though I wouldn't know for myself, since you never bring her around. But I can sense she's special to you. She's the full ride. The chance at a happy relationship." She takes a moment. "The thing that's scary as shit."

"She is."

"If it doesn't work out, it's gonna hurt like hell. But I don't know if you've noticed, Em. You're not exactly thriving as is."

I chuckle into the phone. "Oh, really? I thought I was killing it."

She laughs, too. It sounds light and nice. "I'm glad you called. And I'm here for you always. But I think you know what to do."

The owl hoots again, and I grin. "Yeah. I think I do."

"One more thing."

"Yeah?"

"Hang on tight, okay? Things tend to get a bit messier before they get better. I should know," she says.

"I will. Good night, Andy."

"Night."

I walk back inside with a fresh confidence—one I used to know so well—and sit with Coach and Julie.

"All good?" Julie asks.

I nod. "So much better, yes." I look at Coach, who watches me with a curiosity in her gaze. "I want to start."

She tilts her head, seemingly confused. "Okay. Well, like I said—"

"At shooting guard. I want to start at shooting guard."

Coach looks to Julie briefly, then back to me. "You're sure?"

"I haven't been surer of something in a very long time."

She leans over the table to squeeze my shoulder and smiles. "I'm very proud of you, Emma. And if you ever want to talk more about teaching or coaching, I'd be happy to sit down with you. I have a lot of resources to share."

"Thank you." I'm on a roll of honesty, so I before I can think better of it, I spill it. "Also, I think I should tell you that I have feelings for Lake." Coach's brows rise in apparent surprise, but I push forward. "And not just animosity. I care for her. Want to be with her, and I think, deep down, she wants to be with me, too."

Coach and Julie stay quiet, and I begin to think that I may have overshared. Should've stopped while I was ahead. Then they both burst into laughter and ease every worry I had.

"Wow, Emma," Coach says. "I don't know why I'm so surprised, but holy hell, that came out of nowhere."

"Did it, though?" Julie asks through a smile.

Coach chuckles again, hand on her stomach. "Yes. I mean, I guess I didn't know Lake was into women."

I grin, too. "To be fair, a lot of times, it doesn't matter with me."

"Oh, a bit cocky, are we?" Coach says in a teasing tone.

I shrug. "It's just the truth."

"Well, listen," she says. "Lake is a very special young woman, and I can understand why you feel that way about her. Just keep it professional, please." She brushes imaginary dust from her shoulder in a show of feigned arrogance. "I don't want some young love messing up my debut season as head coach."

I laugh in relief. "I promise."

"But in all honesty, Emma. She's been through a lot, I'm sure you know by now." I expect her next words to be a warning to treat her right, to be delicate with her. To not be the asshole that I expect Coach thinks I am with women.

"Yeah. I know," I say, preparing myself for what she says next.

"So it would be fantastic if she wound up with someone as lovely as you. I'll be rooting for you."

I stare at her, dumbfounded and silent. I feel my mouth open, but no words fall out. I shake my head.

"I told you in my office, I see you, Emma Wilson." She watches me and nods, her hands clasped under her chin. "I see you. And you are *good.* Okay? You're bright and funny and caring and deserve it all. Don't forget that."

I stand and throw my arms around her in the tightest, most awkward hug I've ever given. She pats my arm because she can't hug me back. "You don't know what that means to me," I say, not letting go until she peels my arms off her shoulders and stands.

"Okay, okay. Now a proper hug, yeah?" She opens her arms, and I collide into her.

She tightens me up, and I bury my face in her shoulder. I don't cry, but I'm overwhelmed with the relief of being seen and accepted. Coach thinks I'm *good* and deserving, too. Thinks I have talent and a bright future. "Thank you," I mumble into her shoulder.

"Everything's okay, Emma." She rubs my back one more time before pulling away, and I instantly miss her. She's doomed herself for a season of hugs now. She grips my shoulders and stares into my eyes. "You hear me?"

I nod. "Yeah. I hear you."

As I drive home, I'm extra careful around the dark curves. I have nothing in my life figured out, the girl I'm falling for hates me, and I am no longer the point guard for the Alder Lions. But I'm worth it.

Chapter Seventeen

Our first game against Pine Grove is tomorrow. It's a home game, which is a relief because I'm very nervous. A kind of nervous I haven't felt about basketball in a long time. There's a wild urge in my gut to win, and I will do anything in my power to make sure we do. But before the game, there are a few things I need to take care of.

"Weber, hey." I drop my bag in my chair and meet him at his desk. I'm very early to class, on purpose this time.

He gives me a tentative smile, seemingly unsure what he's going to get from me today. Prelaw Emma, who storms out of rooms? Confident Emma, who calls him a dick with love? Who knows?

I know.

"How are you, Emma?"

I unzip my jacket and let a little air in. "I'm good. Really good, actually."

He nods, looking unamused. "Okay. That's nice." He fiddles with some folders on his desk as if he doesn't know what else to say. I'm sure he's still angry with me. I've kind of avoided talking to him after the incident in his office.

"Running out on you like that was extremely selfish of me."

He looks up, his thick glasses sliding down his nose.

"Not feeling ready to meet with a recruiter is one thing. To completely bail on a meeting that you took time and resources to set up for me was wrong. I know I strained your professional relationship with that recruiter, and I cannot apologize enough. I'm really sorry, Doug."

"Thank you." He takes a deep breath through his nose and releases it through his mouth. It seems I've driven him to learn breathing exercises. "I've been your professor for three and a half years, and I've never seen you as stressed as you were that day. I can't imagine what you must have been feeling to make you react that way." He grimaces. "You okay?"

I nod and zip my jacket again, my body stuck between hot and cold. "Yeah. I'm okay. I think you probably figured this out from me literally running away from my future, but law school is out."

He smiles now. "Officially?"

"Officially."

He walks out from behind his desk and gives me a big hug. "Doesn't that just feel incredible?"

"It really does."

"What's the plan, then? And how can I help?" He lets me go and perches on the edge of his desk.

"The plan is grad school. I want to be a teacher and a coach." I smile at the thought. Smile at how good it feels to *know*. I'm going to be an incredible teacher.

"Perfect." He grins. "So we're going to take the GRE instead. Let's look into—"

"Weber. Stop." I touch his shoulder. "It's the GRE, man. I sign up. I take it. All I need from you is to continue to be my friend and favorite professor."

He shakes his head. "What about grad school? I still have connections and can help with the admissions process."

"I haven't narrowed down the programs I want to apply to yet, but if it turns out I need help, I promise I'll ask."

A few students walk in, but he wraps me in another bear hug. "I'm happy for you," he says.

"Me, too."

❖

I get out of my last class early so I can make it back to Griner before Lake leaves for practice. Normally, I go straight to the Den, but I need to talk to her. I asked Coach to let me tell her about the position. Do I hope it helps to thaw us? Hell yeah. It's the only hook I have. The only reason for her to agree to talk to me.

I peel off my jeans and coat and trade them for our team sweats, then sit on my bed and listen for the bathroom. I look around my room. It's spotless. When I got home from dinner at Coach Jordan's, I had all this weird energy I didn't know what to with, so I cleaned. A lot. Now this space brings me peace. I hear the bathroom door open, and I fly off the bed and fling my door open.

Piper stares at me, confused. "Oh. You can go first. Looks like it's an emergency."

"It's not. I"—I try to peek into the room behind her but don't see anyone—"where's Lake?"

"Oh, she just left for practice."

I turn and run, throwing an apology over my shoulder for Piper. It's too early to leave for practice. She couldn't have gotten far. I'd text her, but given she never responded to my last message, I know she won't respond now. When I hit the steps down to the basketball arena, I see her opening the door.

"Lake," I call. She turns to find me jogging down the concourse and waits. I'm surprised she doesn't keep walking. I catch up and hike my bag up my shoulder. Run a hand through my hair. I'm nervous.

"What?" Her tone is harsh, as it should be. She slouches one shoulder, looking bored.

"You're very early," I say, a little out of breath.

She rolls her eyes. "Yeah, well I have to talk to Coach about the starting position because we completely failed to give her an answer, and I don't want to look bad."

"No, we didn't."

"Excuse me?" She crosses her arms and glares. "What do you mean 'no, we didn't'? If I recall correctly, instead of finishing our game, you lost it and *yelled* at me about attachment issues and my dead brother. Or do you not remember?"

I shake my head, wanting to forget. "I remember." She turns to leave, but I catch her arm. Her gaze drops to my hand, her eyes narrowed in disgust. I release her quickly. "Ten minutes. We have ten minutes to talk. Then, we're playing for the position after practice. The court will be ours, and we'll settle it. Okay? I already talked to Coach. She's cool with it."

"Our first game is literally tomorrow, Emma. That's no time for her to prepare and—"

I hold up my hands. "I said I already talked to her, okay? It's fine."

She stares at me for a moment longer and sighs. "Fine. We'll play for it after practice. But why do I have to talk to you? I really don't want to."

"The team," I spit out. "Our first game is tomorrow, and you know our vibe on the court has been shit, and it's because I've been shit, and we're a total mess. We need to patch it up before tomorrow, or we're going to sink."

"*You* need to patch it up. I didn't do shit."

"Let me, then." She looks off in the distance, her face shifting from angry to sad. I take her hand, and thankfully, she doesn't rip it away. "I need you to know there are no excuses for my behavior. And those things I said…" I shake my head. "They were about me grasping anything I could get my hands on to stay above water. They weren't about you. And I'm so very sorry." I let her hand go and wait.

"Fuck, Emma." She sighs as if I'm the most frustrating thing she has ever experienced. "Fuck you. *Fuck.*"

"So…" I shift my weight to the balls of my feet. Up and down. "Is that a yes?"

"Just come on." She walks to the bench on the side of the pathway, and I follow.

The metal is cold on my ass as I sit next to her. She stays quiet, and that's fair. I'm the one who needs to fix this. "You were right about a few things in the yurt," I say, not quite sure where I'm going with this. The hope is, muscle memory will kick in and maybe a little luck. She doesn't protest, so I continue. "I am a roller coaster.

Was a roller coaster. I'm definitely a mess. But what you said in the morning, it really hurt me."

She scoffs. "Don't you dare try to blame me for this. You really want to talk about things that were said to hurt someone? Come on."

"Lake," I turn to her. "I'm sorry. I'm not trying to erase what I said, though, damn, I wish I could. Just listen to me, okay?"

She stares at me and shakes her head. "I'll play you for the position after practice. But if you think catching me ten minutes before I need to be wrapped is the way to go about this conversation, then you're either clueless or manipulative. Just because we don't have the time doesn't mean I'm going to sit here and nod along with whatever bullshit excuse you have prepared. I don't owe you that." She stands. "I don't owe you a damn thing, Emma."

She walks to the arena and disappears through the door. I drop my head against the back bar of the bench and watch my breath turn white in the cold. "Well, that went well," I say into the breeze. I don't know why, but I'm not freaking out, not disheartened. This will be okay. Answering my dad's call after the LSAT I'm not going to take on Friday…that may be the end of my life as I know it. But one thing at a time.

I walk into the training room as Lake hops off the table. She gives me a curt nod and hustles by. I hop onto her table next to Rachel.

"What's up, Em?"

"Hey. Feeling ready for tomorrow?"

Suzy doesn't look up from Rachel's ankle.

"Been ready. What about you? You and Lake figure out who's starting?"

"We will tonight."

She shrugs. "All right. Well, good luck with all of that."

"Thanks."

Suzy rips the final piece of tape. "You're all set, Rachel. Have a good practice."

"Will do. Thanks." Rachel slides off the table and grabs her Gatorade. "Catch ya out there."

Once Rachel leaves, it's only me and Suzy in the training room. She doesn't say a word, doesn't look up at me. She rolls down my sock and grabs the prewrap. "Wait," I say.

She looks at me, annoyed. "Why?"

I want to sigh at the shattered mess I've left myself to clean up. "I'm sorry." She puts down the prewrap, so it seems like my shot at getting out of this conversation alive is astronomically higher than my conversation with Lake. "I've been attracted to you forever. Clearly. I mean, have you seen yourself? You're gorgeous." A hint of anger slips from her face. "And I love our flirty banter. I should have been clearer about what I wanted. I didn't want a relationship. I honestly just think you're ridiculously cute and sexy and wanted to touch you. Wanted to have sex with you, and I knew you wanted to do the same with me. But I was only open to casual fun, and I should have told you that."

She takes a moment with my words. "Casual fun," she repeats, and I struggle to catch her tone. Not sure if she's about to shrug it off or slap me. She shakes her head. "Look, I'm not trying to date you, either, Emma. You're a little immature for me and not exactly my type." *Okay, ouch.* "But yeah, I wanted you to fuck me. Had this whole big fantasy about it, and you didn't disappoint. But it's not about you not wanting more. Or *me* not wanting more. The next day, you acted like a complete asshole. *You* were the one who made everything weird and changed our vibe."

I'm momentarily speechless. "What?" *How is that right?* She was weird and standoffish and—

"Literally, the next time you saw me, you could hardly look at me. Meanwhile, I treated you exactly the same. I can do casual hookups, but I prefer to have them with people who are mature enough to handle them."

"Wow."

She shrugs. "I'm not trying to offend you. I'm just being honest." She picks up the prewrap again and wraps it deftly around my ankle. "If you didn't want it to happen again, I would've appreciated you just telling me."

I sit quietly while she wraps and switches to tape. "That all makes a lot of sense." She rips the tape, and it's not too tight at all. "I think I've hurt a lot of women by only wanting something casual and just assumed—wrongly assumed—that you'd be hurt, too."

"Well, you did hurt me. But not because of that."

I nod, and she wraps. "I'm sorry, Suzy. Clearly, I am immature."

"It's okay. I get it." She chuckles as she finishes my wrap. "It was fun, though. You and me." She meets my gaze, a little twinkle in her eyes.

I grin. "It was better than I could've imagined."

She piles her tape rolls together and leans back. "Now that we're on the same page, if you ever want to do it again, I'd be open to that. If you promise to not get so weird about it."

"Oh man." I laugh. "That's a generous offer. And I normally would accept. But weirdly, I'm not looking for casual right now."

"Is that right?" She smiles.

I nod. "It is. Yeah."

"Well, good luck. I hope you get what you're looking for."

"Everyone has been wishing me luck with everything lately."

"And are you feeling lucky?"

I hop off the table and grab my bag. Suzy watches me with curiosity. I am very grateful for her. "A bit. Yeah." I wink and leave for practice.

Chapter Eighteen

Lake and I linger awkwardly as everyone drinks water and packs their bags after practice. They all know what we're up to at this point. Word spreads fast, and though I don't think Rachel told anyone, I can tell people know. There's probably a bet on who the starter will be. Hope no one put too much money on me. Lake and I shoot a round, avoiding getting too close to each other.

I shoot a brick and chase my ball down to the bench next to Rachel. She pats me on the back and says, "You got this, Em. Give her hell."

"Thanks. Maybe I'll pop over after." I bend to get my ball, and my heartbeat rushes in my ears. Rach says something, but the whooshing is too loud. I straighten. "What'd you say?"

"I said good luck." She smiles.

"I'm always lucky."

She drops her head back and laughs, a trail of sweat running down her neck. "Finally. Welcome back, dude."

I wrap her in a quick, disgustingly wet hug and jog back to the court. After the last of our teammates leave, and the door closes behind them, Lake turns to me, getting straight to business. "Okay. Same deal. Play to eleven. Win by two." She walks to the top of the key and nods for me to drop my ball. "It's one to four. Your lead. My ball."

She checks the ball, but I don't check it back. "No, no. This is a new game. It's zero, zero." Not only do I believe we should have a clean slate, but I want her to win. I already told Coach that she's the starter. This game is just to dot the i's and cross the t's. It's semantics.

She levels me with a look of absolute disdain, but it rolls right off me like the sweat from my brow. Lake likes me. Lake cares for me. And I was a complete shithead to her. She's just hurt the way she hurt me.

"No. It's one to four. When I beat you, I don't want an ounce of second-guessing. I want it to be crystal clear."

It's not like I'm going to throw the game. I don't believe in that kind of stuff. But I was hoping that I'd get lucky, and Lake would beat me fair and square. Starting off with such a big lead is not ideal, but I nod. "Okay. One to four," I say and check the ball.

My feet are heavy, legs sluggish as sweat continues to drip down my skin. I'm exhausted on every level, and though practice was good today, it drained me. Lake seems to be moving just a bit slower than usual, so I imagine she's a little drained, too. That doesn't stop her from driving on me, her damp skin slipping over mine as she pushes off and pulls up for a fadeaway off the backboard.

She passes me the ball at the top of the key. "Two to four," she says. She doesn't meet my eye. She's focused on my core. Focused on playing defense. I don't really have a plan for this play, and it shows. I drive to my right and cross the ball between my legs to the left, but Lake picks it off and takes it to the hoop uncontested.

"Three to four," she says. I drag my ass back to the top of the key, wishing we had picked a lower amount of points to play to. As I walk by Lake, she pushes the ball into my gut like a handoff, and we both stop for a moment, staring at each other. She smirks. "Better perk up, Wilson."

Her left brow inches upward. Even though she hates me right now, I can still feel our connection. Can feel her. As she stands, pushing the ball into me, I can smell her honey and orange skin. It's fresh for being as sweaty as me. It makes my stomach ache. "I know," I say.

The next few plays pass by in quiet competition, the awkwardness fading with every shot until it feels like we're kids playing at the park. Lake is a joy to play against, her varied skills keeping me on my toes as much as her sass. I drive her to the block and pick up my dribble, stuck on my pivot foot with her behind me. She keeps her hand on my hip as she waves the other to block me. I steal one of Rachel's post moves and back into her to create space, then spin away and shoot. She gasps as the ball swishes through the net.

"Maybe I'll play post instead of point," I say, fighting a grin. "My moves are fire."

She rolls her eyes as I pass her the ball. "You must be confused. We're trying to have a *winning* season."

I wink. "Nine to eight, you."

We get dirtier and more physical with every play, grabbing jerseys, holding, and hip checking until we each end up with our backs on the court at some point. I try to catch my breath. We're tied at ten, but the rules are win by two. Lake tries to pull up on me, but I block her shot, and the ball rolls slowly across the court to the sideline. We sprint after it, trying to knock into one another and pull each other back until we're both close enough to dive for it.

She slides a bit farther than I do and gets a better hand on the ball, but I'm still right there with her. I get a fistful of her jersey and tug her down as we tussle for possession. Our grunts of effort fill the otherwise quiet court as she tries to free herself from my grip and rip the ball from me. But I'm bigger—a bit stronger—so even though she had the better position, I'm going to come away with it. I tighten my grip and rip, twisting all the way over onto my back.

Lake doesn't let go. She lands on top of me with a groan, our legs slippery against each other, the weight of her all over me. Orange and honey all over me. Her sweat all over me. I forget to fight as she anchors on my hips and rips the ball out of my hands, almost falling completely off me. She catches herself with the ball against the floor, chest heaving like mine, trying to catch her breath as she straddles me.

"Shit," she says through her labored breathing. Her hand casually rests on my stomach, and with every deep breath of mine, her body rises and sinks until the pressure of her hits a particularly sensitive area, and I squirm. She looks down and smiles. "My ball," she says as she slides off me, and it feels like she knows exactly what effect she just had on me. Her smirk hints at it, at least.

She stands and offers a hand, pulling me off the ground. "Damn, Lake," I say as I assess my limbs for damage. "You crushed me."

She ducks her head and catches my forearm, turning it to expose my raw elbow. "Ouch. Got yourself a stinger. Careful."

It's as if her words ignite the flames of the court burn. "Ah shit." I blow on it like that would help. "Oh well." I shrug.

She winces and takes my hand, tugging me to the top of the key. "Come on, Em. I still have to beat you." Her vibe has completely relaxed, and I think it's because she knows she's going to win. Even though we're tied, and even though I'm arguably as good of a player, she has this cool confidence about her. Like she's on fire and knows she can't be stopped. It looks good on her.

She scores a quick layup on me, and it becomes clear to me that she's going to win, too, given I can barely move my feet at this point. I walk slowly to the top of the key, trying to gather any energy I have left to give this game my all. I'm a lot of things. Sometimes, I'm a lot of *questionable* things. But I love sports, and I always play to win. Even when I feel like I don't have a shot. Even when I don't want to win.

"Game point," Lake says.

Once I feel like I've gathered enough energy to take her to the hoop one more time, I check the ball. She sinks into her defensive position, her shorts creeping up her smooth slick thighs. And before I stare a little too long, I take off at a sprint, Lake shoulder to shoulder with me as I charge the basket. She has me beat, but I don't try to pull up for a fadeaway or change course. I only have enough energy for this, not for some finesse move. We launch together toward the basket, me trying to get the ball in the hoop, and Lake trying to get a hand on the ball.

I get the shot off before I slam into the padded wall behind the basket, and Lake slams into me with a thud, her body pinning mine to the wall. I barely register the ball bouncing against the rim and falling off to the side. I missed. Lake just needs to make her next basket and—

"Shit," Lake mutters as her hands find my hips. It's an odd place for her hands to be since the play is dead. My pulse quickens when it should be slowing. She looks up at me, her lip trapped under her teeth, before she drops her gaze and pushes away from me.

I take a deep breath and start to follow, but she whirls around and shoves me hard in the chest. I stumble back and thud against the padding again, the breath leaping from my lungs as she leans against me, her warm chest heaving into mine and her hand curling around the back of my neck.

Her breath is hot against my neck, and it takes every ounce of willpower I have to remain still. "Kiss me," she whispers.

I sling her around into the padding, and she gasps when I push my hips against her, pinning her in place. Hooking up with a teammate underneath the hoop after practice, still in our uniforms, is so typical of me. But when she tugs me even closer by my jersey, and I press my lips to hers, there's nothing typical about it. Nothing familiar or standard.

She groans into my mouth as I slip my tongue over hers. I've been with a million girls. But kissing Lake makes me question if I've ever truly kissed a woman before. Even when I knock my teeth against hers in my eagerness, she brushes her fingers over my cheek and chuckles softly into my mouth.

And it solidifies it: I'm a fool for Lake Palmer. But more than that, I'm a lover for her, too.

She wraps both arms around my neck as I deepen our kiss, eager to claim every corner of her mouth. She tastes like Gatorade and salt from our sweat. Our lips slow when we both lose the breath we barely had to begin with, until I'm just a puddle in her arms as we catch our breath together.

"We have to finish the game," I whisper. Do I want to finish the game? No. I'd much rather tell Lake to take the position and keep kissing her. I'm too tired to play anyway. But she said she wanted to earn it outright. And I want to respect that.

She nods against my shoulder. "Whose ball?"

"Yours. Game point," I say.

"That's right." She peppers soft kisses down my neck, finishing with a nip on my collarbone. "Game point." She walks slowly to retrieve the ball, as if she doesn't quite trust her legs to stay stable. I feel exactly the same way as I follow her.

The last play is swift. She drives to the left and pulls up for a quick jumper at the elbow. She sinks the shot and wins the game. Wins the starting position, too. I don't think I'm meant to, but I hear her sigh in relief.

"Congratulations." I give her a high five. "Lake Palmer. Starting point guard for the Alder Lions. Communications major. And *major* cutie."

She shakes her head and chuckles. "Good game. Gave me a run for my money."

"You only beat me because you found my kryptonite and used it against me." I shove her gently in the shoulder, and she knocks my hand away, tugging me against her.

She gives me a soft kiss. "I don't like to leave things to chance." I grin and hold her close, but she pulls back. "Look, I know that must have been confusing after our talk earlier. And I know we have our first game tomorrow, but when can you talk for real? I promise, I won't cut you off and storm away."

"I don't care. Now?"

She shakes her head. "We really need to shower and eat."

I smirk at the thought of showering with Lake in the locker room. The mere image of her naked, water splashing over her skin and soap suds slipping over her breasts, has me on a whole new level of turned on.

My soaked jersey chills my skin, and I shiver. "Yeah. I could use a hot shower," I say, peeling the cold wet penny over my head.

Lake lets her gaze roam down my stomach. "Mm-hmm."

"Come on." I tug her to the bench and rack the ball.

I pull off my shoes and tuck them in my bag, relieved to slip into my slides. Lake does the same. "Even though I'm, like, super stoked to start, I still care about you. How are you feeling about it?"

"I am starting. At shooting guard."

She tilts her head and stares at me. "Did you throw the game?" Her voice is high and harsh.

I stand and squeeze her shoulder, limping a bit as I step in front of her. I look at my useless legs. "Does it look like I threw the game?" She looks down my spent body and shrugs. "Throwing a game isn't in my blood. I hate that I lost to you, but I'm glad you won." She nods, seemingly satisfied with my defense. "I want you to start. Plus, I know you'll do a good job feeding me the ball when I get hot, which will be always."

She laughs and shakes her head. "Cocky even in defeat."

"Gotta love my consistency."

We walk back to the locker room and shower—separately, unfortunately—then walk back to Griner Hall. When we reach our rooms, we stop.

"Pop over if you want to talk tonight," I say.

"How about after the game tomorrow?" She brushes my fingers with hers and smiles. "I'm beyond exhausted and don't think I'm even capable of forming words."

I chuckle. "I feel that."

To my surprise, Lake leans in, tilting her jaw upward for a kiss. I lower my mouth to hers and give her a gentle peck.

"Good night, Emma," she says.

"Rest easy." We each let ourselves into our rooms, and I flop on my bed, letting Lake use that bathroom to brush her teeth first.

I replay kissing her against the padded wall. Over and over and over again. Replay her grin and her chuckles. How she tasted like sweat. How making out with Lake Palmer was the last thing I expected from today, especially after she refused to speak to me. But we'll talk tomorrow after our game.

I dream of her.

Chapter Nineteen

Why are their jerseys so gross-looking?" Nicky asks, looking horrified as we watch the opposing team warm up. She's right. Their new jerseys are an unfortunate pea-soup green that makes me nauseated.

"That would be a deal-breaker if they were recruiting me," Lake says.

I do a double take. She didn't say something wild or anything; it's her joking around with the team that takes me off guard. Even a small joke is an investment, a little building block of connection. Something to lose.

I give her a little nudge. "I thought that was your favorite color."

"Hell. No."

"Come on, Lake. I bet you could pull it off," Rachel chimes in with a big grin.

Lake shakes her head, laughing. "If you ever see me in that color, please take me to the doctor because something ain't right." She touches my arm briefly. "Hey. Thoughts on a team activity tonight to celebrate our win?"

I swallow, her fingertips on my skin making me buzz, distracting me from her question. "Um. Yeah. I could think of something."

"Dude," Rachel interjects. "I told you we're going to Ashley's party tonight." She taps my head, and I swat her away. "Where have you been, Em?"

Truth is, I don't remember her telling me about the party at all. But hey, saves me from having to plan something. "Okay, okay.

Get out of here with that. We'll go to the party." I look at Lake, who looks so damn good in her maroon uniform. "Does Ashley's party sound good to you?"

She shrugs. "These people are cool?"

"Oh yeah. They're the best," Rachel says.

"All right. We'll all go," she says.

After we run through our last warm-up drill, Coach Jordan gathers us in a huddle, and we converge around her, arms linked. "Okay. Listen up, ladies." She draws the zone we've been practicing for the last week on the tablet. "Felicity Harmon is going to try to separate herself on the baseline every play. Take it away from her. If we can shut down her production, they don't have much else to rely on. Set the pace on offense, and be aggressive on defense. Understood?"

"Yes, Coach," we respond in unison.

We take our seats as the lights in the stadium dim. I look over my shoulder to try to find the softball team in the stands. They're easy to spot in their matching white team shirts. I wave at Maya and Andy, and they wave back with smiles.

Maya whistles loudly with her fingers.

"Go, Emma," Andy shouts.

Lake shoots me a grin and knocks her knee against mine as the announcer begins his pregame hype routine:

"It's a lovely evening here in the Lion's Den, and we have a special treat for you all tonight. A showdown between division rivals, Pine Grove and our own Alder Lions." The crowd cheers as he announces the starters. "Coming in at an intimidating five feet and four inches, from Atlanta, Georgia, a transfer from Georgia State, we have our starting point guard, Lake Palmer."

Her name booms through our small arena, filling me with a pride I've never felt for another person. She squeezes my knee and runs through the tunnel of teammates to fist-bump the referees and receive the rest of the starters at the top of the key as we're announced.

"From Atlanta, Georgia, at five foot nine, we have guard, Emma Wilson."

I run through my teammates, giving everyone high fives, fist-bump the refs, and meet Lake on the court. I lean against her. "What, did you pay someone off to give you an extra two inches on your stats?" She pushes back against me. "No way you're five four."

The announcer's voice booms through the building, but I don't hear the words.

"And how would you know? You've never measured me."

"Not yet." I wink. "I'll bring a tape measure tonight."

As Nicky jogs to join us, Lake says, "Just 'cause you had your tongue in my mouth, doesn't mean we're totally good."

"I know. We still have a lot to talk about," I say. Nicky jumps between us like a Ping-Pong ball, and we receive her with high fives and fist bumps.

After the pregame announcements, we all take our positions on the court. Rachel wins the jump, and we start the game with a positive energy. Because we technically didn't know who was starting until yesterday, Lake and I have rarely played on the same team together, usually each a point guard for opposing practice squads. But as Lake sets up our motion and I roll off the pick to the *outside*, I sense an opening for a three-pointer. Lake senses it, too, and launches me a perfect pass right as I'm turning to shoot. *Swish.*

Turns out we have chemistry on the court, too.

We run back for defense, and I smack Lake on the ass as I pass. She looks shocked for a moment, until she apparently remembers that we're on the same team, and it's a totally normal thing to do. "Sweet assist," I call to her before dropping into my position in the zone.

Felicity Harmon loses Nicky and posts up for a three on the baseline. I try to pick off the pass from the point guard, but I miss by an inch, and she sinks her shot. Coach Jordan screams from the bench, "Nicky, you shut that down, or I'll put in someone who can." Her face is as red as her suit.

Her intensity sets me on fire, and the next defensive possession, I bail on my post in the zone to make sure Felicity gets taken out of the play completely. I'm trying to send a message to Nicky, to Felicity, to everyone. *Shut her down.* The player in my zone gets a shot off, but it's a brick, and we rebound it to drive down the court. "That's what I'm talking about, Emma," Coach shouts, and my chest swells with pride.

The game passes in a blur but is a wild success. I've never witnessed our team play so well and so cohesively. Not to mention, I put up twenty-three points. Half of which are thanks to Lake and her incredible talent to set up plays and read defenders. She'll probably break the Alder record for assists. Rachel had a double-double, and Nicky got the picture and held Felicity to fourteen points.

Our locker room is a pit of chaos and loud music reverberating from wall to wall. I wipe my face in the towel that hangs in my locker as Lake walks to me. "Good game," she says.

I toss the towel in the team hamper and smile. "You, too. Seems like we've been missing out playing against each other instead of with each other."

She nods. "It would seem that way, wouldn't it?"

"You know, I think I really like shooting guard. You and I have something special out there. We'll be quite the force to be reckoned with this season."

"Oh yeah?" She squeezes my arm. "So you like how I run things on the court?"

"You could say that." I wink.

"About tonight—"

"You have to come. I'm enforcing it as team captain," I blurt with zero chill.

"I wasn't even aware we had a captain." She shakes her head. "Whatever. Listen. I'm going, but I was wondering if maybe you wanted to share an Uber. I don't have a car and—"

"I do. Have a car," I clarify. "But, yes, let's go together, and let's Uber to be safe."

She grins. "Cool."

"Cool."

Coach cuts the music, and we turn our attention to her. "Listen up, everyone. Great work tonight. We just have lifting in the morning, then we'll watch this game tape at six. No practice." The locker room hums with activity until Coach hushes us for the second time.

"I hear everyone is going to a party tonight. Is that correct?" We all nod. "I love that you are hanging out as a team and celebrating, but be safe out there. If anyone gets arrested, I swear to God, I'll—"

"Franny," Coach Fulton stops her from telling us what she'd do to us with a hand on her shoulder.

She looks at him with a bit of distaste, then back to us. "Well, let's just say you don't want to find out. Am I understood?"

"Yes, Coach," we yell back.

"Congratulations, everyone, we are officially undefeated."

I sit at my desk and wait for Lake and Piper, who caught the sense we were up to something tonight and promptly invited herself along. Yeah, it annoys the shit out of me, but I feel bad for her. She doesn't exactly have the most friends, and it kind of makes me want to cry when I think about it. She's a nice person; I just don't want to prioritize her. But whatever, she's coming.

I fiddle with a pencil and stare at my schedule, barely taking anything in. *LSAT* is written in red on tomorrow's date. I expect the little letters to fill me with dread, but I feel nothing. I shrug. Maybe I'm even a little relieved. Talking to my father will be hell, but having a different idea of what my professional life could look like if I'm not a lawyer brings me peace and the strength to face him. At least, I hope.

Lake and I have so much to talk about, so much unsaid between us, but knowing there's hope with her brings me even more strength. I turn at the sound of the bathroom door cracking open. Lake steps into my room looking criminally beautiful in high-waisted black jeans and a cropped purple sweater that leaves a peek of abs. She's rocking my favorite glasses, her hair side-parted and down. My eyes drop to her shoes, and I gasp.

"Holy shit. When did you get those?" I walk over to get a better look at her navy and maroon Blazers.

"Came in the mail last week. Had them special made in Alder colors. You like them?"

My gaze bounces between hers and the shoes. "Like them? They're the best shoes I've ever seen." I chuckle into my hand, still shocked. "Damn, you're really leaning in, huh?"

"I'm a Lion, baby." She shrugs as if she always has been, and I try not to melt at her use of "baby," even though I know it wasn't really meant for me.

I grab her hand and hold it away from her body, making a show of looking her over. "You're devastating," I say. I lower her hand, but keep it in mine. "And so fucking hot."

She laughs and swats me away. "Well, you already know how I feel about your looks." Her gaze falls over me. "And you're looking good tonight, too."

I'm wearing one of my favorite fits: a boxy black T-shirt that looks good with my tan, an old canvas work coat I got from Goodwill, my go-to bright orange beanie, gray pants, and white Nikes. I don't know why, I just feel fucking great in it. I know I look good, but that doesn't stop me from blushing like a fool at her simple compliment.

I reach for her hand again, and something in her eyes tells me she wants me to. Her skin is warm as her fingers interlace with mine, pushing my stomach into free fall. If life is random, there are infinite paths that Lake could've taken to end up somewhere other than Alder her senior year, but in my heart, I believe there are infinite paths she could've taken to end up right here with me. Any path, any way. We would've still wound up in my dorm room after our first game, her hand squeezing mine and me leaning in for our second kiss.

I bend to her ear and whisper, "When I'm with you, I feel—"

"Who's ready to party?" Piper shouts as she flies into my room.

Lake and I jump apart. Not because we're scared to be caught, but because five seconds ago, we were the only two people who existed in the entire universe, and Piper barging in scared the shit out of us.

I press my hand to my chest. "Christ, Piper. If I wasn't in college, you would've given me a heart attack."

Lake takes a step back, tugging her sweater down and smoothing her hair. "You got us pretty good, girl."

"Shoot. I'm sorry, guys. Didn't mean to scare you," Piper says, her gaze bouncing between us. She narrows her eyes. "Were y'all kissing?"

"No," Lake says at the same time I say, "Yes." She stares at me with a brow raised and a sexy smile on her lips.

"Well, we were about to," I amend.

"Presumptuous," Lake whispers through her smile.

I shoot her a grin. "More like accurate. I thought I proved on the court tonight that I don't miss."

Piper takes a step backward, eyes wide. "Whoa. You two are like"—she pinches her fingers and drives them together in front of her face, making a fake explosion—"ignitable."

"Ignitable?" I ask.

"You know, like you have a lot of chemistry." She looks between us. "Clearly. Anyway, I'm not mad that no one told me y'all are together, but—"

"Whoa, whoa, whoa." Lake raises her hands in protest. "We're not together. Just"—she shoots me an apologetic look—"fooling around a bit."

I know it shouldn't gut me, but *fuck*. I bite my lip to keep from saying something so typically Emma. Something that would push Lake's buttons to hurt her the way she just hurt me. It'd be quick, almost imperceptible. Instead, I keep a sharp grip on my lips and nod.

"Whatever. You guys are totally cute, together or not." She hikes her purse up her shoulder. "Should we call an Uber?"

CHAPTER TWENTY

Ashley's house never changes. It's like walking into a dark humid greenhouse where all the plants are having a party. Rachel, Andy, and Maya cross the dance sea of the living room to greet us.

Andy throws her arms around me, and I receive her with a groan. I'm pretty sore from whupping Pine Grove's ass. "Congratulations on a fantastic first game," she says, then pulls out of my arms to give Lake a hug, too. She looks a little shocked but wraps loose arms around Andy. "You both were fantastic."

Maya gives me a fist bump and introduces herself to Lake. Then, Rachel wraps an arm around my shoulder and speaks into my ear so only I can hear it. "You need to catch me up on you and Lake, like, yesterday."

I push her away and adjust my beanie while she hugs Lake.

"Where the hell did Piper go?" I ask, realizing she's disappeared.

Lake points to the makeshift dance floor with a grin. Piper is already getting loose with some random guy to "Pony."

We all laugh. "Oh, man," I say. "I am way too sober for this. Drinks?"

Everyone nods, and we walk to the back deck where the keg usually is. Even though we were only inside for a minute, the crisp November air feels like heaven. I press my hand to Lake's back and walk with her to the keg and stack of cups.

"Oh my God," Andy calls to a group standing in the grass. "I didn't know you guys were here already." She hops down the couple of steps into the backyard and greets everyone in the group. Maggie and Olivia first, then Tessa and Ashley, and Bailey and Noelle. "I thought you weren't back until spring semester," she says.

"Not technically. But wanted to pop by and say hi," Maggie says, her arm around Olivia's waist.

Maya is quick to follow Andy. She embraces Maggie and Olivia, then the rest of the group. "Where are you off to next?" she asks Olivia.

"Seattle. I'm so excited. Then home for next semester."

Lake tugs my sleeve. "Are those your friends?"

I pour two beers as I watch the group chat and reconnect. I hand her one and shrug. "More like acquaintances. I never really got involved with AQF, and that's kind of what brought them all together."

She takes a sip. "What's AQF?"

"Alder Queer Fellowship. Bailey and Robert, who's inside, started it freshman year. It's a club that lobbies the school for protections and equal rights. Mostly, they're trying to become a school-sanctioned club."

She pulls me closer so the sides of our bodies are flush together. "Sounds like we should join."

"I think I have." I shrug and sip my beer.

"I also think you should introduce me." She looks up at me with a smile, and I take her hand, guiding her to the crew.

"Hey, welcome back, you two," I say. I hold up Lake's hand in a brief presentation. "This is Lake Palmer"—I make sure I have her eye contact as I say the next part—"starting point guard and also my friend. She just transferred from GSU. Lake, this is everyone."

Maggie gives me a curious look and whispers something to Olivia, who smiles sweetly at us. "Aw. Welcome, Lake. This must be a big change from Georgia State."

Lake nods. "Yes. In the best way, though."

"What's your major?" Tessa asks.

"Communications," I answer for her and shoot her a grin. "She's going to be a sports broadcaster when she retires from the WNBA."

"Fuck yeah, Lake. Get it," Maya says.

"It's really great to meet you all," she says. "Oh, and Bailey, I'd like to sign up for AQF whenever possible."

Bailey smiles and fishes her phone from her pocket. "We can make that happen right now. Do you mind giving me your number?" Lake takes her phone and types her number, then hands it back. "Perfect. We're glad to have you. It's going to be a *big* year for AQF."

"Oh yeah?" I say. "Is this the year?"

Noelle grins and squeezes Bailey's hand. "We have some exciting things in the works. Don't want to jinx ourselves, but you may even be involved in one of them."

"Whatever it is, I'd be honored."

"We'll keep you posted." Bailey raises her cup. "Here's to Maggie and Olivia gracing us with their presence, to meeting Lake, and of course, to AQF."

"Cheers," everyone says and knocks their Solo cups, sloshing beer down all our hands.

It's true, I would be honored and should probably ask some follow-up questions in the spirit of fighting for our rights and all, but I can't focus on anyone or anything other than *her*. Lake laughs as she holds her beer away from her and tries to lick the liquid off her other hand. She's radiant. And happy.

"We'll catch you guys soon," I announce and grab Lake's sticky hand. She shoots me a questioning look, but I tug her away as the group says good-bye to us. "Let's rinse off."

I lead us through the bumping party, desperate to get Lake alone. I'm needy and weird and not like I've ever been before. Not like with Andy. Something about Lake feels inherent to me. Like I was born to float until she showed up and filled me with all this heavy…love. She follows me quietly.

I knock on the bathroom door. No one replies, but it's locked. *Shit.* And I'm not the kind of person to go in some random person's room. Well, I am definitely that kind of person. But not with Lake. The hallway becomes crowded with a constant flow of people headed from one side of the house to the other, and the music shades in the gaps between us, filling every empty space with its thumping beat. Something smooth. R&B, maybe.

I stop and turn to Lake, who looks at me like she'd follow me to the ends of the earth. But there's nowhere to go. Not right now. Shoulders of strangers bump into us as we stare at each other. The entire house could be engulfed in flames, and I wouldn't care. Wouldn't even know. I place my hands on her hips, on the skin that her sweater fails to cover, and she reaches for me, too, interlacing her fingers behind my neck. Another stranger bumps into my back and is about to bump into Lake, but I turn her into the wall, her back flush against it.

She pulls me to her mouth, and I sink into her kiss. The chaos around us fades into a humming white noise, and I can't discern anything but the way her lips feel against mine, how her tongue is cool from the beer, and how she drops her hands to my waist, pulling my hips harder into her.

Lake groans into my mouth as I pin her to the wall. People graze my back and bump into us, but we're completely unfazed, making out in the middle of this raging party without a care in the world. That is until Piper finds us, of course.

"There you guys are," she shouts from the other side of the hallway. "Come dance with me."

I pull away from Lake, the frustration mounting in my chest. She grimaces as she tugs my shirt. "Be nice," she says.

I roll my eyes and groan. "I just want you. It's all I want. And I can't find one fucking moment to be alone with you and—"

"Hey." She tugs my shirt again, and I focus on her. "A little patience, babe. You don't have a roommate, remember?"

I completely melt into her, her words liquifying me into a sappy lovesick mess. I brush my lips over her ear and enjoy the way it makes her shudder in my arms. "You've made a mess of me, Lake Palmer. I'm a complete fool for you. I…" I press a gentle kiss on the soft skin just behind her ear. "I need you."

"I don't need you, Emma." She pulls me down so my mouth is an inch from hers. "But fuck, I want you," she says, and presses her words to my lips with a hard kiss, then lets me go. She walks to the living room, leaving me alone in the hallway, stunned and digesting every piece of what just happened.

She wants me. But does she want to *be with me*, or does she just want to take a ride like every other girl? I slip off my beanie, run a shaky hand through my hair, and smooth my shirt. I can't lose my nerve now. We haven't even cleared the air from before. Lake is right, I need to be patient.

I find her at the edge of the living room resisting Piper's attempts to lure her into the dancing mob. "Oh, come on," Piper heckles as she gyrates, looking as if she doesn't have a care in the world. Guys glance at her with apparent interest. Piper is cute as hell, and her energy is contagious. Well, when she isn't interrupting me and Lake, it is.

I know Piper has had a couple hookups during our last three years as suitemates, and from the looks of it, she may get lucky tonight, too. I don't feel the need to protect her or whatever. She's a grown-ass woman, stone-cold sober, and has bigger guns than any of the weenies checking her out right now.

I tuck away my insecurities and bob over to Lake. "What? Don't like to dance?" I do a silly shimmy during which my small boobs are definitely not shaking.

She smothers a chuckle in her hand. "Wow, Emma. And here I thought you might be good at everything."

"Oh, I am. This is just the bait." I take her hand and try to coax her onto the dance floor, but she tugs away, staying planted where she is. I sigh. "See the thing about you, Lake, is you gotta loosen up a little." I take both her hands and swing them back and forth. "You were loose on the court today, and it was incredible. Now you gotten loosen up here and dance a little. Let it all hang out."

She shakes her head, but she's laughing. "You are ridiculous, Emma."

I nod. "What'd I just tell you? I'm a fool for you. So won't you dance with me?"

She makes a dramatic show of rolling her eyes, then takes a step forward. "Fine. But only 'cause I like it when you beg."

I tug her along. Let her get away with all her little power moves because I know she wants me. She wants me as desperately as I want her. And yeah, she may not *need* me, but no one really needs anyone. She needs me in the way I need her. The need to stay in this light we turned on together.

Lake's movements are rigid as Piper and I bounce around in our silly dancing. I try to loosen her up, but she seems unable to let herself go. So stuck in her head. I move behind her, and even though the song is fast and loud, I put my hands on her hips and pull her against me. She doesn't push me away, so I sway, moving her hips with mine.

"See?" I say into her ear. "Dancing isn't so hard."

She shakes her head and leans back. "You're so off the beat, it's ridiculous."

"Moving how I want with you till a slower song comes on. I know you like it." As if to agree, she pushes back into me, and I tighten my grip. Apparently, we're quite good at building our own private world within this one.

We dance out of rhythm with Piper until Jules cuts the lights, leaving us in the dim glow of the patio lights. He cuts the fast song, too, and plays something slow and smooth with a strong bass. One of the guys dancing around Piper wraps his hands around her waist, and she spins into him for a dance.

Lake melds to my body in the extra privacy, and I'm no longer guiding her to the beat in my head. She pushes into me, and we hit every beat together. It's slow and loud and hot as I bow over her, enveloping her. I brush my teeth over her warm neck, letting the salt from her sweat tickle my tongue. When I nip at her skin and suck a bit of flesh into my mouth, she spins in my arms and looks up at me, a little dazed.

"I want you to take me home," she says, and there's no mistaking what she wants. What she *needs*.

"Piper," I call. And she looks up from the guy she's dancing with and grins. "We're calling an Uber. Wanna come with us?"

She whispers something into his ear, and he nods. "Yeah. We're coming."

Oh. Get it, but also, this is going to get very awkward very fast.

❖

After the brief history of Brad's entire life, the Uber drops us in front of Griner Hall. We all walk to our rooms, Lake and I quiet, and Piper and Brad anything but. When we reach our doors, Piper looks at Lake.

"Is it, um, cool if Brad and I use our room tonight?"

Lake leans away like the mere mention of anything sexual happening with Piper in their room makes her extremely uncomfortable. "Oh. Yeah." She waves in front of her face. "Um, it's all yours." I'm pretty sure she would sleep in the basement just to avoid further discussion of the matter, but she looks at me. "Can I crash?"

"I think that'd be okay."

When I close my door behind us, the jokes stop, and the reality of the night falls on us with all its weight of anticipation and desire. I flip on my small lamp, but it's still dark enough to give us confidence. I hang my coat on my chair and sit on the edge of my mattress. Lake steps between my thighs and holds my face. The sweetness of it makes my chest ache, the sharpness of regret stabbing me. Regret for ever making her feel anything but spectacular.

"If I could have it all back..."

"You can't," she whispers. She presses a soft kiss to my mouth. "That's the thing about life. And death...you don't get anything back."

I wrap my arms around her and pull her close. "But I have so much regret, and I want to talk about—"

"I know." She takes my hand and flattens it against her abs. I feel her breaths deepen as she pushes it up to her bra. "But not tonight."

"But—"

She squeezes my hand over her breast, and I shudder, dropping my head against her stomach. Every part of me wants to throw her down on my mattress and show her just what she's been missing. How good I am at this and how incredible I can make her feel. Even with Andy, I said fuck it and fucked her with abandon. But this isn't Whitney, isn't Suzy, isn't Andy. This is *Lake*. "Before we go further, I need you to know that—"

She pushes down the cup of her bra, and everything goes hazy except for the feeling of her soft warm breast in my hand, her nipple hardening under my palm.

She sighs in my ear. "Trust me. Trust that I know. You think I'd be here if I didn't?" she whispers. She lifts a leg over mine and groans as she settles her weight on my thigh. When hers lands against my groin, I groan, too. I pull her harder into me with my free arm as she grinds against my leg. "I've wanted you so badly," she says.

I lift her shirt and brush my teeth over her tight nipple until she cries softly into my ear. I pull back. "I want you in every way possible. Want your body all night long and in the morning, too," I say, then suck her breast into my mouth as she groans and sinks harder onto me. I release and give her nipple a quick lick. "But most of all, Lake, I want you to be mine." I gently push her away so I have enough to space to undo the buckle on her jeans. I swear I almost come from the sound of pulling down her zipper.

I slide my hand down the front of her underwear, straight into her wet heat, and she cries quietly again, dropping her head back. "*Ah.* Emma, fuck." She regains control enough pull back and brush her lips over my ear. "Been yours." She moans. "Always."

The magic words. A promise that when she wakes up in my arms, she'll stay. A promise that she knows who I am and wants that.

I spin us and throw her on my mattress. It's easy really, her being so small. She bites her lip as her eyes go almost black, watching me curl my fingers into her waistband. As I'm about to rip off her jeans, a loud moan echoes through my bathroom door, and the very loud squeaking of a mattress follows.

I turn back to Lake, whose brows are raised in amusement. "I swear to God, if they are on my bed, I'm going to kill her," she says. And I burst into laughter, abandoning her pants and collapsing on top of her. She holds me as we laugh together, chests heaving and eyes watering.

"Wow. I don't think I can do this knowing Piper is getting railed next door," I say.

"Ugh." Lake wiggles out from under me and buttons her jeans. "Damnit. I'm so turned on right now."

I grin. "I know."

She takes a deep breath. "Okay. I'm going to clean up, then let's go on a walk or something."

"Okay."

After we both use the bathroom, we walk hand in hand into the night.

CHAPTER TWENTY-ONE

"Okay, but you definitely should have just trusted me enough to share what was going on," Lake says, her hand squeezing mine.

The night is cold, and we huddle together in the amphitheater, passing time until Piper and Brad are finished with their evening. I don't know how to tell Lake everything I want to tell her. How I wound up such a mess this semester is hazy at best. It kind of feels like one day, I woke up and lost control of my entire life. "I know. But it's all so stupid compared to what you've been through and—"

"Hey." She cuts me off with another squeeze of my hand. "These things aren't a competition. I have my pain, and you have yours. And we are both entitled to feel our feelings, whatever they may be. You've had a really hard semester. I know. Turning away from a life path you've been working toward for three years is a big deal. And extremely stressful." She swallows and looks at the dirt between her feet. "Getting your heart broken by the girl you've loved for almost a decade is also a huge deal."

"I'm over her, Lake." I've told her this multiple times, but I know my actions this semester hinder the weight of my words, however true.

She gives me a half-smile, half grimace. "I know. It's just, you scare me, Emma. I don't want to be just another girl you hook up with. I want to be *your* girl. And the things you said to me were horrible, but it's not *what* you said that freaks me out." She shakes her head, looking to the sky. "It's *why* you said it. Like you don't trust yourself to be good to me."

I chew on my lip. "You're absolutely right. I didn't even trust myself to know what time it was." I scoff. "Literally. I felt like I had no control over anything, and with you, I just wanted you so badly that it scared me. Because what did I have to offer you, Lake Palmer, starting point guard of the Alder Lions, future WNBA player, and woman of my dreams?" I twist my shoe into the dirt and sigh. "Nothing. I had nothing."

"I just need you to be here. That's literally all I need from you." She rubs my back. "Stop trying to run away."

I hold her gaze. "I promise."

"And for the record, I think Coach Jordan is right. You'd be an incredible coach and teacher if that's what you decide to do."

I grin. "I think it is."

"You haven't told your dad?" I shake my head. "It's okay. You will when you're ready, and I've got your back."

"Thank you." I plant a kiss on her cheek. "So what's up with your recruiter? How's it been looking for you with the draft and stuff?"

She grins. "It's looking good. Promising. I don't have anything concrete, but I should know more after winter break."

"Are you still going to want me when you're a hotshot pro athlete?" I ask.

"I don't know. Depends on how good you are in bed." She laughs and bumps my shoulder.

I clutch my chest in mock horror. "Ouch. Right through the heart."

She takes my hand again and looks at me. "In all seriousness, I think you know I don't do casual. Which is why I had a lot of hesitation about getting with you, Em. You have quite the reputation around here."

I grimace. "Yeah. I know."

"And you were kind of right about me having attachment issues, a fear of abandonment because I lost my brother so suddenly. But I'm working through those things with my therapist. Last year, I wouldn't have even looked at you knowing your reputation and the fact that it's our senior year. Really, we have a lot going against us. But here I am, holding your hand and forgiving you for being the biggest asshole I've ever met." She chuckles. "Here I am falling in love with the team I'll only be on for a year. And here I am falling in love with you." She blows out a deep breath. "Shit. It's terrifying."

"You're…falling in love with me?" My words are clumsy.

She nods. "I am."

"And you haven't even seen my moves yet." I laugh. "Oh, you are so fucked, Lake."

"Hey." She hits me hard in the shoulder. "Can you not be avoidant right now by making a dumb joke? I was just ridiculously vulnerable, and I'm already freaking out because—"

"Lake." I drop to a knee like I'm going to propose. "I think I might love you." I kiss her hand like a weirdo. "Be mine. For real." I shake my head. "I know I can be…a bit of a scoundrel. But I've never wanted to be with anyone the way I want to be with you. I want to sit next to your parents at your first WNBA game and watch them smile that smile that you dream of. I want to be there with you when things feel dark and insurmountable. Let me show you what it's like to actually be with me, the real Emma Wilson. Because she's way more than anyone thinks."

"I know she is." She takes a shaky breath. "I know you gave up your position before we played for it, but did you throw the game? Really?"

I chuckle, my legs sore from the game earlier and being on one knee. "I'd trounce a five-year-old before I throw a game."

She winces. "I kind of love that about you, but maybe don't say it to anyone else."

I drop my head back and laugh to the moon, feeling more relaxed than I ever have. Feeling more *me* than I ever have. "Fuck, I love you." I stand and pull her up with me. Kiss her cheek. "Be my girlfriend."

She rolls her eyes. "Maybe if you ask me nicely."

"Oh my God." I sigh. "Lake, please. Will you do me the complete honor of being my one and only?" I ask in my sappiest voice.

"I guess so."

"Aw, come on." I groan.

She chuckles. "I know you haven't done this before, but you really gotta work on your delivery."

I pull her toward to the dorms. "I think I know how I can win you over."

"There's my cocky girl."

We walk back to Griner with an electricity humming between us. Having sex with Lake would have been great before. But now, knowing she's mine and I'm hers, is going to make it mean so much more. Something I've never had before. Something I've never done before. None of the other girls actually cared for me or wanted to know me. Everything feels so right in this moment…

That is, until we walk back to my room and hear Piper and Brad going for round two. Or maybe three at this point.

"I'm going over there and—"

"No. No, you're not." Lake tugs me away from the bathroom door. "Piper has just as much right to a night of fun as we do." She slides my coat off my shoulders and hangs it over my chair. "And because you're my girlfriend and don't have a roommate"—she leans close to my ear—"you can have me just about whenever you want," she whispers.

I groan. "Except tonight because the universe hates me."

She tilts her head as if she's she seriously considering my words. "Does it, though?" She peels off her sweater and hangs it with my coat, leaving her in just a sexy black bra. I swallow as she unzips her jeans and kicks them off, placing them neatly on my desk. "I'm going to brush my teeth. Then, we're going to bed."

As she closes the door to the bathroom behind her, I shimmy out of my clothes and throw them in my closet in a rumpled mess. I momentarily panic about what to wear. *Nothing? Pajamas?* I opt for an old Alder basketball tee with no bra and my soft boxers.

She walks back into my room as I'm plugging in my phone. "Your turn," she says as she slips into my bed.

I brush my teeth so fast, my dentist is probably shaking her head at me. I wipe my mouth clean and open the door to the most beautiful thing I've ever seen: Lake Palmer in my bed, my quilt hitting just below her bra.

I slip in next to her, the twin mattress not allowing for any space. As she rests her head on my chest, the sounds from next door seem to fade away, and we're tucked in our own little world again.

Lake tells me stories of her and River when they were young, running around their neighborhood, wreaking havoc with all their little friends. Of her high school girlfriend on the track team, Bethany, and how she struggled to break up with Lake after River died, so she drew out their relationship for another six months. How Lake only had one relationship after that, but her parents didn't like the girl, and Lake broke up with her within the year.

I tell her more about Andy, not in a way to make her jealous. In a way to make her close. Tell her about the backhand I can still feel on my cheek. About late nights in the driveway shooting hoops with my brother and friends. The bits of my life that I imagine would flash before my eyes when I die.

I stroke her arm as she nuzzles into my chest. "I got a full ride to Alder," I say.

"Damn, girl. Coach Carson must have really—"

I clear my throat. "For softball."

She pulls up and looks at me. "For softball? I didn't know you were that good. I thought you just played in high school for fun."

I fuck with the corner of my quilt as a hot flash of shame roars through me. "I did play for fun, but I was really good. All-state my senior year and broke the school record for home runs in a single season. Won defensive player of the year, too." I laugh because, wow, why don't I play softball? But something must have gone right because I'm exactly where I'm supposed to be: with Lake and Coach Jordan, building something together.

"Go on," she says.

"Coach Clayton offered me a full ride, and I hid it from my dad, from Andy, from everyone." I shake my head. "I just couldn't be that. Wasn't ready."

"It's truly terrifying, isn't it?" She rubs my forearm. "To have it all on your shoulders. And what if something goes wrong? Being the best makes you stick out from the rest. Makes you more vulnerable. More responsible. I totally feel that."

I sigh. "Yeah, except, you handled it, and I didn't. And I'm pretty sure that's why I avoided everything with Andy and every other girl for that matter. Shit, tried to do it with you, too."

She bows to kiss me on the cheek. "You've figured it out, Emma. Look at you, leading our team in a currently undefeated season, thank you very much. And making yourself vulnerable enough to accept love." She lies on her back next to me and holds my hand. We stare at the ceiling in a peaceful quiet.

"I think I felt the same way as you," she says. "After River, I was so scared to lose that I never wanted to gain again." I turn on my side and kiss her shoulder. "It took a long time and a lot of healing and therapy to actually realize."

"To realize what?" I whisper.

She turns, and our lips are so close, I can feel her warm breath on mine. "Life is so tenuous, isn't it? There's nothing divine or karmic watching over us. A life ahead of you or a life behind you means nothing. Being young and golden means nothing. Death is just a lottery. Now I know, I want to love while I'm here instead of fearing the inevitable loss. Because the loss always comes, but the love you have to fight for just to have it exist."

I take a moment to digest her words and reach for her face. Brush the backs of my fingers down her soft cheek. "Why is it all so terrifying?"

"And what would life be if it wasn't?" She chuckles and turns to kiss my palm. "It'd be like a slice of stale bread or something. Nothing to look forward to. No beauty in the triumph. Bland."

"I love eating mass amounts of food, but you, like, *love* food. Don't you?"

"I do. I'll cook for you sometime."

"Deal."

❖

At some point, we drift to sleep in each other's arms. I think it was somewhere between discussing our favorite professors and the merits of Cool Whip in Southern desserts. I wake to Lake stirring next to me, her legs and arms vined around me just like in the yurt. Her breathing is deep and otherworldly, and I hope she's dreaming of something sweet. I reach for my phone, trying not to disturb her. Double-check I have my alarm set for seven. We have game film to watch, and I have a fake LSAT to take.

I put my phone facedown on my desk and snuggle into Lake, thankful I don't have to pee this time. She shifts to her back, pulling my arm with her, and I turn on my side so it stays in its socket. She is ridiculously gorgeous, from her long lashes to her full lips. Her breasts rise and fall with every breath, and I want desperately to free them from her bra. To feel Lake's naked body next to mine.

I wiggle out of her grip and run my fingers up and down her stomach, trying to ease her out of her dreams. She doesn't stir, so I run my hand higher, over the cup of her bra. The lacey detailing feels ticklish against the pads of my fingers as I focus on her nipple hardening underneath and her lips plucking open. She takes a breath that's sharper than the rest as I feel her grip my shirt. Suddenly, I'm a volcano of desire for her.

"Don't stop," she whispers. She pushes up on her elbows just enough for me to reach behind her and flip loose the clasp of her bra. I peel it off and toss it to the floor. Her breasts are even more beautiful than I could have imagined. She runs her fingertips over my bottom lip. "What do you want?" Her voice is breathy and low, as if she knows exactly what I want.

"I want you in my mouth."

She gasps when I brush my knuckles over her nipple. "What time is it?" she asks in a shaky voice.

"Four."

"Take this off," she says, tugging on the hem of my shirt.

I pull it over my head and throw it toward the closet, feeling more naked—more exposed—than I ever have. Never have I bared myself this way to anyone. My skin feels like a map drawn just for her. My failures. My hopes. My insecurities. It's all for her to see. Only her.

She stares at my small breasts and holds one in her palm. I shiver. "You feel amazing, Emma. And you are so, so beautiful. You have an alarm set?"

I nod and lower myself, pulling her tight nipple into my mouth and sucking. She moans a little too loud, so I clasp a hand over her mouth. She bucks against me, trying to press her hips into me.

"So impatient," I whisper in her ear as I give in and slip a hand down her panties. "I should really tie you up."

I get distracted by the feel of her wet heat on my fingers, slippery and thick, and pull my hand from her mouth. "Emma," she gasps. "I've never been this turned on before." She tangles a hand in my hair and tugs, and *fuck*, it makes me shake with pleasure.

"I've never felt this way either," I say as I sink down her body, kissing and licking and nipping my way to her waistband. I don't waste time. Not fucking around tonight. Not with her. She's wet and needy and wants my hot mouth on her now. I pull off her panties and try to memorize how they look, wet and bunched up, sliding over her smooth thighs and sharp knees, down to her delicate ankles.

She squirms as I watch her breathing heavy and grasping for me. *Not fucking around tonight.* I lick a trail up her inner thigh until I can feel the heat of her on my lips and her tremble on the tip of my tongue. She moans as I lap her up, indulging in every corner of her folds and her sweet, sharp taste, sucking on her long lips as my fingers explore the rest of her, getting nice and slick before I ease them in.

I push two fingers inside, and she instantly tightens around me, pulling me deeper. "Yes," she gasps. I slide in and out in long, deep strokes that match the pace of my tongue on her clit. She moves her hips to my rhythm and squeezes her breasts as I push deeper. She's stunning.

I would slip in a third finger, but she continues to tighten around me, and I know she's close. I roll my tongue over her clit and push harder into her as her entire body begins to reverberate. My fingers still. She's clamped around them so hard, I can't move them anymore, so I hold her as she rides out her orgasm. When her body relaxes and her grip loosens, I pull my fingers from her, and a trickle of hot liquid follows.

I'm careful to avoid her sensitive spots as I gently lick her clean.

"Come here," she says, her arm draped over her face. I crawl up her body and collapse next to her. "I've never felt so loved in my life." She kisses me gently. "And I've definitely never come so hard, either."

I grin. I can't help it. "You are mind-blowing to me, Lake. Everything about you. Your looks, the way you play basketball… how you fuck." I bite my lip and shake my head, wanting to go again right now. "I want you in my mouth again. Want you to come for me over and over until we have to shower and leave for the Den."

She presses a finger to my lips to shush me. "And what? I just don't get to touch you?" She looks down to my boxers. "You must be so wet." Her hand slides down my stomach and pushes into my waistband. My toes curl when she slides through me, her breathing heavy, and I squeeze my eyes shut, trying not come in under five seconds. "Just let go, baby."

With that, she slides my boxers off and lowers herself between my thighs. I last maybe ten seconds with her fingers filling me and her warm tongue stroking me, until I completely lose it, shaking myself undone. She doesn't speak, just kisses me thoroughly so I can taste myself on her lips and cuddles next to me.

I don't speak either. There's nothing to say. We hold each other and slip in and out of sleep for the next hour.

❖

We wake a half hour before my alarm goes off, and Lake slips into the shower. "Get in here with me," she says.

I watch as the water splashes against her skin and groan. "I can't." I shake my head. "If I get in with you, it will be at least an hour before we get out, and we can't be late. I promised Coach Jordan I'd never be late again."

"Suit yourself." She shrugs and closes the shower curtain while I brush my teeth.

My phone rings from my room, but I let it go to voice mail as I spit toothpaste in the sink and rinse my mouth. It rings again, and I sigh, going to pick it up. It's my dad, and I don't know why I answer, but I do.

"Hey, Dad."

"Big day, Emma Bear. Big day. How are you feeling?"

Oh shit. It's LSAT day. I take a deep breath and try to focus on the call and the lie I'm supposed to tell. "Ready as I'll ever—"

"What's that sound?" It takes me a moment to figure out what he's talking about. A moment too long of him listening to the water splashing against tile. "Is that a shower? Where are you, Emma?"

Fuck. Pure panic floods my system as all the blood drains from my face. I feel woozy. "Dad, calm down. I can explain, I just—"

"Calm down? You're supposed to be in the lobby of your test taking center." I hear the shift in his voice. He's gone. "I'm going to ask you one more time. Where the fuck are you, Emma?"

Tears sting my eyes, and I hate it. Hate how I was just on top of the world, and he reduces me to nothing in two seconds. I try to gather myself, refusing to cry on the phone with Lake in the shower. *Wait,* I don't hear the shower anymore. I turn to find Lake standing in the doorway with a towel wrapped around herself and her brows scrunched in concern.

"Emma, I swear to God. If you don't..."

My dad trails off in a mess of threats and profanities. It all sounds like white noise that doesn't matter to me because I'm looking at her. The thing that actually matters to me. She sits, her warm hand on my back, and nods as if to say *you got this*.

"Dad. Dad, stop. I'm not taking the LSAT, and I'm never going to because I don't want to be a lawyer." His voice barrels through the phone, and I cut him off again. "I love you, but I can't talk to you when you're like this." I hang up.

My hands shake, and my ears hum. *Holy shit.* He knows. My dad knows my big lie, and now, everything is in the open. The starting position is sorted, I chose a career path I'm going to love, my dad knows about the LSAT, and Lake is mine.

Lake squeezes my thigh. "Are you okay?"

"Yeah." I can feel a huge grin spread over my face. "I'm going to rinse off. Then we're getting breakfast before film." I snag my towel from the hook on my closet door. "Eggs and French toast and bacon. I'm starving, aren't you?"

She raises a brow. "Um. Yeah. Starving."

"Great. I'll be out in a minute."

I shower without a care in the world. I don't think about my dad or the profanities he threw at me. Nope, that shit's for the birds. Today, I'm going to get breakfast with my girlfriend and show up to film and maybe hang out with our friends later. Who knows? Who cares? It's a lovely Friday, after all.

Chapter Twenty-two

Everyone gets in position for the tip-off against Covington, the biggest rival in our conference. It's an away game, our last before our brief winter break, and I want to go out on a win. Keep this positive momentum going in my life. I eye their point guard, Blaire Haines. Hate that—

"Ay, if it isn't Lake Palmer. Feel more comfortable on a losing team, huh?" she heckles Lake.

I take an aggressive step toward her, but Nicky tugs me back. "Hey. Get your head straight," she says. It's been two weeks since Lake and I made it official—still get chills thinking about that night—and our team took it in stride. No one cares about teammates dating when literally half the roster is queer. As long as you keep it professional and in your pants around the crew. Which I'm apparently struggling to do right now. The professional part.

I'd like to shove my foot so far up Blaire's ass that it comes out her nose. As I was saying, I hate that bitch. She looks like me, plays like me, has an ego like me, but is completely evil. Like, she gets her jollies from being straight up mean on the court. She doesn't exactly seem nice on social media either, carrying her shit talk from the court to the Gram.

And she apparently has it out for my girlfriend, who is handling it way better than I am.

Lake rolls her eyes and sways into the Covington player's shoulder next to her. "I see Blaire is still obsessed with me." The

Covington player scoffs and takes a step away. "Hey, Rach." Rachel turns to Lake as the ref walks to center court. "Get this one to me," she says.

Rachel winks, then squats in preparation for the tip. It warms me to see the two of them getting along so well. Lake really won her over the last couple of weeks with her efforts on and off the court with the team. Not to mention the fact that Lake and I are together, and Rachel is obligated to like her now.

Rachel tips the ball straight into Lake's hands, who takes off like a rocket down the court. Blaire cuts her off before she can score an easy layup, but Lake pulls up for a jumper at the elbow and sinks it. *That's my girl.*

The first quarter trudges by with copious amounts of fouls, elbows thrown, and jersey tugging. I've hit the floor hard three times already, and Lake has a cut down the side of her eye like a teardrop from someone clawing her face. We're up nineteen to sixteen, but the momentum shifts every possession, and it's anyone's game.

We gather at the end of the quarter, and Coach Jordan and Coach Fulton argue over a play Coach Jordan drew up on the tablet. "Just, not now," she says in frustration, then directs her attention to us. "Listen up. We're doing great on offense. Keep taking those open shots. On defense, we need to batten down the hatches. If they get an opportunity at the basket, it better be because they beat you, not because you were playing loose. Do you understand me?"

We nod and say "Yes, ma'am."

"I know it's a dirty game out there. Keep it tight. I don't want any stupid mistakes costing us the game because someone couldn't keep their cool on the court."

"Yes, ma'am."

"Hands in," Coach says, and we pile our sweaty hands on top of each other. "We've been working hard, we trust each other, and we have more heart than Covington will ever have. Let's get out there and defend our winning season."

We holler, "Lions," on three and take the court for the second quarter.

Rachel smacks Lake's butt and says, "Keep killing 'em, girl."

"You, too," Lake says.

I stand next to her while we wait for Covington to take the court. "I swear, if Blaire throws hands one more time—"

"Chill, Em." She tugs on my jersey as if holding me back from something. "She's gonna throw hands all night, but you have to listen to Coach. No dumb mistakes."

I nod. "Okay. Okay, fine."

Halfway through the second quarter, Nicky gets fouled taking it to the hoop. She misses her second free throw, and everyone crashes the boards. Seconds after Rachel secures the rebound, Blaire winds up her elbow and clocks Lake in the face over her shoulder. Lake crumples to her knees, holding her face in her jersey, the navy of it turning black at the collar from the blood rushing out of her nose.

No foul. *No foul. No foul?*

Suzy rushes to Lake with gloved hands and a chunk of gauze to contain her bloody nose. Hot rage flashes through me as I jog to the ref. "Hey," I shout. I don't mean to shout, I just…*what the fuck*? "The ball wasn't even for grabs, and number twenty-four just broke our point guard's nose. And that's not a foul?"

The ref crosses his arms and stares at me. "I didn't see it. Can't call a foul out of thin air."

I spread my arms in exasperation. "Well, what the hell were you looking at? Because it sure as shit was a foul, and it sure as shit was as clear as day. Like, five feet from the ball, too."

He raises his brows as I lose my temper, my voice hitting the high notes of my anger. "Easy now," he warns.

But I can't stop. "Fuck you." I regret it the second the words escape my mouth. The ref blows his whistle in my face and chops his hands together in a T.

"Technical foul," he shouts. "Number thirteen."

I shake my head as Coach Jordan absolutely loses her shit on me from the sideline. She screams my name until she's redder than I ever saw Coach Carson, and I finally walk over to accept my fate.

She gets me by the scruff and stares hard at me. "What the hell did I just say? Did I say run out there and get a technical foul?" I blink. "Did I?" she yells.

"No, ma'am."

She ducks her head to maintain eye contact as I avoid hers. "Did I say to run out there and lose your head and make a stupid mistake?"

"No, ma'am."

"Play smart, Emma, or I'll bench you the rest of the game. You understand?"

I nod. "Yes, ma'am."

"Now get back out there. You're at point."

I meander back to the half court line as Covington's shooting guard takes the penalty free throws. "You okay?" I mouth to Lake, who sits with the gauze under her nose, her head tilted back. She looks down at me and gives a thumbs-up.

"Shame. She's so pretty, too," Blaire says, sidling up to me as her teammate sinks her first shot.

I shake my head, trying not to engage. Trying to be good. Her teammate sinks the second shot, and Blaire leans even closer. "It landed a little high, if I'm honest. Was hoping to shatter some teeth."

She jogs away before I even have the chance to tackle her to the ground. Which would be lucky for me if I was anyone else. But I'm not. I'm me, and there's no fucking chance in this universe that I'm letting Blaire Haines get away with this shit. With hurting Lake on purpose. They have a quick possession on offense, which ends with a brick from Blaire and a rebound for Rachel. She passes it to me, and I push up the court, eager to get it out of my hands.

Covington is in a two-three zone, with Blaire on the left elbow, so I pass it to Nicky and run to the baseline. Blaire squats in her defensive position, her back to me. I wave for Nicky, trying to catch her eye. *Come on, Nick. Over here.* She finally looks my way, and I hold up my fist, the universal sign for a pick, and quietly approach Blaire's blind side. When Nicky gives me a little nod, I charge full force at Blaire, who turns to chase Nicky. I crash into her with such force, she hits the hardwood about five feet away from me with a thud and a groan.

Another instant mistake but no instant regret. Except, I wish there was blood.

"Fuck, dude," Nicky says. I think I hear Lake say my name from the bench.

I shrug, staring at Blaire trying to catch her breath with disdain. The same ref blows the same loud whistle in my face. "Technical foul. Second of the game. Number thirteen is ejected," he yells, making the stupid little T in front of my face again.

I walk to the exit of the gym, but Coach catches my shirt. "We're going to have a nice long chat about this when we get back to Alder tonight. Do you understand?" I nod. "Lake's nose isn't even broken."

I shrug as if I don't know what she's talking about. "I was just setting a pick. Accidentally hit her blind."

She tightens her grip in my jersey and pierces me with her stare. "As I've said before, I see you, Emma." She lets me go, and I walk to the visitor's locker room.

I grumble to myself down the hallway. I'm not, like, having a meltdown or anything. She fucking got what was coming to her. I burst through the door of the locker room and throw my jersey in the hamper. Fuck Blaire Haines.

"Stop by my office before you leave tonight," Coach says.

I nod as I walk by her on the bus. Lake stops in front of me and sits in a seat a couple rows back from the front. I slide in next to her. She moves slowly, careful to avoid any contact with her nose.

Once everyone has settled and the driver cuts the lights, I turn to her. "How does it feel?"

"Like a swollen mess, but it's fine. Not broken or anything." She gently dabs it with the ice pack.

She flinches as I reach for her slowly. "It's okay. You just have a speck of blood still." I brush my thumb over her upper lip and smear the tiny bit of red. Getting hit in the nose is weirdly painful, and hers looks especially tender and bruised. "You're going to have a black eye, maybe two."

She chuckles. "Well, what can ya do?" She shrugs. "Lucky I've already wooed you."

I nudge her shoulder. "Get out of here with that nonsense." She squeezes my hand, interlacing our fingers. "Why haven't your parents been to a game yet? I want to meet them."

"Yeah. I want you to meet them, too." She sighs, dropping her gaze to our hands. "They will in the spring. They don't want to drive through the mountains at night and don't want to rent a hotel room, so they'll pick a couple of important games and just go to those."

I rub my thumb over her hand. "They don't like driving in the dark?"

"Hate it." She brushes her fingers over my cheek to tuck a loose lock of hair behind my ear. "What about you? Why haven't your folks come up yet?"

I chuckle. "Besides the fact that my dad hates me right now?"

"He loves you. He just doesn't always show it in a healthy way. But, yeah, besides that."

"I know." I sigh. "He loves me a ton. And I love him, too." I pick at a fluff ball on the knee of my sweats. "People are so weird. And my dad is one of the weirdest, but, yeah, we'll figure it out."

"You will." She pushes herself up to kiss me on the cheek, and I still, not wanting to accidentally hurt her nose.

Her kiss leaves me feeling warm and full again. "It's just hard for them to swing it with three kids still. Just like yours, they'll come for a couple of big ones in the spring."

"I can't wait." She tugs my arm to catch my gaze. "And don't think you're just magically off the hook for what happened tonight."

"Off the hook?" I shake my head, incredulous. "The person who's *off the hook* is Blaire. She's lucky I didn't fucking break her teeth the way she wanted to do to you. I swear to God, if she even says a word to you the next time we play, I'm going to—"

"Stop, Emma." She shushes me. "You can't keep getting technicals and being ejected from games. Not okay."

"But—"

"Wickedly sexy, yes. But no more. Understand?" She looks at me with a raised brow, her gaze dropping briefly to my mouth, making my whole body hum.

"Nuh-uh. Nope. Don't give me that look, Lake." I shake my head, breaking the spell of her seductive eye contact. I drop my voice, "Your nose is all fucked-up. We can't even make out. And all of this"—I wave a finger at her eyes then mine—"is just going to leave me wanting things I can't have."

"Come here." I lean down so my ear is close to her mouth. "Now don't move." Her hand runs up my thigh as her lips brush over the sensitive skin behind my ear. "Like I said," she whispers, her hand inching higher and higher, making it more and more difficult to stay still. "Don't move, or you're going to hurt me."

Her words are hot on my skin, and I close my eyes, trying not to squirm as she squeezes my thigh and runs her tongue down my neck to where it meets my shoulder. "Careful," I whisper. "We could hit a bump, and—"

"I said you're never allowed to do that again, and you're not. But *fuck*, Emma. Seeing you put that bitch on her ass for me made me want to follow you into the locker room and let you take me right there on the bench." She punctuates her admission with teeth on my skin, and it takes all my willpower to stay still. For her and for our team, though pretty much everyone is asleep or has headphones in.

I clear my throat. "You're in big trouble when we get home."

"Good."

After a few minutes of quiet, Lake dozes off with her head on my shoulder, and it's adorable because she's not in big trouble when she gets home. We're both bone-achingly exhausted, and when we get home, I'm tucking her in with a glass of water and two Tylenol. I know what I did on the court was wrong. I know it was a mistake. But I would do it again a million times. How could I not? I love her.

Since day one. Since she stared at me from the doorway of the bathroom. An instant force. Lake is wicked smart, confident and sure-footed, and always up for a challenge. Someone who stands up and fights. Someone who sees me for all my potential.

I'm the luckiest son of a bitch in the universe.

When we arrive, I meet Coach Jordan in her office even though I really, *really* don't want to. I've been so good and on top of things with life and basketball lately, and I hate that I've disappointed her again. Her opinion means a lot to me.

"Emma, have a seat."

I slink into the chair and set my bag on its partner. "I know I fucked up. I'm sorry."

"You aren't sorry." She shakes her head. "Don't give me that bullshit, Emma. You'd do it again in a heartbeat." I stay quiet as she leans on her elbows on her desk. "I know you have feelings for Lake, but what did I tell you? Keep it professional, right? Nothing about what you did to Blaire—"

"Coach." I lean forward. "I would've done the same thing for literally anyone on the team. Don't get me wrong, I was out of line, and it especially pissed me off that it was Lake. But you're always saying you know me. Well, don't you know if that pitiful excuse for a human laid a hand on Rachel, Nicky, Quinn, anyone, that I'd have laid her out all the same?"

Coach stares at me for a moment longer, then shakes her head. "Christ, Emma."

"I'm not religious." I wink.

She flattens her palms on the table and narrows her eyes. "Was that a joke?"

"What, you didn't like it?" I chuckle. Can't help it. I love Coach Jordan and am super comfortable with her, even when she's pissed.

She shakes her head. "No. It was bad."

"Tough crowd." I shrug.

"You sure are something." She sighs. I know I'm exhausting to her, but I also know that she loves me deep down. She wouldn't have invited me to dinner if she didn't. "Just don't do it again, okay?"

"Cross my heart." I draw an X over my chest.

She leans back in her chair. "How are you doing? You seem…" She looks to the ceiling, swiveling in her chair. "Lighter."

"Yeah. I'm feeling good."

"Going home for the short holiday break?"

I consider it. I was planning on it, but now… "She doesn't know it yet, but I think I'm going to crash at Rachel's house."

She nods. "Okay. And you're always welcome at ours, Emma. Whenever."

"Thanks, Coach. I really"—I shake my head, lost for words—"I'm so lucky you took the job. You mean a lot to me."

Coach crumbles a Post-it Note and throws it at me. "Get out of here before I change my mind about liking you, Wilson." I grin and grab my bag. "Merry Christmas, Emma." Her words are gentle.

"Merry Christmas, Coach."

Chapter Twenty-three

I wait at our spot for Lake to get back from winter break. Okay, it's not technically "our spot" since we've only been here once, but I'm making it our spot now. I could've just waited for her in the dorm, but that's no fun. Plus, it's snowing, and Alder is a special kind of beautiful in the snow. Magical. And there's no better view than from the roof of the library.

I pull my beanie down to cover my ears and take a deep breath of the icy air. My short break was nice and exactly what I needed to recharge for this coming semester. For my *last* semester at Alder. I shake the thought out of my head. It makes me ache to think about losing this place and the unknown that follows. Instead, I replay my time with Rachel and the Dunstons, the chillest, most loving family in the entire world.

We ate nonstop, saw a silly Christmas comedy in the theater, and slept until ten every morning. My folks were less than pleased that I didn't come home for the holidays, but I called them on Christmas morning, and things were civil. Except with Gracie… she was pissed, but I made it up to her with a stout AMC gift card.

I turn at the sound of the door creaking open. Lake pops her head out of the opening, and I jog over, careful to not trip over the maze of pipes and drains. "You're here," I say. I grab her hand and help her up.

She stands before me looking beautiful as ever in her plaid wool coat and her signature glasses. We just stare for a moment, neither of us speaking. Though we texted and called each other over the short break, the tiny bit of distance wormed a bit of insecurity into my brain. Like, what if things are different when we get back?

She shivers, snowflakes dusting her dark hair and lashes. "Shit, it's cold."

Her voice melts any inkling of question in my mind. She's mine. Always has been. "It's January in the mountains." She crosses her arms, her expression matching the one from the first time we met in our dorm. "But don't worry. I run warm." I open my arms for her.

She collides into me. "Ugh, I missed you," she says.

"It was only—"

"Five days, I know. But I can't help it, okay? I miss you even when I'm just in class," she mumbles.

I pull away to see her adorable face and squeeze her shoulders. "You didn't let me finish. It was only five days, but I missed you like hell, too." I keep her at arm's length. "How's the nose feeling?" There's still bruising under both her eyes.

"If you think I'm not going to kiss you, you're delusional."

I laugh. "Last time we were up here, you swore up and down that you didn't want to kiss me."

She grins. "No. I swore up and down that it wasn't a date. I was dying to kiss you." She steps into my arms. "And my nose feels so much better. Just be gentle."

I lean in, careful to avoid her bruises, and run my tongue over her bottom lip. She shoves me in the chest.

"Ew. What was that?" She wipes her mouth, and I laugh.

I point at her nose. "You said be careful. I didn't want to risk it."

"Don't be weird about it, Emma. Just kiss me, damnit."

I take her hand and walk to the edge where we talked during our "not" date. She takes in the scene of Alder covered in snow, her hands gripping the cold rail. "Wow," she says. "It's gorgeous."

"Yeah. And quiet, too. I like it like this."

I tug her so she spins to face me, then push her gently against the railing. "You want me to kiss you?" She nods, her lips slightly parted. I duck my head and kiss her neck, but she gets a fistful of my coat and pulls me into her. I accidentally brush her nose, and she groans, but she presses her mouth into mine. She's warm and tastes exactly how I remember. I'm careful to keep my head tilted far enough to avoid her bruises and slip my tongue against hers.

She sighs, and I push her a little harder against the railing. She breaks from my mouth to say, "I met with Cheryl, the recruiter Coach Jordan knows." Her words are choppy and breathless, and she crashes into my mouth again.

"What?" I pull back, keeping my grip on her hips. "How was it? You have to tell me everything."

"She says I'm on the league's radar. Thinks I could be a second-round pick if we keep winning and if I keep playing the way I'm playing." She flattens her hand against my chest. "Which means you need to keep putting up those points for me, baby. Keep my assists high."

"Lake." I pull her into a tight hug. "This is huge." Excitement over flows me, and I think I'm holding her too tight because she wiggles out of my grip. But I can't help it. I want her to achieve everything she dreams of, and she's on her way. I'm so relieved I got out of it.

She chuckles. "I know. I know, but it could still not work out." She leans against the rail, and I join her, taking her hand in mine. I can't not touch her. "Like you so kindly pointed out last semester, there are only 144 roster spots, and not all of them get filled because of salary caps. Being drafted in the second round doesn't guarantee I'll play."

"You will." She half grins, but it looks more like a wince. "I'm not kidding, Lake. I didn't know you as a player before, but now I do. You play like you're dancing. I swear to God, you have the most beautiful rhythm I've ever seen."

She squeezes my hand. "And you play like you're playing in my driveway after school, under the garage light, and my mom is about to call us in for dinner. With joy and freedom and ease. Like nothing in the world matters except play."

I would do anything to have that memory with her. And I'm lucky to be able to play with her now. "I know a place we can do that."

"Me, too." She grins. "Hey. You used to say I play like a robot."

"You did. Must've been nervous or something."

She scoffs. "Well, yeah. I wasn't expecting"—she waves around her head—"all this." Her lip quirks up in the corner. "I wasn't expecting you. Not only did you have me all twisted in my gut, but you're obviously an incredible player. I was scared for my spot, for sure."

Hearing her admit that makes me want to hug her. "It was always going to be you, Lake."

"No. No, it wasn't. You may not have thrown the game, but I feel like maybe something deep down held you back."

"Nothing about you has ever held me back." I chuckle and shake my head. "I'm a fucking incredible shooting guard. Better than I was at point, and I would have never known. I love it."

"You could probably enter the draft, too."

I scoff. "No way in hell. I'm not good enough."

"Emma, you're as good as me. It's totally possible. We can talk to Coach and call Cheryl. She said—"

I squeeze her shoulder to stop her rambling. "It doesn't matter, Lake. I don't want to. Have zero interest. I just want to teach and coach. Wear a whistle around my neck and be a part of a school community. I literally can't wait."

A warm smile spreads over her face. "I literally can't wait either. You're going to be amazing."

"Thank you." I pop a quick kiss on her lips. "Let's go get some dinner. I'm starving."

Lake bumps Rachel's arm. "Nicky's grinning like she got away with something," she says. We watch Nicky stroll into the gym with a goofy smile on her face and her limbs loose. She looks high.

"Oh, that girl is definitely up to something," Rachel says.

I turn away from Nicky to watch the two of them, Lake and Rachel. They stand under the hoop with the exact same posture. Arms crossed, weight on one leg, and a skeptical look on their faces. Only Lake hits at five-foot-three, if we're being generous, and Rachel is six-six. They're adorable standing together like that. And it warms my heart to see Lake build all these connections and relationships. Even if they may not last past graduation.

Nicky walks to us with a silly smile on her face. "What's up? Why are y'all staring at me all weird?"

"Why are you looking like you just got away with robbing a bank?" Lake asks.

Nicky rolls her eyes. "Come on. Don't make me say it."

"Oh, shit." Rachel covers her mouth with her fist and leans away. "She can't quit Brian's dick."

I pass her a ball. "Luckily, no one's asking you to," I say.

Lake tilts her head, considering her. "Is it maybe possible that your feelings run deeper than his dick?"

Nicky smirks. "Not much runs deeper than his dick." She waggles her brows, and I shove her in the shoulder.

"Gross, Nick."

Lake raises her brows, and it makes me want to lie her down every single time. "Hmm," she says, a finger to her lips. "Avoiding the question with a joke. Suspicious."

Nicky's gaze tags her basketball shoes.

"You're booed up, aren't you?" Rachel asks.

"Ugh. Screw you guys." Nicky bounces the ball in apparent frustration, then looks at Lake. "Don't tell Coach. Please? It's fresh and not worth the trouble."

Lake glances at me, then walks to Nicky and gives her shoulder a gentle squeeze. "Of course I won't. It's not a big deal. What's he gonna do, anyway? Wash your jersey with extra love?" Everyone chuckles at how low-stakes Nicky and Brian are. "It's not a big deal. I promise."

Coach blows her whistle, and we all turn our attention to center court. "Let's huddle real quick before warm-ups."

Our team gathers around the coaches on the painted roaring Alder Lion. Lake stands next to me, our arms pressed together from the proximity of our teammates. I finger her hand, and a small smile pulls on her lips.

"I know we have endless meetings and watch endless film, and you're probably getting tired of hearing my voice, but I want to say a few things before we hit the court. We went into winter break with a huge win against Covington, and we've continued our winning streak for two weeks now. Our energy is light and fun, and I'm loving it." She smiles, and it's contagious. Our whole team is grinning.

"As we get into the meat of our season, carry on that energy. Basketball is a game. Play it. No one expected us to have a winning season, and we're proving them wrong. No one expects us to make it to the tournament. Prove them wrong." She pops her hand on her hip and looks around our team. "I just want you to know that I believe we're a championship team. Continue to play like it, and let's see how far we can take this thing. Bring it in."

Lions on three.

We always take practice seriously—we're division one athletes—but today, we practice like we truly believe what Coach Jordan said. Like we believe we could go all the way, and we'd do anything to get there. I sprint harder than I ever have in practice, sink more shots, and defend like I'm defending the last of the human race. It's the first time at Alder that I've felt like I'm playing *for something*. And it doesn't scare me anymore.

Lake tucks the tail of her jersey down her waistband and gathers her locs in a bun. She looks sharp and beautiful in her all-white uniform, white socks that hit at her calf, and her white basketball shoes. She notices me watching and gives me a small smile. A nervous smile. I walk around Quinn, who jams out to something on her phone, and sidle up to Lake. Rub her back.

"You okay?" I ask. There's a lot happening today. The softball team did a big promotion with a giveaway in an effort to fill our stands tonight. And knowing Andy and Maya and the relationship between Coach Clayton and Coach Jordan, the stands will be full. We're playing Chelsea Mountain, who is wicked good this year. Even if we've been on a hot streak, they could easily beat us if we're not on our game. And the cherry on top: it's Valentine's Day, and both of our parents are here.

Lake nods, fooling with the hem of my jersey. "Yeah. There's just a lot today, you know?"

I pull her in for a hug, and she wraps her arms tightly around me. "I know." I kiss the top of her head, confident no one is paying attention, not really caring if they are. "One thing at a time, okay?" She nods under my chin. "First, we need to take care of Chelsea Mountain. Then, you're going to meet my parents, and I'm going to meet yours."

She pulls back to look at me. "Should we, like, all get together or something?"

"Um, we could."

"What?" Her brows meet in a vee. "You don't want to?"

"It's not that I don't want to, and we totally can. It's just that, I still haven't really talked to my dad since the whole LSAT thing, and I didn't come home for Christmas. I would just hate for your parents' first impression of my family to be me and my dad having a moment."

She gives me a sad smile. "It's going to be okay. But I get it. We'll play it by ear, okay?"

"Okay." I plant a quick kiss on her cheek. "Happy Valentine's Day, Lake," I whisper.

She brushes my fingers with hers. "Happy Valentine's Day," she whispers back. "Never been one to celebrate, but maybe if we're not too tired later, we can give it a try."

A heat blooms in me. Lake and I have spent many nights together at this point, but I only crave her more. "I think we should definitely find out what all the hype is about."

She pushes me away. "Don't spend all your energy on the court." She winks.

I walk back to my locker feeling unstoppable.

❖

We're down by twelve with seven minutes left, and we've only held the lead twice briefly. Chelsea Mountain is kicking our asses, and we struggle to gain back any kind of momentum. I try to catch my breath as Coach Jordan screams at the ref about a missed call. The stands are full, and the Den is louder than I've ever heard it before. It's like playing at UGA or South Carolina. I wipe my face in my jersey as Lake jogs by, getting in position for the throw-in.

Of course my dad comes to the game where we're losing and playing like we're half-dead. I haven't found my parents in the crowd yet. Gave up after a minute with how many people are here. Wouldn't want to see my dad's face, anyway.

"Hey." Lake walks up behind me, her hand on my sweaty lower back. Coach continues to yell at the ref, buying us some time. Lake is out of breath, too, but she seems steady. Confident still. "One thing at a time, remember? Don't worry about the noise. Don't worry about your parents. Don't worry about losing." I glance to the scoreboard, and she tugs my jersey, forcing me to look at her. "Just play with me, Emma. We've got seven minutes until my mom calls us in for dinner."

I grin, instantly at ease. "Okay. Let's play."

"And, Emma?"

Coach stalks back to the bench, and the ref blows his whistle. "Yeah?"

"Get me my assists."

I watch her walk away, her shorts riding up and exposing all of that thigh and muscle. How does she know the exact words to say to me? I wink as I walk past her to my spot in the zone.

The Chelsea Mountain girl throws it in, and it's game on. They run through their form of motion, the flow of which has become evident to me. I wait. *Wait.* The next pass should be coming right to—

I pick it off, and as if she knew I was going to, Lake is already at half court. I chuck her the ball and sprint to the hoop as defenders run to cut her off. But I'm fast and make it to the key just as they collapse on her. She hits me in stride with a beautiful behind-the-back pass, and I sink the layup. And just like that, the momentum swings.

"That's what I'm talking about," Coach screams as she runs down the short length of the bench with us. "Don't let them fucking breathe."

Next possession, we force them into a bad shot, and Rachel launches through the air for the rebound. We set up our offense, and I hit her on the post. She's been fighting hard against the Chelsea Mountain center, and I want her to get more points. She shakes left and spins right in a beautiful post move for a basket, cutting their lead to eight.

We fight hard, scrappy and eager, whittling away at their lead slowly but surely. We're down by three with fifty seconds left. The crowd is so loud I can barely hear myself think. Nicky rolls off a pick, and Lake passes her the ball for a jump shot. Down by one.

They kill time on offense. Too much time, but it's fine. All we need is one more shot, and the game is ours. The shot clock hits two seconds, and their point guard drives to the basket. Lake gets a step on her and plants herself in the way of her drive. She hits Lake hard, and they both thud against the ground.

Whistle blows, and the ref signals a foul on Lake. And now, they get to shoot free throws. *Fuck.*

I pull Lake off the floor. "Shit," she says, wiping her brow. "My feet were planted, I swear."

I grab her by the shoulders. "It doesn't matter. She's going to make these, but that only puts us down by three. I'm on fire. Drive to the basket and dump it to me for a three. We got this."

She nods, and we watch Chelsea Mountain's point guard sink her free throws. Lake takes the throw-in, and I run down the court. *I got this.* There's just enough time, and I've been on fire this quarter. Lake crosses over and drives hard to the left as I shuffle along the three-point line to keep in her line of sight. She throws me the ball at the last second, and I shoot it as a defender barrels toward me. The ball bounces from one side of the rim to the other. Bounces. Bounces. Then falls off the side as my back hits the court. I missed.

I missed.

"Foul!" Coach Jordan screams. It pierces my ears at the same time as the ref's whistle.

That's three free throws. *I get three free throws.* It's not over. I slip around in my sweat until Nicky pulls me off the ground and smacks my butt. "Wouldn't want anyone else on the line but you. Bring it home, Em."

I walk to the free throw line, the crowd a fuzzy mass of motion behind it, until a group of students gives the signal for everyone to quiet down. Then it's just that. *Quiet.* The ref passes me the ball, and I spin it in my hands. It's the same ball. Same smooth leather, with the same soft goose bumps. As I sink into my shooting motion, things go a bit hazy in my peripherals. But I shoot anyway.

And miss. It's short an inch and hits the front rim before ricocheting into Rachel's hands. The crowd's disappointment crashes over me in a one big collective sigh. Someone shouts, "Come on!"

Lake meets me on the line and wraps an arm around my waist, pulling me tight against her. "Listen to me, Em." I scan the restless crowd, scattered and in disbelief. I can't believe I missed. *I missed.* "Emma." She pulls me even tighter, and I bow my head so she can speak in my ear. "Make or miss it. It doesn't matter, baby. All you have to do is take your shot."

She sinks down from her tiptoes and walks away. "Lake," I call. She turns, her expression all fire and ease, her brow slightly quirked. She's both to me: passion and comfort. "I love you."

"I love you, too, Emma Wilson." She winks.

I turn back to the basket, bolstered. *Make it or miss it.* She says it doesn't matter. All I have to do is take my shot.

Swish.

The crowd cheers, and I sink my third shot. But it's not enough. We're still down by one with only five seconds on the clock and—

The Chelsea Mountain guard can't find an open player to throw in to and panics. She tries to get it to their point guard, but Nicky comes off her player to double-team her and gets a hand on the ball. It bounces across the key, and I dive for it, sliding on top of the ball before the Chelsea Mountain player. I throw it to Lake, and she pulls up for the jumper.

The buzzer fills the stadium. We won.

Lake flies into my arms, wrapping her legs around my waist as our entire team swarms us, and the crowd loses their damn minds. "We fucking did it," Rachel screams. It feels like we made the playoffs. We overcame and found a way to win. We found our inner strength.

Our team disperses, and Lake gets pulled to be interviewed by a reporter.

"Hey. Good game, thirteen." I turn to find Chelsea Mountain's point guard. She's my height, with dark skin and a cute grin. She's definitely attractive, and something in her words makes me feel like she's flirting. But I'm not interested.

"Oh hey. Thank you. It was a tough one. Y'all played hard," I say. Simple with nothing that could be interpreted as flirting, but she takes a step closer and gives my jersey a little tug. Apparently, I'm still emitting some weird bat call I have no control over.

"We don't leave until morning, and I'm not really one for curfews." She winks.

"I, uh, my folks are in town, and I'm not really available." I run my hand over my ponytail.

"Hi. I'm Lake." Lake is next to me in an instant, her arm around my waist. Chelsea Mountain girl uncurls her fingers from my jersey, and I exhale in relief. "Good game. You guys have quite the team this year."

She nods. "You, too."

"Come on, Em. Let's go celebrate." She pulls me away, and I leave the opposing point guard with a wave.

Suddenly, I'm worried about what Lake thinks happened between us. I've never had a serious girlfriend, but I assume she could be jealous. "I didn't do anything to make her—"

"I know." She wraps me in a quick hug. "That's not what I thought at all. But I'm still going to interrupt thirsty women trying to get at my girl." She pulls away, her gaze dropping down my body. "It's not your fault you can't turn it off."

I release all the tension I've been carrying all game. All the worry, too. "Come on. Introduce me to your parents," I say.

Chapter Twenty-four

We make our way through the bustling court to the opposite baseline where Lake's parents stand holding each other in excitement. They smile and whisper to each other. Her mom wears an Alder basketball T-shirt and dark blue jeans. She's around my height, and Lake's dad is well over six feet. They look nice, if a little reserved.

I nudge her. "Does it bother the hell out of you that you didn't inherit your parents' height?"

She shoves me hard. "Oh, shut up. You love that I'm short. Plus, it makes me kind of hard to guard."

"And easy to throw around," I say right before we hit earshot.

"Emma. *Shh.*" She smacks my arm.

Lake's mom takes two quick strides and wraps her in her arms. "Lake, baby."

"Hey, Mom. Thanks for coming." She pulls her dad into a hug next, and I stand a step away, waiting for my intro.

"Amazing game. And the winning shot. That's our girl," her dad says, pride dripping from his words.

"Thanks, Dad." She pulls out of his hug and takes my hand, giving me a little tug forward. "Guys, I want you to meet Emma, my girlfriend and obviously an incredible player."

I feel an instant burn in my cheeks, my usual confidence with meeting parents—with meeting anyone—completely vanishing because I've never met her parents. *The* parents. Parents that I hope will be my in-laws someday. Oh shit, I have it so fucking bad for Lake.

"Mr. Palmer, it's nice to meet you," I manage to say, though my tongue feels swollen and awkward on my words.

"Emma, what a game. You have some real talent." Her dad holds out his hand. "Call me Chris, please."

"Yes, sir." I turn to her mom, who ignores my extended hand and gives me a hug, instead.

"Oh, it's so good to finally meet you, Emma. Lake has been nonstop about you."

I grin, the nerves fading with the warmth of her mom. "Oh yeah? Hope it was mostly good."

"All of it. I promise. I'm Luz, by the way."

Lake lays a hand on her mom's shoulder. "Mom, please. Can you not?"

She pulls her daughter in for another hug. "Oh relax. I'm sure I'm not telling Emma anything she doesn't already know."

"Emma." I turn at the sound of Gracie's voice. She jogs across the court, her navy foam finger held high. I extend my arms just in time. She jumps into me, and I spin her around until I get dizzy.

"I didn't know you were coming, Gracie." I take a moment to let the wobble in my body stabilize, then present my sister to the Palmers. She looks exactly like me, just more girly and twelve. "Everyone, this is my youngest sibling, Gracie. Don't tell the others, but she's definitely my favorite. And, Gracie, this is Lake and her parents, Chris and Luz."

She shoots me a toothy grin. "Hi, it's nice to meet you all." Gracie's gaze lingers on Lake as if she knows exactly what she means to me.

They wave at Gracie with sweet smiles, but there's something just a little vacant about them now. I think I see what Lake is talking about. Like there's a downward pull or something. A heaviness in there somewhere. Of course there is.

My mom and dad walk up a minute later. My mom hugs me. "Great game, sweetie."

I look at my dad, waiting for him to speak so I know how to react. He looks older and a little tired, his hair thinner and grayer than I remember. Kind of looks like I could take him. "Come here, Emma Bear," he says and pulls me into a hug. I let him. "I love you and am so proud of you. No matter what you want to do with your life," he whispers. I pull back, but he keeps his grip on my shoulders. "You hear me?"

"I hear you." And though I do hear him, I also know him. I know he'll erupt at me again. It's not a problem we can fix right now but one I want to commit to fixing in the future. The next big conversation I have with my father will be asking him to go to family therapy with me. "I love you, too." Enough of this. I turn to the Palmers and introduce them to my parents.

They shake hands and exchange all the pleasantries. "Your daughter is lovely. We're so glad Lake found someone like Emma," Luz says.

My folks tilt their heads, clearly confused and in the dark.

"Lake and I are together," I say quickly, hoping to avoid any unnecessary awkward comments or questions from my parents.

"Are you now?" I jump at a hand squeezing my shoulder from behind.

I gulp. "Coach Jordan. Hi." *Shit.* This party is getting just a tad crowded. She looks between Lake and me with a skeptical gaze.

"Congrats, you two." The hard line of her mouth breaks into a smile. "And fantastic game." She hugs Lake's parents. "So good to see you both again. Luz, how's the sourdough going?"

Luz touches her chest and chuckles. "Oh, Franny. I think we both know that starter is long gone."

Coach introduces herself to my parents, and everyone compliments each other on the game, the coaching, the playing, until Coach finally pulls us away for our post-game meeting. We say good-bye and make plans to meet our parents after. Separately.

After we shower and are released, Lake and I walk together through campus until I need to turn left toward the library parking deck, and she needs to turn right to the upper deck. "I'll text you when we're done," I say.

She gives me a kiss on the cheek. "It's nice to see my parents and all, but I can't wait to spend the rest of the night with you."

"Me, too."

My parents treat me to a late dinner at the one Italian place in town. I eat two entire meals. And dessert. I love my parents. They're fine. But the best part is exchanging secret eye rolls and silly looks with Gracie. When dinner is over, they drive me home, and I thank them for taking me out. Mostly, I just want to get home to Lake. Even though I'm beyond tired, I don't care. I want to stay up all night with her.

❖

I lie in bed, waiting for what feels like forever, but is only forty minutes, until Lake knocks quietly on the bathroom door and crawls into bed next to me. It's already ten, but again, I don't care.

I turn on my side to face her. "Hi," I say.

"Hi." She smiles, but it stops short, not reaching her eyes, and her tone is low. Sad sounding.

I cup her cheek. "What's wrong? Are you upset?" She takes a deep breath and rolls on her back, covering her face with her arm. "You can tell me," I say softly. My stomach tightens in anticipation. I have no idea what's up, and it's making me nervous.

"I'm sorry," she says, her words muffled in her arm.

I gently pull her arm away from her face so I can see her. "For what? What's going on, Lake?"

She shakes her head, tears welling in her eyes. "I think being with my parents made me nervous."

"Okay." I rub my thumb over her cheek. "Nervous about what?"

"I told them I entered myself into the WNBA draft, and they were obviously really excited, and we talked about that for a while."

"It's official?" I ask. My words as high as I feel.

She nods, but she doesn't seem excited. "I mean, yeah. But it doesn't mean anything yet."

"You're in the WNBA draft. What's not exciting about that? You're probably a second-round pick, too. Especially after you won us that game."

"What about us?" She shakes her head. "I just found you, and the end of the season is around the corner. Then graduation. Then what?" She wipes a tear that hasn't quite fallen yet. "And you could have anyone, Emma. So many women want you. How can I compete with that when I'll be traveling for work, and we may not even live in the same place? I just"—she takes a sharp breath—"can't help but feel like I'm setting myself up for this giant loss, and I don't know if I can handle it."

I squeeze her hand. "Hey, it's going to—"

"No." She flips on her side to look at me, her eyes full of worry. "Don't promise me things you can't be sure of." She drops her voice to a whisper. "I just don't want to end up like them. Don't want to be sad for the rest of my life."

"Lake." I tilt her chin to capture her gaze again. My room is dark, but the campus street lamps give just enough light through my window for me to see. "I can't promise you anything, and you know that. The world is wild and greedy and will take and take and take from you. From us. It will ruin our plans and torch our dreams. But that's the only way to get to the place truly meant for us." I take a deep breath, hoping I'm not rambling too much. "I bet you didn't plan to play your senior year at Alder, but here you are with me."

She pulls me down for a soft kiss. "Here I am," she whispers.

"And we may not live in the same place for a while. Maybe things will be rocky. Shit, maybe things won't work out. But if you give up now, there's zero chance. I know in my gut that it's you, Lake. And I've run down every possible road to find you. To find us. No matter what twisted course life lies for us. I will find you. That's what I can promise. I will fight to find you." I cup her cheek, needing to hold her. "Someone once told me, make it or miss it. It doesn't matter. All you have to do is take your shot." I lower my lips to her ear. "Take a shot."

She turns to capture my lips. Her kiss is slow and deep, as if she's trying to communicate all her feelings through the brush of our tongues and the firming of her grip on the back of my neck. I slide on top and push a piece of hair from her forehead. Let my mouth drop to her neck and confess my love against her pulse.

"I love you, too," she says, peppering praise between kisses. "Your brightness." *Kiss.* "Your swagger." *Kiss.* "Your compassion."

I slip my fingers under her shirt, and her warm skin is like a jolt to my system. Her words like a zap. Each of her breaths fills me with this vastness. An overwhelming feeling of gratitude. I take a sharp inhale, suddenly wanting for oxygen.

She pulls me down, pressing my face to her neck. "You're trembling, Emma."

I nod against her, finding comfort in her warm citrus scent and the harmony of her pulse with her breathing. "I know," I whisper.

"Come here." She gently rolls us so I'm on my back, and she kneels over me. She pulls her shirt over her head, and I can't help but reach for her. Brush my knuckles over her soft breasts. "You, too," she says.

I lean forward and tug off my shirt. Then push my shorts down my legs. Lake gathers them from my ankles and drops them on the floor. She adds her own shorts to the pile of discarded clothes, then lies her naked body over mine. I shudder when her breasts skim over my nipples. I've always been sensitive that way.

Our thighs interlock, and our breathing is deep, though we don't kiss or tug or nip. We hold each other tight as if trying to forge one body from ours. A body we could inhabit together. Shared skin and blood and heart. At least, that's what I feel—what I desire—when I pull her against me: her body in mine, mine in hers.

She's always gotten under my skin.

And I know I've always been under hers.

She pulls up and swings her leg over mine, straddling me. She sits, her wet warmth low on my stomach, her gaze raking over my body. I ache for every inch of her, but she pushes my arms down. Instead, she palms my breasts, her hands warm and demanding. She groans with me, my nipples hardening between her fingers as she grinds against me.

"Lake." Her name coasts from my lips as she massages me. I don't know if she has ever used a strap-on, but this moment feels right. "If you want to try, I bought a strap-on for us."

"Yeah?" Her voice is breathy, and she grinds harder into me, as if the idea turns her on.

I nod. "Only if you're comfortable with it. Only if you want it."

She lowers herself and pulls my nipple into her mouth. I smother a groan of pleasure as the sharp sensation of her wet mouth and hard teeth rockets through me. Then, she kisses my neck, making me squirm. Making me so, so wet for her. "I want you to wear it."

"Okay." I gently roll her off me and slip out of bed. I grab the bag from my dresser and go to the bathroom. It only takes me a minute to situate myself before I walk back into the dark of my room.

Lake stares at me—at the silicone between my thighs—and crooks her finger. "Come here."

I lower myself on top of her, letting the small dildo push against her hips and belly, letting her get used to the feel of it on her skin. We make out with it between us, and she strokes it, trying to tug it between her thighs. "Wait a second." I grab her wrists and pin them to the mattress, but it only seems to exacerbate her need. Her chest heaves, nipples hard and begging to be sucked.

"Emma. Please, can we do this?" She lifts her hips, trying to find pressure. Relief.

"Of course we can. I just"—I let her wrists go, and she strokes my shoulders—"have you ever done this before?"

"No. Is that a problem?"

I shake my head. "Not at all." It's not a problem, I've just never used a strap-on with someone I love. I've only ever used it as a device. To fuck someone with. Or to be fucked. I've never done *this* before.

"I trust you, Emma. Just go slow."

I look into her eyes and nod. "Okay. You have to promise to tell me if I go too deep or if it's just too much, okay? Even if it's not huge, it's a lot to get used to."

"I said I trust you. And I promise to communicate." She pulls my mouth against hers for one of the sweetest kisses I've ever experienced. "Do you trust *me*?"

I straighten and gently push her knees farther apart. "With everything." Her folds glisten in the dim orange glow of my room, and my mouth waters as I take her by the hips and slide her down my bed to meet me, the tip of the dildo lying just under her belly button.

I grab the head and push it down, sliding it over her wetness, letting it slip through her, over her entrance, over her clit. She moans, and I know I could give her an orgasm just from this. But she wants me inside, so I run my fingers through her and rub her wetness over the tip. It's plenty of lube.

I lower it to her entrance and press against her. Not sliding in but adding some pressure so she knows I'm about to. "I love you," I say.

"Emma, I love you so much." She touches her forehead. "Please, I'm so ready."

I ease into her, and she groans. Her walls are tight, and I hit resistance right away. I pull out and lower myself so I can kiss her. I suck on her earlobe. "I know you want it," I whisper. "But try to relax before you pull me in. Let yourself get used to it first."

"Okay. Okay, I'm ready."

I brace myself on an elbow and reach for it again, rubbing through her folds until her breaths quicken. Then I ease back into her inch by slow inch. She gasps, and I kiss under her jaw, waiting for her to tell me to stop or give me a sign. "Stay there," she whispers.

She rocks her hips gently, exploring the sensation of the strap-on inside her. She moans and reaches for my hips. I can feel her trying to pull more inside. "Ready for more?"

"Yes."

I pump my hips, slowly pushing deeper, until she releases the sexiest moan of pleasure I've ever heard. Then I slide out and back in, exploring different paces and rhythms, indulging in learning how my girlfriend likes to be fucked. I hit the right spot over and over until I feel a tremble building in her legs and rising through her body like an avalanche. I don't stop. She reaches for me, grasping at my back, scratching down my shoulder blades.

Until she cries out and I let her. I don't try to smother the sound for Piper. Hopefully, she's fast asleep, and I don't want to mute it. It's the most beautiful thing I've ever heard. Lake's body goes rigid as I hold her, and she hiccups on the last waves of her pleasure.

"Oh my God," she gasps, then falls back against the mattress. I slip out of her, and rub my fingers over the length of her. Over and over. "Oh. My. *God.*" Her breathing is fast again, and I add more pressure. "Emma, I'm gonna—oh my God, I'm gonna—" A gush of hot liquid flows from her, and she crumbles, panting, and reaches for me.

But I can't move. I'm in complete awe.

After a minute, she says, "Shit. I'm sorry." She pushes herself upright and runs a hand over the giant wet spot on my sheets. "It's never happened before. I didn't know—"

"Lake." She finally looks at me, the worry on her face melting away. "That was the most beautiful thing I've ever experienced." I press her hand over my heart. "Ever."

She takes a shaky breath. "I'm sorry about the mess. I have an extra pair of sheets. I can get them right now—"

I kiss her, cutting off her nonsense. "You can do that again in my mouth," I whisper. "That's what you can do right now."

She reaches for the buckle on my harness and pulls it loose. I tug it off and let it drop to the floor. Her hands run up and down my body, dipping into me and dragging my wetness over my skin. We're everywhere. "In your mouth?" she repeats.

I roll us over so she's straddling me again, and I slide down my mattress, until I can feel the heat of her on my lips. "In my mouth," I whisper against her folds and grip her hips, pulling her down to me.

Lake sleeps in my arms, her breath deep and slow. I kiss the top of her head gently, imagining she feels at home with me holding her. Imagining she feels at home with *me*. Last night changed us. I swear the chemistry of my blood is different. Like I was just a blank slate before her. And whether I get to call her mine forever or not, she's already given me so much. Showed me my depths. My colors.

Gave me the courage to take my shot.

CHAPTER TWENTY-FIVE

I grab an everything bagel and a pack of cream cheese from the breakfast spread in the front of the Den. My coffee balances awkwardly in the crook of my elbow as I reach for a butter knife. I'm definitely going to spill. Not that I care for coffee, but it's a necessity sometimes.

"I got it." Lake takes the cup from my arm and walks to our seats in the front row.

Rachel comes up behind me and moans. "Bagels. Yes." She grabs two, one cinnamon sugar, one asiago, and piles packs of cream cheeses in her pocket. "Bagels are life," she says sleepily and sits on the other side of Lake.

I add an asiago to my plate, jealous of Rachel's, and slide into my chair.

"I should've gotten two," Lake whispers.

I tear my asiago and slide half onto her plate as Coach walks in front of the whiteboard. Lake squeezes my thigh in thanks and takes a bite, closing her eyes in apparent pleasure.

"Good morning, everyone."

"Morning, Coach," we respond in unison.

"I have some exciting news to share with you." The sound of crunching wrappers stops. "March is a week away, and with it comes conference championships and the NCAA tournament. Now, I have some connections in the world of women's basketball and feel confident that we'll be picked on Selection Sunday for a First Four game."

The Den erupts in cheering. "Holy shit," I say, squeezing Lake's shoulder. "This is real?" I never even considered that playing in the NCAA tournament would be a possibility for our team. But here we are, talking about the First Four over Einstein's.

She flashes a confident grin. "It's real."

"We have one regular season game left." Coach scans the room, seemingly taking in all our faces. I wipe my mouth in case I have cream cheese on it. Her gaze stops on me, and I swear I see a hint of a smile on her lips. She's up to something. "One game left that doesn't have an impact on our bid. We could lose to Ridgeland by fifty points and still make it to the First Four."

We shoot confused glances at one another. I'm completely lost.

"And Ridgeland has nothing to gain by beating us. They have no shot at the NCAA tournament, much less the conference championship. So I have a proposition for you. There is a population of students and faculty at Alder University—a pride of Lions—who don't have the same protections and rights as their fellow Lions. Raise your hand if you're familiar with the Alder Queer Fellowship."

A nervous tangle fills my stomach as the entire team raises their hands. This moment feels big. Important.

"I am a queer woman, and I coach queer players. You have queer professors and queer friends. And at Alder, I could be fired for having a wife whom I *have*. You could lose a scholarship for being openly queer and not following the core 'values' of the university. You could start a club as a safe space for our queer population here and be told time and time again that you don't belong. The university refuses to recognize AQF as a school-sanctioned club. And this is not only happening on our campus but across the country.

"This is your team." She waves over us. "And all of you get to decide. Ridgeland's head coach and I have agreed to forfeit"—the Den collectively gasps—"in protest to these archaic principles. AQF has coordinated with multiple sister clubs across the Southeast, and we will not be the only ones refusing to take the court if you agree."

Murmuring fills the Den, and Coach hushes us. "Quiet, quiet." She gives us a moment to calm down. "Some things are bigger than a game. And this is one of those moments. I propose that we show up in uniform with Ridgeland and sit silently on the bench the entirety of our televised game. AQF has sent me a public statement that we can use, or we can write our own. Coach Fulton and I are going to leave for a half hour. Take that time to discuss. When we come back, I want an answer."

She nods and walks out.

The room is silent. Half-eaten bagels lie untouched in front of us. I hear Lake swallow next to me, and she nudges me with her knee. When I look at her, she nods to the front of the room. But this isn't my thing. If anything, Rachel is way more involved with the AQF crew.

"Rach," I whisper, and shit, it sounds so loud. She looks at me, brows raised. "Did you know about this?" She shakes her head, but I find it hard to believe Andy didn't let it slip. "Come on." I nod to the front of the room like Lake did and slide out of my seat with Rachel. Lake remains sitting. Not sure why she thinks she's not coming up with us. "You, too." I tug her hand until she follows.

The three of us stand in front of our shocked team, and again, I don't feel like I'm the leader of this. Rachel is. We all are. I nudge her.

"Um," she says. "Our whole team is basically queer, huh?" The room fills with laughter, and the tension—the uncertainty—vanishes. Her chuckles fade away as she steps in front of me and Lake. "In all seriousness, this type of opportunity for peaceful protest, for change, is a gift. To fight for each other's right to exist..." She shakes her head. "I don't know how we can turn away from that. Sports has never just been sports. Sports is culture, our society, and it has *always* been a vehicle for social justice."

"She's right," Lake says. "I actually wrote a history paper on this last year. Protesting in sports goes all the way back to chariot racing." She chuckles with the rest of the team as my chest fills with pride for the two of them. She looks to me as if trying to give me the floor, but I step back. She turns her attention back to our team.

"It's our civic duty to take hold of opportunities like this and try to change our environment for the better." She shrugs. "I vote for sitting through the whole damn thing. Because I'm a lesbian and believe I should have the same rights and protections as straight students at Alder."

"Exactly," Rachel says. "By sitting, we take a stand."

"I also vote that we sit out," I say.

"Raise your hand if you vote to sit," Rachel says.

There's no deliberation, no discussion or panicked glances. Our teammates' hands shoot in the air. We know what's *right*.

"Can we eat our bagels now?" Nicky asks, and the whole room bursts into laughter.

"Yes," Rachel says. "Eat your damn bagels."

We eat and chat, a relaxed joy about us. "Damn, Lake," I say. "I didn't know you were going to be our future president."

She shoots me a grin and wipes her mouth in a napkin. "Public speaking is, like, going to be my whole career, Em. I'm pretty fucking good at it."

I stare at her, completely in awe. "Yeah. Right."

We turn at a knock on the door, and Coach Jordan walks in. She stands in front of us, seemingly taking in our light energy. "So?" she asks.

"We're sitting it out," Rachel says.

A wide grin spreads over Coach's face. "I am so wildly proud of all of you. Congratulations. I'll call Ridgeland's coach and let him know. Be here at one tomorrow so we can prepare ourselves before the game. Now get out of here and enjoy your day."

We walk out together. The air is still winter crisp, but the sunshine is warm, and little bits of spring peek out from every corner; birds chirp, a bee swarms by, and tulips protrude from the dirt in colorful pops. There's an energy to campus. Something building.

❖

"It's simply unbelievable," the reporter says. She stands on center court as her cameraman pans in on our bench, then

Ridgeland's. "Both teams are refusing to take the court." She shakes her head in apparent disbelief. "I've never seen anything like this."

Coach Jordan grins. I think she took pleasure in not responding to the reporter's question. She's not a sports broadcaster but someone from the local news we don't know. She's loud and arrogant and seems mad at us. The sports broadcaster, Deidra, on the other hand, was given written notice of what is happening. She speaks quietly into her microphone, respecting our silence. Respecting our protest.

The stands are abuzz with confusion. Everyone seems confused. That's the whole point, to draw attention. Everyone watching this on the news will have no idea what's going on until Deidra's story breaks. We'll gain attention, then *boom*, it's conversation time. And sure, the Right will call us disrespectful little brats, but we will stay strong and *respect* ourselves and our peers.

AQF sits silently in solidarity with us right in our line of view, wearing matching rainbow shirts. I'm kind of surprised they haven't been thrown out yet, but the university seemingly has no idea how to handle this. They've done literally nothing except try to get us to speak, but Coach just sits there in silence, risking her brand-new job for what she believes in.

The minutes pass surprisingly quickly as we sit and do nothing. Until the final buzzer sounds for the fourth quarter, and both teams line up to shake hands. "Congratulations," I hear the opposing coach say to Coach Jordan.

"You, too, Nathan. You, too."

Coach told us before the game not to linger. To go straight to the locker room, change, grab to-go meals she had prepared for us, and go straight to our dorms and stay there the rest of the night. "If I so much as catch wind that you've set foot outside, you will not play a single second in the conference championship. Am I clear?" she said.

She was clear.

We walk straight to the locker room, where an armed officer stands sentry at the door, quickly change, grab our meals, and walk together to Wilder where we'll stay with Andy, Maya, and Rachel for the evening, not wanting to be alone.

The door closes behind us, and we all take a big exhale of relief. What we just did was *big*. I can still feel the adrenaline in my blood. Andy and Maya stand to gives us hugs. The idea of sharing a room with Andy and Lake together would've bothered me at the beginning of this year. Would've turned me into a jumbled mess. But as I plop on the sleeping bag next to Rachel's bed with Lake, I feel completely at ease. We're just with our friends.

"Wow," I say.

"Yeah," Lake says. "Who knew sitting on the bench the entire game could be more exciting than playing?"

"You did perfectly," Andy says. She pulls out her phone and types something. "Bailey says the news is blowing up. You guys are getting tons of attention. So is AQF."

"Should I pull it up on my laptop?" Maya asks.

Rachel sighs as she flops onto her bed. "I don't know. I'm all jacked up still and starving and just don't feel like I want to know all the shit people are saying about us. Not tonight." I think the phone calls with our parents was enough drama for the evening. They were all supportive, but I think they find it hard to have their kids in this kind of critical spotlight. They're worried, if the ten texts from my dad with an increasing amount of question marks in each one has anything to say about it. The annoyance I sense in his messages is agitating, though. It feels like he cares less about our safety and more about how tonight affects our record. He probably thinks something like social justice isn't as important as the results of a college basketball game.

But then, I'm starting to not care so much what my dad thinks.

I pop open my container of food. It's cozy being locked in Rachel and Andy's room together, but there's a heaviness in the air. We're locked in here for our safety as the rest of the nation fights over what we did tonight. "Yeah. I'm cool with just chilling. We'll handle everything tomorrow."

"Bailey's on it, anyway," Andy says.

Maya opens a giant pizza box. "Didn't know you all had food. I got pizza for everyone."

Rachel plays music on her laptop. "Well, good. Now we can hole up for days if we need to."

I squeeze Lake's hand to comfort myself as much as to comfort her. We spend the evening eating and chatting about life and sports and love. About Andy and Maya's season opener in a couple of days. I revel in the ease with which Lake interacts with everyone. Especially Andy. When she asks Andy questions about her life and shares her condolences for her father, I know she trusts me.

As it gets later, we get sillier and sillier, sharing stories of our first kisses and first times—stories of the dumbest things we've ever done—until the importance of the night feels faraway and otherworldly. Until Rachel drifts to sleep first, and we follow shortly after.

Chapter Twenty-six

I blink in shock as Lake flies into my arms, knocking me to the floor. This moment is the complete opposite of the game we refused to play. This moment is loud, it's raucous, and it's just for us. Coach Jordan runs to center court where our team has become a mosh pit of celebration. Even Coach Fulton does a few little hops of joy.

Winning the conference championship is blissful.

We earned this moment. As Coach Jordan passes the trophy to Lake, everything becomes very real. Sure, we are officially champions of some sort, but we knew we would take home the conference. The thing that makes winning this title so special, so important, is that with this win, we officially make it to the first round of the NCAA tournament.

"We're in," Lake yells. She thrusts the trophy in the air as we gather around for a photo. For a thousand photos.

The game wasn't even close, and that gives us hope for progressing in the tournament. Our success also gives Lake much deserved national attention. She's the starting point guard and leader of the team that hasn't had a winning season in four years and is now conference champions and on their way to the big tournament. Her draft prospects are rising by the day, and I can't wait to watch her on TV next month to see which team is lucky enough to snag her.

Then, we graduate.

I take a step away from the chaos of celebration. *Then, we graduate.* I look at my hands as if checking where all my time disappeared to. Then, I look at Lake, the smile on her face so bright and brilliant, and I feel at ease. It's not Alder. Not that damned stone or the cavernous dining hall or the comfort of the mountains that surround us.

It's Lake. And it's me. That's what I need to keep. Not this place.

I am complete and ready to face anything. But with Lake, I feel like I've already arrived. Whatever winding roads or twisted paths life puts me on, I can carry her with me. At least, that's what I will fight for every day. For this home I've found.

She finds me on the periphery and pulls me into a hug. "You okay?" she asks, looking at me with concern.

I pick her up and give her a spin, replacing whatever expression I had with a big grin. "Of course. Just needed a minute."

She rubs under my collarbone. "It's a bit overwhelming, isn't it?"

"It's perfect. Congratulations, Lake. You deserve all of it." I bend to kiss her cheek.

After the celebration, we shower and pile back onto the bus. The drive to our hotel is fifteen minutes. Fifteen minutes until I get to fall asleep with her in my arms. In a queen-sized bed. I squeeze her hand in the dark bus, and she shoots me a sexy smirk. Okay, maybe more like an *hour* and fifteen minutes until I fall asleep with her in my arms.

Weber passes me a piece of paper as I walk by his desk. It's contact information for someone who works in the College of Education at UGA. "Ready for Saturday?" he asks.

I hold up the paper. "Should I call them today?"

He grins, his chunky glasses slipping down his nose. "That's a big change of tune from when you were looking at law school."

"Yeah." I fold the paper neatly and put it in my back pocket for later. "I'm excited for teaching. And I'm…" I shrug, no epic explanation popping into my head. "I don't know. I'm just at ease."

He walks around his desk to wrap me in his thick arms. I'll miss these hugs. "I can't believe you're about to graduate." He pulls away but holds me by the shoulders, staring hard at me. "You were my most annoying student. And the student I'm most proud of."

I roll my eyes. "Stop. You're going to make me cry." I collide against him for another hug. "Thanks, Weber. This year was, like, kind of terrifying, and I don't know if I would've made it through without your support." My turn to pull away and stare at him. "Just knowing that someone on this campus cared about me and was looking out for me made all the difference." I shake my head, literal tears welling. "You and Coach Jordan…you just…"

He squeezes my shoulders. "I know, I know. And now you get to go be that to a bunch of wild little Emma Wilsons. Good luck. You're quite the pain in the ass."

I shove him. "Ugh, you're the worst."

"Go sit down. We still have a month of class left, you know."

I hike up my bag and groan. "I know, Doug. I know."

I sit through Weber's class and let it all soak in. Maybe I'll go to UGA and get a master's in education. I like the idea of staying close to Atlanta, especially since all the mock drafts have Lake being selected by the Dream. That is *the dream*. Half our friends are from Atlanta: Andy, Maya, Ashley, and Rachel. Both our families live there, and it's one of the coolest cities to live in right now.

Class ends before I can finish daydreaming of what my life will look like in a few months. I walk past Weber. "Pay attention next time, Wilson," he calls after me. I give him a middle finger as I walk into the hallway. The afternoon is warm, the air thick with fresh blooms and pollen. The spring air is sweet, and I close my eyes to the sun, basking in it for a moment before I walk back to Griner to pack for our trip to Atlanta where we'll play in the first round of the NCAA tournament on Saturday.

Lake greets me when I walk into my room. She's always over, and somehow, she's never over enough. She sits on the edge of my bed, swinging her legs, and I give her a push so her back hits my mattress. I kiss her long and hard. "Hi," I finally say.

She smiles and interlocks her fingers behind my neck, pulling me down for another kiss. "I missed you."

"I daydreamed about the draft and living in Atlanta all through Weber's class."

She chuckles. "I'm sure he loved that."

I pull the paper out of my back pocket to show her. "He gave me the contact information of one of his friends in the College of Education at UGA. It's not too far from Atlanta if you wind up with the Dream, and their master's program is highly rated." I shake my head, excitement swelling in my chest. "I just can't wait for life with you."

She kisses me, cupping my cheek. "This is life with me, baby. Right now."

"I love you."

"I love you, too." She pushes me off and sits up. "Now, let's pack."

❖

"Good luck," Piper yells as our team files onto the bus. She stands in a group with Andy, Maya, Bailey, Noelle, Maggie, and Olivia. They clap, and I watch them through the windows until I reach the back of the bus with Lake.

"They're the best," she says, pushing her bag under the seat in front of her.

"They really, really are." I continue to watch them as they cheer for us, homemade signs in hand and smiles on their faces.

Earlier this week, we met up with Bailey, Robert, and Ashley in the basement of Wilder Hall to talk about our protest and the national coverage it received. It was *huge*. We made it into all the major publications and have been a hot-button topic of national debate. Apparently, it was the kind of pressure the Alder administration needed to reconsider its policy on LGBTQ+ students and faculty and the merits of having a club such as AQF.

The university is getting major heat. Now it's just a waiting game to see how they respond. But that's an issue for next week because tomorrow, we play in our first NCAA tournament game. And *that* is my focus.

And Lake's hand in mine.

"You nervous to play your old team?" I ask.

"Not at all." She pushes her glasses up the bridge of her nose and lays her head on my shoulder. "I already have everything I want from this season. Everything else is just the cherry on top. Plus, GSU is super nice. You won't have to get any technical fouls this game."

I sigh in relief. "Thank God. I want to go out on good terms with Coach Jordan, given she's, like, my hero and all."

"You're such a softie, Emma Wilson."

"Through and through."

I've never played in such a big arena with so many people in the stands. I have a feeling the turnout has something to do with the attention we received for the game we didn't play. Coach Jordan gave several interviews defending us and our right to play against the countless bigots calling for our disqualification from the tournament. She didn't allow any of us to be questioned. I think it was her way of keeping us safe and focused while she took the brunt of the consequences. One such consequence being an intense meeting with Dr. Lymer, the head honcho of the board of trustees. But the trustees must have their hands full because from what we can tell, Coach has yet to be fired.

Regardless, this place is bumping. The butterflies in my stomach are in full swarm as we warm up, cameras flashing and recording us live. Lake wanders to the other side of the court to greet her old team as I fidget with the tail of my jersey and try to ease my nerves.

Then, it's time.

The announcer introduces our starting lineups in his booming voice, echoing in time with the flashing lights. I feel like a performer instead of a basketball player as I run through the tunnel of teammates.

"Just go out there and play. Do what you've done all season," Coach Jordan shouts, and we take our positions for the opening tip-off.

I give Lake a nervous glance that beckons her over. She squats next to me. "Hey. This is just a game. *Play*," she says, gripping the back of my jersey. "Also, number twenty-four has been in a funk with her three-pointers. You can play a little looser on defense with her." She tugs me closer. "And have fun, baby. This could be it."

"Oh shit. This could be my last game ever." I straighten and pull her in for a hug, not caring about all the eyes on us.

"As a player," she says and plants a quick kiss on my cheek that I'm pretty sure is going to blow up the queer basketball social media world tonight.

Rachel loses the tip.

We spend the entire game swimming against the current that is GSU dominating us. They seem to win every rebound, sink every shot, and get every call from the refs. It's just one of those games where everything seems to go wrong, and the score reflects that.

We're down by fifteen at the start of the fourth quarter. Down by fifteen with *zero momentum*. But weirdly, I'm having fun.

I backpedal as the GSU offense pushes down the court. Try to memorize how it sounds to play in such a big stadium with fans who are here to see us. I want to burn the image of Lake in her white Alder uniform in my brain. And the image of her squatting, back to me, ready to steal the ball.

My last game as a player. But I'll always be a baller.

And my wife—my *future* wife—has many games ahead of her, and I'm going to try to make as many as humanly possible. As many as my teaching schedule allows.

But right now, I have four minutes left to *play*.

❖

When we arrive back in Alder, the same group of students and professors who saw us off welcome us home, except for Andy and Maya. They're in Tennessee for a game today, surely kicking some poor team's ass. We grab our bags and walk off the bus to chants of, "Go Lions," and, "Great season."

It was a great season. Thanks to Coach Jordan, we had the opportunity to be part of a program overhaul that future classes and teams will benefit from. It's only the beginning for the Alder Lions women's basketball team. And next year, they're going to crush GSU if given the opportunity.

Chapter Twenty-seven

Rachel points at my laptop. "There she is, there she is," she shouts.

I try to find Lake among the big group of WNBA draft members, all in glamorous suits and dresses, but the camera pans out, and I apparently miss her. "Where? I don't see her."

"She was right there," Andy says, pointing to the corner of the screen.

Maya passes around a bowl of popcorn, and Bailey and Piper discreetly pour beer into Solo cups. We've turned the basement of Griner Hall into our own little draft watch party. It kills me not to be with Lake and her family in New York, but I couldn't miss this Monday of classes. I had a quiz and two papers due, and as it turns out, I really care about doing well.

"You can try FaceTime. If you want to get your eyes on her and say a quick hi," Noelle suggests.

I pull out my phone as the host of the draft steps up to the podium. "You think?" I ask. "I don't want to be a burden or distraction." I frown at my phone.

Noelle lays a hand on my back. "If you were there, wouldn't you want a quick call from Lake just to say good luck?"

I hit the FaceTime icon under Lake's contact information in my phone and give Noelle a small smile. The screen cuts to a view of Lake's breasts and under her chin. Her phone must be in her lap. "Hey," she whisper-yells as she looks at the screen. She is *stunning* in her new shimmering gold dress and a matching gold pin that her mom gave her for good luck holding back one side of her beautiful hair

I almost cry at the sight of her. "I just..." I wipe at the very real tear falling down my cheek. I am *definitely* crying. "You're gorgeous. Wanted you to know I'm right here watching with the crew. Good luck, and I love you, Lake Palmer."

She smiles down at her phone and takes a long breath. "I love you, Emma. Fingers crossed for the Dream."

"Fingers crossed. Enjoy every second."

She blows a kiss and hangs up. I flit my gaze right back to the laptop, and there she is, smiling at her lap like a complete fool, her mouth moving over the words, "I love you, Emma." There must be a delay on the live feed. Getting to see that moment was a gift.

Andy walks behind me and wraps her arms around my shoulders, her mouth next to my ear. "You've always been bright. But I've never seen you on fire. I'm so happy for you, Emma."

I stand and pull her into me. It's a tight hug, full of complete love, unhindered by what-ifs and unrequited crushes. A hug I've never shared with her before. An *intimacy* I've never shared with her before. "Look at us. Exactly where we're supposed to be." I squeeze her even tighter until she laughs and squirms to get away. "You'll always be my best friend, Andrea Foster. Always."

"You'll always be mine, Emma." She plucks at the sleeve of my T-shirt. "You've never changed your laundry detergent."

I raise a brow. "Oh? Okay." I chuckle, confused.

She smiles, and it's full of so much comfort and love. "Don't," she says.

I stand a little straighter. "I won't."

Maya groans and tosses a piece of popcorn at us. "Fucking finally," she says, walking up and throwing an arm over both of us. "It only took almost two years for you guys to figure this shit out." Andy shoves her away and promptly pops a sweet kiss to her lips. Maya melts against her, and I don't turn away. I smile.

"It's back on," Rachel calls.

We crowd my laptop and watch the first round of the draft. Women we know, some who we've played against, take the stage and accept their jerseys with a handshake and big smile for the camera. Everyone is stunning, their athletic bodies displayed in a different light tonight.

"And with the nineteenth pick, the Seattle Storm select"—the host looks at the notes I assume are on the podium—"Lake Palmer, guard, from Alder University." The camera focuses on Lake as she hugs her parents, a wide smile on her face. She walks up the stairs to the stage with all the composure in the world and shakes the host's hand. Then, she grabs a corner of the green Storm jersey and holds it up for a photo.

"Seattle," I say, letting it sink in. "*Seattle?*" I stand and grip the back of my chair. "Seattle is dope," I yell and jog around the room in a victory lap, hugging and high-fiving our friends. "We're going to Seattle, baby!"

"Whoop, whoop," Rachel hollers. "Your girl just got drafted into the WNBA."

"Holy shit. Congratulations, Emma," Maya says.

Bailey squeezes my shoulder. "Seattle is awesome. You're going to love it there."

"Is that where you'll go to school?" Piper asks.

I calm my breathing enough to process the question. "No." I run a hand through my hair. "No, I think I want to go to UGA. But the WNBA season is mostly in the summer, so it should work out. It *will* work out. I'll move up after I graduate. And who knows? She could move teams, too." I shake my head. "But whatever. This is fantastic news."

"The best news," Andy says.

After the show ends, Lake calls me on FaceTime, and I walk to the other room to talk in private. "Lake," I yell, completely unable to contain my excitement. "Congratulations! The second round. Incredible."

She takes a deep breath, the smile never leaving her face. "I'm so happy. I think I'm in shock still." Her brows narrow as she stares at her phone. "Seattle, though. I really thought it'd be Atlanta, and I know—"

"Seattle will be amazing. We've been googling it over here. Have you seen photos? They have a giant mountain with snow and the Space Needle," I ramble. I'm nervous, yes. It will be hard, yes. But Lake and I can do this.

"What about you?" she asks, worry creeping into her voice. "You were so set on UGA, and Seattle is literally across the country."

"I'm going to UGA, and you're going to Seattle. The master program I'm interested in can be completed in a year and a half." She nods, her eyes watering. "Those are happy tears brewing, right?"

She nods again, more emphatically this time. "I'm really proud of you."

"Proud of me?" I laugh. "Lake, you're going to play in the WNBA. I'm so wildly proud of *you.* Now, wipe those tears and go spend the evening getting spoiled by your parents, okay?"

"Okay."

"We'll talk more about it when you get home. I love you more than anything, Lake. Congratulations."

She sighs and wipes her eye, careful not to smudge her makeup. "I wish you were here."

"Me, too."

"Okay. I should go. I love you."

She hangs up, and I take a moment alone before I join our friends in celebration again. Everything is going to be okay. I'm going to be a teacher. My girlfriend is in the WNBA. And we're in love. At the beginning of this school year, I couldn't have imagined sitting here, in the basement of my dorm, with this encompassing feeling of joy. With the feeling that I have everything to look forward to in my life.

I rub my face and send a quiet thanks to any higher being that may exist out there, then walk back to the common area. "Oh," I say, shocked by Noelle and Bailey lurking in the corridor of the bathrooms. They pull away from their tight embrace, red coloring their cheeks. "Sorry, I didn't mean to," I stutter, feeling like an intruder.

"No, it's okay," Noelle says. "Bailey was just telling me some good news."

Bailey tugs her hand and shakes her head. "Yeah, but nothing that needs to be shared tonight. Tonight is for celebrating you and Lake."

"Mm-hmm," I say. "So AQF got the green—"

Bailey holds up a hand. "Like, I said. Nothing that needs to be discussed tonight." She piles her hands in her pockets, a big grin taking over her face. "Even if it were that, I'd probably want to officially announce it at the gala we're hosting in the forestry department." She winks.

"Holy shit, you guys." I take two quick strides and pull them in for a hug. "Oh my God, Bailey. Congratulations."

"Thank you. Thank you." They hug me back.

"Okay." Noelle pulls away. "Let's go crush some beers."

❖

Okay, I'm romantic as fuck.

I think I always knew this about myself, but now that I have Lake, I'm like Casanova, full stop. I step back to admire my work. Is it against the rules to set up an entire fancy dinner of pizza and red wine, with lights I strung myself and a candle in the middle of a blanket…on the roof of the library? Yeah, but I couldn't care less.

I put the final touches on my little date night by scattering rose petals around our spot on the roof because I am one hundred percent that sap. I check my phone. Lake should be arriving back from New York in ten minutes.

I send a quick text. *Meet me in our spot.*

A minute later, she responds. *Be there in fifteen.* She follows her words with a heart emoji.

I crack a beer while I wait since red wine is not my favorite, but Bailey recommended the bottle, and I'm trying to broaden my palate. But for now, I drink an IPA and enjoy the view I love so much. I'm going to miss Alder. The cool liquid feels good down my throat as I sit on the blanket and look at the sky. The stars are bright. Just for us.

Then I hear the door creak.

"Lake," I say. I rush to her, all but pulling her through the hatch.

She climbs me, pulling herself into my arms and wrapping her legs around my waist. Her mouth is on mine before she says a single word. She sucks gently on my bottom lip before pulling back, silently asking to be let go. I put her down. "Hi," she says. She looks over my shoulder, her eyes going wide. "What's all this?"

I extend a hand to present our setup. "Well, since I beat you to the top, I get to decide if this is a date or not. So welcome to our first official date." She walks slowly to the little blanket. "I have pizza and wine. And one beer. I already drank the other."

She pulls me toward the blanket and spins to look at me. Her gaze drops down my body. "I've never seen you so dressed up." She tugs on the lapels of my shirt. "You look…" She shakes her head as if struggling to find the words.

I kiss her and tug her along. "Come sit. The pizza's getting cold." She sits across from me, and I pass her the bottle of wine. "I, uh, forgot cups."

She unscrews the cap and takes a swig. "Don't need a cup." She winks. "You should've told me to dress up. I'm just in running shorts and a basketball T-shirt."

"And your glasses. My favorite." I smile at her. "You're perfect, Lake." I slide a piece of pizza onto her plate. "Please, eat."

"How did you get these lights?" She points to the glowing strand above our heads and takes a bite. "*Mm.* So good. Thank you."

"I bought them." I point to the corner of the roof. "There's an outlet over there." I eat as we watch each other. "Oh." I wipe my mouth and grab the small box in the corner. "I almost forgot to give you—"

The *whoop whoop* of a siren interrupts me. I peek over the ledge and duck. "Oh shit. Campus security."

"What?" Her voice is high.

"The lights were a mistake." I tuck the box under my arm and crawl to unplug them. "Grab the wine. We gotta get out of here now."

Lake grabs the bottle, and we jog to the door, climbing down into the stairwell. We make it down one flight.

"To the top," a campus officer yells, his voice echoing through the stairwell.

"Shit." I skid to a stop on the first landing, Lake running into my back. She grabs the sides of my shirt as the voices grow louder and the footsteps closer. "We gotta go down one more," I say. "I think the fifth floor is all electrical junk. We gotta make it to the fourth."

"But—"

"Come on." I pull her as we fly down the next flight of stairs. They're still below us somewhere, huffing and puffing, their steps tired and loud. I hit the landing and yank open the door to the library. Lake brushes by me, and I close the door slowly, trying not to make a sound. Hopefully, the security guards will be too tired to continue the chase after their slow run to the top.

"Oh my God," Lake says. Her chest heaves but not from running downstairs; she's a star basketball player. She's scared. "What do we do?"

I walk her around a stack of old reference books to get away from the door. This floor—the quiet floor—is pretty dead, which doesn't help us in our escape. I pull her against me and whisper in her ear. "Give me the wine. You take the box." I realize the only real thing they could get us for is the alcohol.

I take the bottle and tuck it behind a thick green book. She tucks the box under her arm. "Careful with that. It's fragile."

"Okay," she whispers.

"I think we should wait a minute before we take the elevator down. What do you think?"

She nods. "Probably a good idea."

"Lake"—I squeeze her hand—"I'm really sorry. I guess I didn't think this all the way through."

She shakes her head with a quiet chuckle. "Leave it to Emma Wilson to get a girl's heart rate up within the first two minutes of their first date."

I grin. "I'm glad we agree this is a date."

She nudges me with her elbow. "How long have you been trying to date me?"

"Oh man." I drop my head against the books behind us. "I mean, when we first met in the bathroom, I wanted you. The way you speak and how confident you are just pulled me in. Then watching you play…wow." I pull her in front of me, needing her hips against mine. "But talking with you in my room. That's when I knew. There was always a different feeling I had about you, but after that, I knew I wanted to be with you."

She smirks and runs her free hand up my side. "And you handled your feelings so well."

I push her gently away. "Hey, now, that's not fair." I'm joking, but I can feel my face fall as a string of the things I said to her—*did* to her—rush through my head like a sickening tsunami. I can't even look at her. "It makes me sick to think about."

"Hey." Her body is against mine in a second, her warm hand on my cheek gently guiding my gaze to hers. "I forgive you. Not only do I trust you, but throughout the draft, I knew no matter where I ended up, you would support me. The things you said back then, those don't exist to me anymore, and I'm sorry I brought it up. Even as a joke."

I grip her hips and hold her against me. "I just feel like I shouldn't have gotten what I wanted after that."

"I disagree." She stands on tiptoes to kiss me, then rubs her thumb over my cheek. "But if it helps, don't you think I *should've* gotten what I wanted after all that?" I nod. "And that was you. So let it go, and let me enjoy this weird date, okay?"

Her words crack me open like an egg, and I ooze into her. I turn and kiss her palm. "You ready to make our next move?"

She nods. "To the dorm?"

"That's not a date," I whine.

"Listen, Emma. While I've had fun, I'm really uncomfortable in this situation, and I hope you can be sensitive to the fact that since I'm Black, and you're not, we're probably experiencing this very differently. Even if it is just campus security, it's still very scary and dangerous. And I want to feel safe. I want you to take me home."

I grab her hand. "Let's go."

❖

We sit on my bed and enjoy a beer together. She sets hers down and pulls the box into her lap. I'm suddenly nervous. It's the first gift I've given her, and it's not good enough. How would anything ever be good enough? She fingers the edge of the box.

"It's a corsage," I spit out. She arches a brow. "For the gala."

She lifts the top of the little white box and smiles. "It's so beautiful. You picked this out?"

I grin. "Yeah. Well, I'm hoping you wear your gold dress from the draft so I can experience it in real life. And I thought this one would complement it and—"

She kisses me, pulling my mouth to hers. I'm worried we'll crush the flowers, so I sneak the box out of her lap and slide it on my desk.

"It's not going to last until the gala," she says between kisses.

"What?"

Her mouth is on mine again, this time with a delicious brush of tongue. "They're fresh flowers, baby." Another kiss. "I'll keep them forever, but there's no way they'll make it past a week." Her words are breathless as she continues her sweet kiss attack.

"I'm ridiculous," I say, a little breathless myself, before I dive back into her.

"No, you're perfect, Emma. And the corsage is perfect," she whispers against my ear, her hot breath only exacerbating my need for her. Her fingers slip under my shirt to my belt buckle, and the sound of her loosening it and unzipping my pants makes me wild for her. Undoes me.

She slinks to her knees, a glint of mischief in her eyes, and I gasp when she yanks down my pants. "Fuck, Lake."

She spreads my thighs. "No. Fuck you, Emma."

Chapter Twenty-eight

The week after our date is finals week. Now that basketball is over and we've had our last meeting of the year—ever, for me—I can focus on other things: studying, enjoying my last week at Alder, and of course, Lake. School has never been hard for me—I thank the universe for it every day—so studying is more of a show of solidarity. I sit next to Lake, Rachel, Andy, and Maya in the library while everyone spreads their books and prepares for exams.

We're on the third floor of the library, and as my friends study, I look around at the most mundane things. The walls are a weird taupe color I've never noticed. It smells like old paper and stale coffee. There are etchings from past students in every wooden surface. I pile my hands in my hoodie and let the nostalgia wash over me.

Alder University has a magic about it. It gave us a place apart from the world, tucked in the mountains, to grow up and find ourselves. To fail and be messy. To build friendships. And fall in love.

"Um, excuse me?"

Everyone looks up from their books at the girl standing at the end of our table. Her long brown hair flows past her shoulders, hitting just under her breasts, and her green eyes are mesmerizing. She fiddles with her hands before clasping them and clearing her throat. She's adorable. Beautiful. "You're Rachel Dunston."

Rachel nods, her eyes wide. "That's me."

"Yeah." The girl blushes and scans us, clearly nervous. "Look, I know my timing is, like, impeccable with us graduating in a week and all." She drops her gaze and shakes her head before smiling and looking right at Rachel. "Guess it just means I have nothing to lose. Rachel, I don't know you, but you are sexy, talented, and have this energy that I'm so attracted to. Will you go on a date with me?"

As Rachel looks at her, we all exchange grins and nudges. I squeeze Lake's hand. This is so fucking cute. "What's your name?" Rachel asks.

"Victoria."

Rachel smiles and scribbles her number on the corner of the page in her textbook, then rips it.

Andy gasps. "Not the textbook. There's paper every—" Maya knocks her shoulder to hush her.

"I'd love that, Victoria. You made my day."

Victoria holds the tiny piece of paper like it's precious and tucks it into her jeans pocket. She grins. "Happy studying."

"Nice to meet you."

Victoria walks away. Once she's out of earshot…

"Holy shit, dude. She's super hot," I say.

"Right?" Maya says. "Like, so hot. And adorable."

"And brave," Lake adds. "That girl just strutted up and did the damn thing."

Rachel smiles, messing with the torn corner of her page. "She was definitely all of those things." She sighs. "But yeah, poor timing. Like, literally the last week of school. I'm off to Kentucky for med school."

"After the summer," Andy says. She reaches for Rachel's hands. "Can't believe you tore that poor page." She shakes her head. "Anyway, I think everyone at this table can attest to the fact that there will always be something standing in the way of you and the thing you want. She asked you, that's what matters. And who knows? Her timing seems pretty perfect to me."

"It's true," I say. "You obviously know nothing about her. She could be from Atlanta, then you have the whole summer. Plus, you may end up hating her, and it will be a moot point. Just enjoy the ride." Rachel deserves a big love. The biggest love, and I hope Victoria is her Lake. Her Maya.

"I can't believe we're graduating. Kinda thought it'd last forever," Rachel says, her voice quiet.

Andy groans. "I can't. I can't talk about this." She flips her book closed and shakes her head. "I'm sorry. It's just really emotional for me—for us all—and I'm a little sleep-deprived. And I just can't think about not having this anymore."

Maya squeezes her shoulder and presses a kiss to her temple. "Everyone shut up about graduation," she says. We burst into chuckles, Andy included. "What's everyone's plan for the gala?"

For the next half hour, we forget about grades and exams and graduation. We talk about suits and dresses, if Rachel will ask Victoria to be her date, and how we're going to sneak in booze. We make a plan to meet at Wilder, pregame in Andy and Rachel's room, then walk over to the forestry building together. It feels like prom. Well, I assume. I didn't go to mine. Instead, I picked up the head cheerleader five minutes in and hooked up with her in my back seat in the corner of the school parking lot.

I didn't want to go to prom. But I've been looking forward to the AQF gala for as long as I've known about it. Lake rubs her thumb over my hand, and I kiss her cheek. There's nothing I want more than to get all dressed up with her, dance to sappy songs, and be each other's date. Just have a couple of exams to take, then we get to celebrate.

And there's so much to celebrate.

"Wow." I take Lake by the hand and give her a spin. "We don't have to go anywhere tonight, you know? We could stay right here, just you and me," I say. She smiles, and it seems to glow. Everything about her seems to glow, from her shimmering gold dress to the clasp in her hair to the silly wilted flowers on her wrist.

No one in the universe is as stunning as Lake Palmer.

"Come here." She pulls me down for a kiss, and I squeeze her hips when her tongue slips into my mouth.

"Careful, or I'm going to make us late," I whisper, dragging my fingertips down her exposed back. "You shouldn't put it past me." I squeeze her ass.

"I'm not trying to," she says. Her breaths are heavy as we deepen our kiss, and things go hazy. "Shit. I want you, but we can't be late."

"Yeah." I take a step away and smooth my jacket. "I want to hike up your dress and make you come all over it, but I really don't want to be late either."

Her eyes widen. "Come on, Emma. Don't do that to me. It's hard enough to resist as it is." I give her a self-satisfied grin, and she shakes her head. "You think you're so funny, huh? Feeling pretty cocky over there?"

I press my hand to my chest. "Me? Cocky?" I gasp. "Not at all, dear."

She crosses her arms, brow raised. "You may find it interesting to know that I'm not wearing underwear. And squeezing my ass"—she steps into my arms and brushes her lips over the shell of my ear—"was very exciting." She gently sucks on the sensitive skin below my ear, and I shudder. "I can play this game, too." She pushes me away and grabs her clutch, her entire demeanor morphing to cheery and disinterested. "Ready?"

I stare at her in shock. "Um." Swallow. Nod.

She grabs my hand. "Don't be so weird. Let's go."

We stroll across the quad, feeling a bit out of place in our nicest clothes in the light of day. I wear my hair down, tight black pants, black loafers with thin gold detailing, a bomb-ass black velvet jacket with a monotone floral pattern, a white shirt unbuttoned past my sternum, and black suspenders. No bra.

And I don't even come close to *her*.

We reach Andy and Rachel's door. "Lake," I say before I knock. "You're the most beautiful thing I've ever seen. I can't believe you're my date."

She smiles. "I'll always be your date, Emma."

We walk into a party. Maya, Andy, and Rachel all look incredible and have a joy about them. Their cheeks are rosy, and the music is loud. Louder than it should be given there's a bottle of tequila on Andy's dresser. A sight I never thought I'd see. I guess that's the beauty of having finished classes. What can they do to us now?

I give Andy a hug. She looks beautiful in a sleek red dress, her hair in a complicated twist. "Never thought I'd see you do tequila shots. Especially during season."

"Oh no. I'm not." She releases me and smiles. "They are." She shoots Maya and Rachel a scandalized look. "And y'all are."

I look at Lake, who's grinning. "I think we are," I say.

Andy hands me the bottle, and I'm momentarily shocked. But why would she have shot glasses? I shrug and take a swig. "Yep. That's tequila." I suck in a sharp breath and cover my mouth with the back of my hand. It's rough on the way down. "Cheap tequila." I pass it to Lake. "Good luck."

She cringes as she raises the bottle. "Well, here's to us. You've all made this a very special year." She takes a deep breath and tucks her hair behind her ear. "Y'all may not know we lost my brother in a car crash when I was a sophomore in high school." She swallows. "And I haven't felt like my feet have truly been on the ground since. Like, I've just been floating. *Ghosting*, really. Until now. My only regret is that I didn't have more time at Alder with you guys." She takes a gulp of the tequila. "*Shit.* That's fire. Fire in my chest." She waves as if she can ease the burn.

"Come here." Rachel pulls Lake in for a hug. "Glad you made it here, Lake. Thanks for sharing that with us."

We turn at a knock on the door. "Who's that?" I ask, not expecting anyone else.

Rachel launches off the bed and pulls open the door. Victoria stands in the threshold looking nervous as hell with a six-pack of beer just out in the open. She wears an emerald dress that matches the green detailing of Rachel's suit. Everyone looks so beautiful tonight.

"Damn, girl," Rachel says, taking the beer. "Walking around with beer just out in the open like that and wearing that dress like it was made just for you." She kisses Victoria on the cheek. "You look incredible, and thank you for the beer. This tequila is nasty." Rachel passes around the beer.

I open mine, relieved to have something that doesn't taste like lighter fluid. "So nasty. Thanks for saving us."

"Want one, May?" Rachel asks.

Maya takes the bottle from Lake and casually sips. "Nah, I love tequila." She cringes. "Not so much beer."

We spend another half hour drinking and chatting before we walk together to the forestry building. The campus is bathed in the dim golden light of dusk, and we're quiet as we walk, probably all trying to burn this memory into our brains. Taking it in together. One of the last times we'll walk this cobblestone as students.

It hurts. But it's sweet, too.

The forestry building is always beautiful with its mostly glass exterior that butts up to the Alder woods. It gives the feeling of being submerged in the wilderness. The atrium is strung with hundreds of glowing lights, and the mammoth live oak in the center is adorned in rainbow lights. It's so beautiful, it makes me want to cry. Everyone has a sense of what's coming, but when we walk in, I *know* what's coming.

The moment we all deserve.

"Wow," Andy says. "Bailey nailed it. It's...beautiful."

There has to be at least two hundred people here, all dressed to the nines and celebrating. I recognize Dr. Martin and spot Coach Jordan in the corner with Julie. A few of the reporters from our basketball game talk with Bailey and Robert by the small stage. "We should go say hi to Coach," I say.

I take Lake's hand, and Rachel follows.

"Look at you girls," she says with a big smile. "I already miss all three of you." She pulls Lake into a tight hug, and Julie squeezes her shoulder. "Congratulations, sweetie. Julie and I cried when you got drafted." She holds Lake by the shoulders, staring into her eyes. "I couldn't be prouder of you."

They hug again before Coach turns to me. "Emma, I know you'll be at UGA. And I expect you to come for dinner next year."

I smile. "Of course. I gotta catch some Alder games. Plus, I'm excited to see Jessa's new moves."

She grabs Rachel's hand. "And Rachel, you have this incredible grounding energy. You're going to be a wonderful doctor." Rachel hugs her, and she laughs. "You three have my heart. Now go celebrate."

We dance and laugh and enjoy the evening together, feeling young and old at the same time. Saying good-bye to everything we've known while being on the cusp of everything to come. It's such an odd sensation. But knowing I have Lake for whatever comes after graduation makes it easier to take. The best part about tonight will be the best part of tomorrow, and if I play my cards right, the best part of every day.

"Excuse me, I'd just like to say a few words." Bailey stands on stage with Robert to her left and Ashley and Dr. Martin to her right. "I'll make it quick because tonight is for celebrating each other, celebrating what we've built here together, and celebrating the fact that the Alder Queer Fellowship is now an official university club." The crowd erupts into applause and sharp whistles.

She holds up a hand to calm us. And damn, I think she could run for office one day. The way she carries herself makes her look like she's already in office. "All of us have worked so hard and been through so much to make this happen. We've defended our right to exist with countless hours of preparation, we've sacrificed games we'll never get back, we protected each other against hate speech and bullies, we used what makes us special and talented to rally together and fight for equality. What I hope for Alder and for AQF is that this is merely a humble beginning. And as I and my fellow founding officers pass the torch of leadership, we look forward to the progress to come. Thank you all so very much. Cheers, my friends."

"We love you, Bailey," some girl shouts from the corner of the atrium, and the entire crowd erupts in applause.

"Wow. This is huge," Lake says.

I turn to her. Her eyes are watering, and she clutches her hands to her chest. The cheering dies down as guests begin to flow onto the dance floor. "Come dance with me," I say. She doesn't hesitate. She takes my hand and allows me to lead her to the space in front of the stage and pull her tight against me. "What a whirlwind."

She nods, her head against my chest. "It was, wasn't it?"

We sway to the slow beat, our arms around each other, no form to our movements. "Would you change anything?" I ask.

She looks up, a smile spreading to her eyes. "I would have kissed you that night on the roof before you left. And in your room before Andy walked in. And so many more times. I would have taken greater care with my words that morning in the yurt and held you even closer that night." She gently guides me down, her mouth on my ear. "If I could, why wouldn't I ask for even more of you, Emma?"

I smile against her neck, then kiss her again and again as if I can make up for all the moments we didn't. "Don't ask me what I would change," I say. "Please."

"Don't change a thing. Look where it got us." She looks up at the glowing lights, and I follow her gaze.

"It's overwhelming," I say.

"What is?"

"How I feel about you." I pull her tighter against me until the warmth from our chests swells. I brush my lips over the soft skin below her ear. "I wish this night would never end," I whisper.

She pulls back and stares at me, her hands clasping behind my neck. "It has to end. How else will I get to kiss you good morning?" She kisses me softly as if showing me how she'd do it. An image of her in *our* bed, white sheets draped over her bare back, flashes through my mind, convincing me this night needs to end, too. "This is just the first quarter, Emma. We have the entire game left."

GRADUATION

Emma and Lake

I drop my fork, the clanking of the metal against ceramic drawing the attention of Lake and her parents. It's the night before graduation, and her parents are treating us to a celebratory dinner. Lake watches me, her eyes wide. "Everything okay, Em?"

"That"—I nod to my plate—"is incredible." I pick up my fork and shovel another bite into my mouth. Shut my eyes and groan. "It's, like…like—"

"It's your delicious," Lake says. I open my eyes to find hers on me. And her smile… *That's the smile.* I swallow and turn to Luz and Chris, but they're not watching me, they're watching her. And they have it, too. They have the smile.

I kick Lake under the table and nod discreetly at her parents. She narrows her eyes, then turns her gaze on them. "Lake," her mom says. She reaches over the table and takes Lake's hand. "Your father and I have waited so long to see that smile again. We *dreamed* of seeing that smile again. After River passed, we were so worried we'd never get to. But looking at you now, baby"—she wipes a tear form her cheek, nodding slowly—"we're just so full of joy, seeing you living. Seeing you so happy."

Lake's mouth drops open, and she stays quiet for a moment. "I…" She shakes her head. "I thought you—"

"We will always hold River in our hearts," her dad says, reaching for her hands, too. "Losing him was the type of pain we never knew could exist. But, baby girl, watching you hollow yourself out…" He chews his lip, seemingly willing away tears. "Well, that just broke us to the bone." He takes a deep breath. "Missed that smile, sweetheart. It's so good to have you back."

Full-on tears stream down Lake's face as her parents hold her hands and tell her everything she never knew. She takes a stuttering breath. "I missed you."

In an instant, they're in a teary group hug in the middle of Pollini's. Students and their parents look up from their meals to watch the Palmers hug it out while I smile and take another bite of my mushroom risotto. Lake sits back down, a little embarrassed seeming from all the attention on her. Then, she takes a breath and looks at me.

I swallow, and though I want to, like, be in this moment with her completely…I pile another huge forkful into my mouth and grin, my lips about to bust open. Lake smiles through her watering eyes and brushes her knuckles gently against my temple. "Same as mine. That's lucky."

"Oh, Emma, just wait until you try ours, baby," her mom says.

"Careful, or I'll be over every night, Mrs. Palmer," I say.

She gives me a huge smile. "Well, since our girl will be across the country, we'll need someone to keep us company. You're welcome anytime."

Lake scoffs. "Are you trying to replace me with my girlfriend?" She waves a hand to where they hugged. "After we had a moment and everything. Ice cold, Mom. Ice cold."

"Oh, come on, baby. We need someone to watch all your games with."

This is it. The perfect moment. "I actually have a gift for you two," I say. "It's not much. 'Cause I don't have a job yet and all." *Fucking. It. Up.* I can feel my cheeks heat. "But"—I pull an envelope from my back pocket and hand it to her mom—"this is for you. Thank you for treating me to this dinner and showing me such kindness." I wipe my brow. "It means so much to me."

Luz tears the envelope and pulls out the card I made. It's bad. Really bad. I'm far from artistic, yet I tried to draw a scene of Lake playing in her first WNBA game in colored pencil. She smiles as she reads the log-in information and password for their new WNBA league pass. "You can watch every game live, even though the Seattle Storm is out of network. And there are replays if you miss one." I swallow. "I got myself one, too."

"Emma," Luz says, hand to her heart. "Thank you. What a thoughtful gift."

Lake squeezes my thigh under the table. "Can you, uh, accompany me to the bathroom real quick?"

I feel my eyes widen. "Now?"

"It will only take a second."

I follow her awkwardly to the restroom in the back of the restaurant, hoping her parents don't think we're about to hook up or something. *Are we about to hook up or something?*

"Come here," she says as she pulls me into a small stall. She shoves me against the graffitied divider, her hands tangled in my shirt, and I lose my breath when my back hits the metal. She stares at me, and I'm not sure I've ever seen her look at me this way before. It's so *deep*. "I need you to know," she starts, then shakes her head. "Are you listening?"

I nod as her grip in my shirt tightens, and she pushes me harder against the stall. "I need *you* to know that I don't carry cash," I say through a chuckle.

"Shut up." She kisses me hard, and right when I begin to pull her closer, she leans back and gives me the same look as before. "I love you, Emma Wilson. And I have this feeling"—she lets go with one hand to clutch her chest—"that I'm never going to stop." She uncurls her fingers from my shirt and flattens her palms under my collarbone. "So please, don't you stop either," she whispers.

I pull her against me, making her gasp. Kiss her until I feel her body melt into mine. "Stop? This is just the first quarter, Lake."

Graduation

Maggie and Olivia

"You think she's close?" I ask for the seventh time. "If we don't leave in an hour, we're going to be late to the Ag Department brunch, and I told Dr. Young that—"

"Maggie," Olivia says gently, her hands on my shoulders, stopping me from pacing my living room. "She said she would be here by nine, and it's quarter till. Okay? And you'll hear her tires in the gravel when she's here." She turns to my brother. "Aiden, can we please get her another mimosa?"

"Someone say mimosas?" Uncle Ward pops in the back door, rosy-cheeked from his shower. His beard is trimmed and clothes ironed. He looks good. It warms me knowing how much he cares about today.

Aiden pulls prosecco and orange juice from the fridge. "Hell, yeah, we said mimosas. It's Maggie and Olivia's graduation. Want one, Uncle Ward?"

"Yes, please." He pinches his fingers in front of his face. "Just a splash of OJ."

Aiden laughs. "I got you. Dad? What about you?"

My dad seems just as nervous as I am, probably more. Olivia and I have gone to visit my mom twice already, but he hasn't seen her in seven years. He paces, a constant hand running through his hair. "No," he says, then shakes his head. "I mean, yes. No OJ."

Olivia gives me a quick kiss and walks to my dad on the other side of the kitchen. “Mr. Hyde.” She takes his hand, and he seems shocked for a moment. “Stop for a second and breathe. You’re going to pass out at this rate.” This earns her a small smile. Hydes don’t often let their guard down, but Olivia is family. She loves us, mostly lives with us, and works with us. She’s Hyde through and through. My dad would trust her with anything, including being vulnerable. “You know Delaney, and she knows you.” She takes the glass of prosecco from Aiden and hands it to him. “Let’s drink these bubbles and take the pressure off, okay?”

He takes a deep breath and downs his prosecco.

“Okay, Hydes,” she says, turning to the rest of the room. “Listen up. I need you all to pull it together because my parents are about to arrive any second, and I need them to believe y’all are normal.”

“Hey,” Uncle Ward says, sounding hurt.

She cuts him a sharp look, her brow raised.

“Who’s normal?” Scott asks, walking into the kitchen in his pajamas.

Olivia shakes her head, hands on her hips. “Nope, nope, nope. Walk back in that room, shower, and get dressed.” She points to the hallway, and Scott disappears as quickly as he came.

I come up behind her and snake my arms around her waist, enjoying how she instantly relaxes into me. “I think our nerves got to you,” I whisper in her ear.

She spins in my arms and hugs me. “I’m sorry,” she says. “It’s all a little nerve-racking isn’t it?” The squall in her blue eyes is building.

I laugh. “It really is. I’m sorry for adding to the stress. This is a good day. All good things happening.”

She nods against my chest. “Yeah. Yeah, you’re right. I just can’t believe today is the day.”

“Today is the day, love.” I take her hand and guide her to the back door as she clutches the rose quartz necklace I got her for her birthday. “Come on. Take a little ride with me.”

“Now?” she asks.

"We'll be quick, I promise." My dad gives me a look as I walk outside. "I said we'd be quick. Don't worry," I tell him.

We climb into the ATV and take off into the orchard, her hand on my thigh. Not out of fear. We've turned Olivia into an adrenaline junky. We race through the peaches, through the Honeycrisps, to the opposite side of the orchard, by the trail up to the firepit. I park in a sweet little spot with a gorgeous western-facing view of the mountains. It's far enough from the apple trees that the hustle and bustle of work won't reach us.

"This is it," I say.

She shakes her head, gripping the crystal again, a frown line forming between her brows. "This is what, exactly?"

"Where we'll build our first home this summer." I skip to the back of the ATV and grab the shovel. "And today, we're breaking ground."

She walks around to meet me, her hand on my cheek and her lips on mine. I groan, and she pushes me into the side of the ATV. It's like striking a match. Everything feels amazing; her warm wet tongue on mine, the sun on my face, even the metal frame digging into my back. She fumbles with my belt buckle.

"Wait. We're going to be late." I say between kisses. "They're all going to meet without us." She yanks my belt loose.

"I don't care, Maggie." She pulls down my zipper. "They're adults. They can figure it out, and I'm done stressing about it." Her hand pushes into my underwear, and a long moan slips out my throat. She pulls back, and I instantly miss it. Her smirk is all fire.

"Come back."

"No." She walks backward, never dropping my gaze. "Grab the picnic blanket and consummate our home with me." The sun kisses her pale shoulders as she slips the straps of her sundress down each of them.

I grab the blanket and jog over.

We make fast love in the early summer warmth, half-clothed and hungry for each other on the very spot we'll call our homebase. We do have a lot of traveling to do…

"I love you, Maggie Hyde," she says, slipping her dress back on. "Look at this life we're building."

I kiss the tops of her breasts, overflowing with contentment. This warm, satiated feeling consuming me. "You're the light I grow toward, and I love you so much."

"Phototropism," she says with a wink.

"Phototropism."

GRADUATION

Andy and Maya

"Okay," I say, counting through my mental checklist. I shake my head, frustrated. "No. No, I'm definitely missing something." I groan. "Why didn't I write this down? I *always* make a list to pack for a game, especially for the conference championship."

I don't often spiral anymore, but there's so much going on today, I can feel the tingling in my fingers creep up my arms as Maya and I pack alone in my room. We graduate today. Which is great, yeah. Whatever. But we also have to leave at six in the morning tomorrow to travel to Charlotte for the tournament. And maybe I haven't entirely processed my feelings about leaving Alder or about graduating or about graduating without my dad. A shiver runs down my spine.

Then, Maya's holding me, her chest flush against my back, her arms looped under mine in a tight embrace. "It's scary. I know, baby." I focus on how her chest rises with each of her breaths. *One breath, two breaths.* "There's a lot going on. Big changes. Unknowns. We have to go apartment hunting soon. But I'm right here. Breathe. Breathe." She times her words with her own breaths, just how I like it. "Ready?" Her question is warm on my neck. I nod. "One," she says.

"One," I repeat.

"Two," she says.

"Two," I repeat.

"Three."

"Three."

She pushes a soft kiss to my pulse, and I can feel two quick beats of my heart under the pressure of her lips. "Swerve," we say together. I take a deep breath before spinning in her arms.

As if I need an excuse to touch her, I brush nonexistent lint from the shoulder of her sleeveless white jumpsuit. "God, you're beautiful." I press my forehead gently to hers. "My Maya."

"Don't make me cry, Andy," she whispers. "My makeup is flawless, and it took me for fucking ever." I chuckle, careful to avoid getting my own makeup on her white outfit. "These heels are killing me. May have to ditch them later."

"Ditch your heels?" I raise a brow. "You would limp home with bleeding feet before that ever happened."

She kisses me, and it sends me. Just like the first time in the training room and every time after that. I wrap my arms around her neck and sink into her mouth. The only mouth I want. I need her tongue on mine, but she pulls back. "You're right." She chuckles. "Only classless quitters ditch their heels."

"Is that so?" I laugh, rubbing her soft cheek with my thumb. "Because you know I'm pulling these off the second I can."

We both look at my strappy black heels. She bites down a chuckle. "And you totally get to because you have me to carry on our heel wearing. I put the team on my back, baby."

"Kiss me," I whisper.

She kisses me exactly how I need her to. Full of longing and promises and eagerness. "Andrea." And when she says my name like that, everything I've always known about us is confirmed. I know she won't follow with more words. It's all in my name. In every kiss. How she treats me every moment of every day.

"Maya. I—"

My alarm blares in my pocket, and we erupt into laughter. "If I had a dollar," Maya says, as she tugs me to the door. "Come on, gorgeous. Grab your cap and gown. Let's go do this."

Graduation

Bailey and Noelle

Noelle squeezes my hand, anchoring me like she always has. As good as I've gotten at public speaking, nothing has felt like this. I zero in on a blade of grass between my brown loafers. But my vision blurs as sweat drips down my back. These fucking gowns are stifling.

"Hey," she whispers. She's as glorious as the day I met her. Her golden hair is down and pinned back on the side. And she's wearing the green dress she wore during Thanksgiving of freshman year, matching green eyes twinkling under the bright sun.

"Hi," I say, my voice a little shaky.

"Luke wanted me to give this to you." She slips me a small piece of paper sloppily folded into an amorphous clump.

It takes me a minute to loosen it and smooth it down.

You can't put the toothpaste back in the tube. And who would want to? Look at us go. Love you, Bailey.

Tears gather in my eyes, and I look at Noelle. "I don't understand what—"

She pushes another folded piece of paper in my hands. "Cassie wanted me to give this to you."

This note is very neat, with crisp edges and sharp corners.

You brought me such joy these four years. We've helped each other grow into the women we are today. Love you, Bailey.

"Noelle, I—"

"From Matt." She hands me a note, and I unfold it. It's the title page from *The Alchemist*.

A poem for Bailey: Fuck The Alchemist *and fuck* Stars Wars, *too. If I could pick a hero, it'd be you.*

Happy graduation. Love, Matt.

I don't even have to ask to know what's next. Noelle slips me a folded piece of pink paper, and I take care to not tear the edges while I unfold it.

Noelle told me to write something light and cute to take your mind off the big speech. I actually think she was kind of depending on me to save the day. I mean, let's be real. Cassie didn't write anything light or cute. Matt? Please. Don't even get me started about my boo's lack of emotional competency. Luke? Yeah, okay. Maybe.

Priya? Yes. One hundred percent. All day.

Only, I don't feel very light or cheery. You've been my family for four years. Slept in the bed next to me for four years. Laughed with me, cried with me, put up with my snoring. The truth is, I'm sad. And I'm scared. These four years have meant everything to me, and I don't want to lose what we have.

But we still have today and tonight. And I can't wait to watch Phillip Fucking Lymer have to introduce you. Bite his fucking dick off.

Love,

Your stunning roommate

I try to smother my laughter in my gown as I look down our row at the people I adore most in this world.

"Better?" Noelle asks.

I wipe a tear of laughter. "Priya told me to, and I quote, 'bite his fucking dick off.'" She laughs as she squeezes my knee. "Do I get one from you?"

She shoots me one of her sexy smirks. "I didn't want to write mine down."

"And why's that?"

"I want you to hear it in my voice." She pulls me toward her, her lips brushing against my ear, making me shiver. "Tonight, when we all switch rooms, and it's just me and you"—she nips at my neck—"I want you to use that special gift I got us on me. All night long."

I swallow, my speech the farthest thing from my mind. All I can think of, all I can feel, is Noelle. Her body trembling under mine. "Hang tight, love. I have a gift for you, too."

"And now, please welcome our student body class president, Bailey Sullivan," Phillip Lymer announces. "Bailey, please come say a few words."

I kiss Noelle. "I love you, baby. Promise you won't be mad."

"Be mad? What—"

I can't hear the rest of what she says because I'm halfway down the aisle toward the stage. I hop up the stairs and stand behind the podium. My mom and Dave wave at me, and I wave back, feeling steadied by their presence. I take a deep breath.

"Thank you so much, Dr. Lymer. I'll keep this short because I know it's hot, and these gowns are like an oven." I pull mine away from me and cringe. The audience chuckles. "I hope that you all feel how I feel today. Like you walked onto those cobblestone paths as a freshman and promptly fell because you didn't know the 'Alder step' yet." This really gets the seniors laughing because we have *all* fallen. "Yep. High knees on the paths. High knees." I grin. "But now we sit here as different people. People who have completed a journey. People who are starting a new journey. And I want to thank you all for doing high knees with me through these four years.

"Because I'm not at all who I used to be. And together, our graduating class has left a mark on this gray stone. And now, Alder isn't what it used to be, either. We've grown together, student and school. So cheers to us. Congratulations, everyone."

The crowd claps at my simple speech or probably the brevity of it. But I'm not *quite* done with my time on stage. I have one last mark to make on this university. "One more thing. Noelle Parker, could you please join me on stage for just one moment?" I hear Dr. Lymer step toward me, but he stops when I pin him with a glare and wiggle the universal sign for "hang loose." "All good, Dr. Lymer. Don't you worry." I wink, and he frowns. *Beautiful.*

Noelle takes a hesitant step on stage, and I don't care an ounce about Dr. Lymer. Don't care an ounce about any of my fellow graduates. I only care about *her*. Noelle Parker.

She glances at Dr. Lymer and the big crowd on the lawn below. "Bailey…" Her voice trembles.

I take her hand. "Remember. You promised you wouldn't get mad."

Her eyes go wide. "I definitely said I would probably be mad," she says through a fake smile.

I grin and kiss her hand, earning a couple hollers of approval from the audience. "Well, I *definitely* didn't hear that part." She looks nervously around. "Hey. Don't worry about anyone else, okay? It's just me and you." I take a step away from the mic so this moment is private. No one can hear me but her. "You okay?"

"Yeah. I love you, Bailey." Her words are breathy, and her eyes begin to water. She seems to know exactly what I'm up to. "I'm ready."

"I've dreamt of this moment since the day I met you four years ago in the dining hall. Only I couldn't see it clearly. I could've never imagined we'd get to do this in front of our Catholic university, with all of our friends and family in the audience." I can basically feel Mr. Parker's eyes lasering into me, but he'll adjust. I know I'm growing on him. "Noelle, you are my first love, and I want you to be my only love." I sink to a knee. I hear Priya gasp, but I push her out of my mind.

Tears fall down Noelle's cheeks, and she kneels with me. "Bailey, I—"

I laugh. I can feel tears on my face, too. "You're not supposed to be down here."

She kisses me hard and long and a little too intimately for our audience. The crowd cheers. "Don't be ridiculous. I'm supposed to be wherever you are. If you're on your knees, I'm on my knees."

I'm full-on crying as I reach under my gown into my pocket and pull out the ring box. Now the entire crowd gasps. I hear Dr. Lymer say something, but I ignore him. Open the box. "Noelle Parker, will you marry me?"

She almost knocks me over with the force of her hug. "Yes." She peppers me with kisses. "Yes, Bailey. A million times, yes. It was always you, and it always will be."

The crowd is like a white noise that barely reaches my ears when Noelle's words sink into me.

I walked into Alder University scared of who I was. Now I'm walking out with five best friends, the legacy of AQF, an acceptance letter to UGA Law, and most importantly, my fiancée.

Oh, I almost forgot…

And a pretty cool little sign we stole freshman year.

About the Author

Ana is an award-winning author of sapphic romance. She worked in the Pacific Northwest wine industry for eight years and now lives in her hometown of Atlanta. She loves all things fermented or distilled, walking the local trails, and eating pastries. So many pastries. She is currently working on her next book and dreaming of a beach trip.

Books Available from Bold Strokes Books

Coasting and Crashing by Ana Hartnett. Life comes easy to Emma Wilson until Lake Palmer shows up at Alder University and derails her every plan. (978-1-63679-511-9)

Every Beat of Her Heart by KC Richardson. Piper and Gillian have their own fears about falling in love, but will they be able to overcome those feelings once they learn each other's secrets? (978-1-63679-515-7)

Grave Consequences by Sandra Barret. A decade after necromancy became licensed and legalized, can Tamar and Maddy overcome the lingering prejudice against their kind and their growing attraction to each other to uncover a plot that threatens both their lives? (978-1-63679-467-9)

Haunted by Myth by Barbara Ann Wright. When ghost-hunter Chloe seeks an answer to the current spectral epidemic, all clues point to one very famous face: Helen of Troy, whose motives are more complicated than history suggests and whose charms few can resist. (978-1-63679-461-7)

Invisible by Anna Larner. When medical school dropout Phoebe Frink falls for the shy costume shop assistant Violet Unwin, everything about their love feels certain, but can the same be said about their future? (978-1-63679-469-3)

Like They Do in the Movies by Nan Campbell. Celebrity gossip writer Fran Underhill becomes Chelsea Cartwright's personal assistant with the aim of taking the popular actress down, but neither of them anticipates the clash of their attraction. (978-1-63679-525-6)

Limelight by Gun Brooke. Liberty Bell and Palmer Elliston loathe each other. They clash every week on the hottest new TV show, until Liberty starts to sing and the impossible happens. (978-1-63679-192-0)

Playing with Matches by Georgia Beers. To help save Cori's store and help Liz survive her ex's wedding they strike a deal: a fake relationship, but just for one week. There's no way this will turn into the real deal. (978-1-63679-507-2)

The Memories of Marlie Rose by Morgan Lee Miller. Broadway legend Marlie Rose undergoes a procedure to erase all of her unwanted memories, but as she starts regretting her decision, she discovers that the only person who could help is the love she's trying to forget. (978-1-63679-347-4)

The Murders at Sugar Mill Farm by Ronica Black. A serial killer is on the loose in southern Louisiana, and it's up to three women to solve the case while carefully dancing around feelings for each other. (978-1-63679-455-6)

Fire in the Sky by Radclyffe and Julie Cannon. Two women from different worlds have nothing in common and every reason to wish they'd never met—except for the attraction neither can deny. (978-1-63679-573-7)

A Talent Ignited by Suzanne Lenoir. When Evelyne is abducted and Annika believes she has been abandoned, they must risk everything to find each other again. (978-1-63679-483-9)

All Things Beautiful by Alaina Erdell. Casey Norford only planned to learn to paint like her mentor, Leighton Vaughn, not sleep with her. (978-1-63679-479-2)

An Atlas to Forever by Krystina Rivers. Can Atlas, a difficult dog Ellie inherits after the death of her best friend, help the busy hopeless romantic find forever love with commitment-phobic animal behaviorist Hayden Brandt? (978-1-63679-451-8)

Bait and Witch by Clifford Mae Henderson. When Zeddi gets an unexpected inheritance from her client Mags, she discovers that Mags served as high priestess to a dwindling coven of old witches—who are positive that Mags was murdered. Zeddi owes it to her to uncover the truth. (978-1-63679-535-5)

Buried Secrets by Sheri Lewis Wohl. Tuesday and Addie, along with Tuesday's dog, Tripper, struggle to solve a twenty-five-year-old mystery while searching for love and redemption along the way. (978-1-63679-396-2)

Come Find Me in the Midnight Sun by Bailey Bridgewater. In Alaska, disappearing is the easy part. When two men go missing, state trooper Louisa Linebach must solve the case, and when she thinks she's coming close, she's wrong. (978-1-63679-566-9)

Death on the Water by CJ Birch. The Ocean Summit's authorities have ruled a death on board its inaugural cruise as a suicide, but Claire suspects murder and with the help of Assistant Cruise Director Moira, Claire conducts her own investigation. (978-1-63679-497-6)

Living For You by Jenny Frame. Can Sera Debrek face real and personal demons to help save the world from darkness and open her heart to love? (978-1-63679-491-4)

Mississippi River Mischief by Greg Herren. When a politician turns up dead and Scotty's client is the most obvious suspect, Scotty and his friends set out to prove his client's innocence. (978-1-63679-353-5)

Ride with Me by Jenna Jarvis. When Lucy's vacation to find herself becomes Emma's chance to remember herself, they realize that everything they're looking for might already be sitting right next to them—if they're willing to reach for it. (978-1-63679-499-0)

Whiskey and Wine by Kelly and Tana Fireside. Winemaker Tessa Williams and sex toy shop owner Lace Reynolds are both used to taking risks, but will they be willing to put their friendship on the line if it gives them a shot at finding forever love? (978-1-63679-531-7)

Hands of the Morri by Heather K O'Malley. Discovering she is a Lost Sister and growing acquainted with her new body, Asche learns how to be a warrior and commune with the Goddess the Hands serve, the Morri. (978-1-63679-465-5)

I Know About You by Erin Kaste. With her stalker inching closer to the truth, Cary Smith is forced to face the past she's tried desperately to forget. (978-1-63679-513-3)

Mate of Her Own by Elena Abbott. When Heather McKenna finally confronts the family who cursed her, her werewolf is shocked to discover her one true mate, and that's only the beginning. (978-1-63679-481-5)

Pumpkin Spice by Tagan Shepard. For Nicki, new love is making this pumpkin spice season sweeter than expected. (978-1-63679-388-7)

Rivals for Love by Ali Vali. Brooks Boseman's brother Curtis is getting married, and Brooks needs to be at the engagement party. Only she can't possibly go, not with Curtis set to marry the secret love of her youth, Fallon Goodwin. (978-1-63679-384-9)

Sweat Equity by Aurora Rey. When cheesemaker Sy Travino takes a job in rural Vermont and hires contractor Maddie Barrow to rehab a house she buys sight unseen, they both wind up with a lot more than they bargained for. (978-1-63679-487-7)

Taking the Plunge by Amanda Radley. When Regina Avery meets model Grace Holland—the most beautiful woman she's ever seen—she doesn't have a clue how to flirt, date, or hold on to a relationship. But Regina must take the plunge with Grace and hope she manages to swim. (978-1-63679-400-6)

We Met in a Bar by Claire Forsythe. Wealthy nightclub owner Erica turns undercover bartender on a mission to catch a thief where she meets no-strings, no-commitments Charlie, who couldn't be further from Erica's type. Right? (978-1-63679-521-8)

Western Blue by Suzie Clarke. Step back in time to this historic western filled with heroism, loyalty, friendship, and love. The odds are against this unlikely group—but never underestimate women who have nothing to lose. (978-1-63679-095-4)

Windswept by Patricia Evans. The windswept shores of the Scottish Highlands weave magic for two people convinced they'd never fall in love again. (978-1-63679-382-5)

An Independent Woman by Kit Meredith. Alex and Rebecca's attraction won't stop smoldering, despite their reluctance to act on it and incompatible poly relationship styles. (978-1-63679-553-9)

Cherish by Kris Bryant. Josie and Olivia cherish the time spent together, but when the summer ends and their temporary romance melts into the real deal, reality gets complicated. (978-1-63679-567-6)

Cold Case Heat by Mary P. Burns. Sydney Hansen receives a threat in a very cold murder case that sends her to the police for help where she finds more than justice with Detective Gale Sterling. (978-1-63679-374-0)

Proximity by Jordan Meadows. Joan really likes Ellie, but being alone with her could turn deadly unless she can keep her dangerous powers under control. (978-1-63679-476-1)

Sweet Spot by Kimberly Cooper Griffin. Pro surfer Shia Turning will have to take a chance if she wants to find the sweet spot. (978-1-63679-418-1)

The Haunting of Oak Springs by Crin Claxton. Ghosts and the past haunt the supernatural detective in a race to save the lesbians of Oak Springs farm. (978-1-63679-432-7)

Transitory by J.M. Redmann. The cops blow it off as a customer surprised by what was under the dress, but PI Micky Knight knows they're wrong—she either makes it her case or lets a murderer go free to kill again. (978-1-63679-251-4)

Unexpectedly Yours by Toni Logan. A private resort on a tropical island, a feisty old chief, and a kleptomaniac pet pig bring Suzanne and Allie together for unexpected love. (978-1-63679-160-9)

Bold Strokes Books
Quality and Diversity in LGBTQ Literature